FIREBLOOMS

ALSO BY ALEXANDRA VILLASANTE

The Grief Keeper

FIREBLOOMS

Alexandra Villasante

NANCY PAULSEN BOOKS

NANCY PAULSEN BOOKS
An imprint of Penguin Random House LLC
1745 Broadway, New York, New York 10019

First published in the United States of America by Nancy Paulsen Books,
an imprint of Penguin Random House LLC, 2025

Copyright © 2025 by Alexandra Villasante

Penguin Random House values and supports copyright. Copyright fuels creativity, encourages diverse voices, promotes free speech, and creates a vibrant culture. Thank you for buying an authorized edition of this book and for complying with copyright laws by not reproducing, scanning, or distributing any part of it in any form without permission. You are supporting writers and allowing Penguin Random House to continue to publish books for every reader. Please note that no part of this book may be used or reproduced in any manner for the purpose of training artificial intelligence technologies or systems.

Nancy Paulsen Books & colophon are trademarks of Penguin Random House LLC.
The Penguin colophon is a registered trademark of Penguin Books Limited.

Visit us online at PenguinRandomHouse.com.

Library of Congress Cataloging-in-Publication Data
Names: Villasante, Alexandra, author.
Title: Fireblooms / Alexandra Villasante.
Description: New York, New York: Nancy Paulsen Books, 2025. | Audience term: Teenagers | Summary: "Seventeen-year-old Sebastian moves to a town that uses technology to prevent hate speech and bullying, only to discover this flawed system is not without its dangers"—Provided by publisher.
Identifiers: LCCN 2024049592 (print) | LCCN 2024049593 (ebook) | ISBN 9780525514053 (hardcover) | ISBN 9780525514060 (ebook)
Subjects: CYAC: Mothers and sons—Fiction. | Psychic trauma—Fiction. | Technology—Fiction. | High schools—Fiction. | Schools—Fiction. | LGBTQ+ people—Fiction. | Romance stories. | LCGFT: Queer fiction. | Romance fiction. | Novels.
Classification: LCC PZ7.1.V548 Fi 2025 (print) | LCC PZ7.1.V548 (ebook) | DDC [Fic]—dc23
LC record available at https://lccn.loc.gov/2024049592
LC ebook record available at https://lccn.loc.gov/2024049593

Printed in the United States of America
ISBN 9780525514053
1   3   5   7   9   10   8   6   4   2
BVG

Edited by Stacey Barney • Design by Suki Boynton • Text set in Mercury Text G2

This book is a work of fiction. Any references to historical events, real people, or real places are used fictitiously. Other names, characters, places, and events are products of the author's imagination, and any resemblance to actual events or places or persons, living or dead, is entirely coincidental.

The publisher does not have any control over and does not assume any responsibility for author or third-party websites or their content.

The authorized representative in the EU for product safety and compliance is Penguin Random House Ireland, Morrison Chambers, 32 Nassau Street, Dublin D02 YH68, Ireland, https://eu-contact.penguin.ie.

*To Tim, for cutting rugs,
facing the music, and dancing.*

FIREBLOOMS

I

Sebas

The 6:40 Greyhound bus from San Marcos approaches the pristine New Gault terminal like it needs to apologize. I see it playing out in my mind: a wide-angle, aerial shot of the dinged-up bus hesitating like it knows it doesn't belong. Correction: The bus is fine. I'm the one that doesn't belong.

New Gault is nothing like any other bus terminal I've been in—and as much as Papá and I have traveled over the years, I've seen a lot of them. Even rich-ass San Marcos has a less rich area. That's where cities like to keep their buses—and their plebes. I'm a plebe. "*Plebeian* means *common worker*—did you know that?" Anaïs, my best friend of six months, said to me before I left. I didn't know then, but I know now. I'm plebe as fuck and proud of it.

I grab my duffel bag from the overhead rack and stand, cracking my back. Twelve hours on this bus, curved like a pretzel without much leg room—now I'm finally in New Gault. Yay.

In the concourse, I look around like a tourist at the gleaming floors you could eat off, the total lack of stained tiles, cell phone fix-it kiosks, and pee-smelling seats. What kind of bus terminal is this? There's a fancy diner selling ten-dollar hamburgers and an athletic clothing store selling items so expensive, I'd be afraid to sweat in them. I shake my head and look for signs to tell me where to go. Before I get the chance to orient myself, a white woman with very smiley eyes practically accosts me.

"Hi, I'm Tamera," she says, which I already know because her name tag says TAMERA. I mean, why wear a name tag if you're gonna lead with announcing your name? "Do you need help?"

I think about floating a joke like, *Yes, I need to get the hell out of this freak show town ASAP, Tamera,* or *Don't all the children of God need help, Tammy?* but I'm pretty sure Tamera wouldn't find any of that funny. I'm too tired to find it funny myself.

"I'm looking for the purple bus?" I say, slipping my phone out of my back pocket and opening the text Mom sent me yesterday. It takes an unreasonable amount of time, like, many, many seconds, for it to load. I blame Tamera, who is excitedly waiting to dance her fingers across her tablet and provide me with some answers.

"We have a violet tram and an indigo tram; do you know which one?"

How could I know? Mom only said to take the purple bus to the last stop, then walk straight until I hit the trailer park. Besides, aren't violet, indigo, and purple basically the same color?

"Whichever one goes to Butternut Flats Road?" I make it a question because I'm tired and awkward. Tamera doesn't notice, she just tappity taps on her tablet. Soon, she's frowning and giving me sad puppy eyes.

"I'm so sorry. I can't find that address anywhere in New Gault." I legit almost feel bad for her, she's so sad about it.

"It's not in New Gault. It's in just plain Gault. Like, what used to be Gault?" There I am again, making statements into questions. Mom said she lives in a scrap of leftover town from when the last wildfire consumed a whole bunch of Northern California a few years ago. They abandoned the handful of buildings that didn't burn and moved the whole town a couple of miles over, built it from scratch, and slapped a "New" in front of it. Ta-da. Insta-town.

Tamera's eyes clear of sadness, thank God.

"Ah! That explains it! Well, I'm not sure you can get all the way there from here. You may have to walk a bit."

"Got it. But how do I get, like, that far?"

"Tram: violet, of course! You can't miss it," she says, gesturing to the sliding glass doors behind her next to a cell phone store—I knew there had to be one—called TECH-ology that's sleek and immaculate. Never heard of the brands in the window displays, and the phones look like they're imported from space.

"Tram: violet is painted—"

"Let me guess, purple."

"—like a beautiful field of flowers!"

I stomp past her as she waves sunnily, and then I turn back to her with a "thank you," because I know Abuela would kill me for being rude, and because I'm a pendejo, I can't even be properly angsty to a stranger.

Outside the terminal, the tram stop shelters fan out in an arc, painted the colors of the rainbow. I walk down the line of Roy G. Biv until I get to the violet tram shelter, which is painted with a field of violets. The tram stop for indigo, next to it, looks like grapes threw up. Honestly, New Gault, stop trying so hard.

I lean against the shelter's glass sides and close my eyes. I wanted to sleep so badly on the long trip up here, to keep my strength up, or gird my loins, as Anaïs would say. But I couldn't stop thinking about, anticipating, what was gonna be waiting for me. Mom. Not *Mamá* like Anaïs's mom, or *Mami*, which is what Papá calls Abuela. Never, if you value your life, would you call my gringa mother *Mamá*.

I snap out of my daze because suddenly a tram appears out of nowhere and opens its doors. It's noiseless, and I realize it's not a tram, it's an electric bus—no track, just wheels. *Tram* is, I guess, supposed to be classier. It doesn't change the fact that this is a bus. I climb on, feeling in my jeans pocket for the collection of change, tokens, and taped-together bills I have in there, hoping that I have something that can be used as fare. If I'm lucky, I can download an app and tap my payment with my phone (my poor, janky, hand-me-down phone, which has had practically no reception for the last hour). If I'm unlucky, I'll have to trek back into the bus terminal, pass puppy-eyed Tamera, and try to figure out payment.

The tram driver is Black and dressed in the same hipster uniform as Tamera. His name is DOUG. Guess how I know.

"Welcome, young traveler!"

Fuck my life.

"Uh. How much?" I don't see a turnstile, a digital reader, or a box for coins. It's just Doug and his toothy, handsome smile.

"For you? It's free!"

My face must say what I'm thinking, because Doug chuckles and closes the tram doors.

"Take a seat, friend."

I sit across from him, nearest the door in case I have to throw myself out of this tram. Being called *friend* triggers me. It usually means someone is real excited about saving your soul, whether you want it saved or not. Two summers ago, Pa and I were in Georgia, working on a building site of a new high school gymnasium. The old gymnasium was creepy as hell and had the inscription ONE WHO BLASPHEMES THE NAME OF THE LORD SHALL SURELY BE PUT TO DEATH over the doors. I can smell religious weirdness a mile away, and I'm on the alert for it now.

But Doug just says, "All transportation is free in New Gault. It's how the city was built. It runs twenty-four hours, it's always free, and—except on the days when I don't have enough coffee—it's always cheery!"

Oh my God, I think. *I'm in Stepford.*

Out of the tram window, I watch the streets—painted white instead of tar black—the trees planted in boxes, a lone person walking their dog. Doug tells me the roads are painted white to reduce surface temperature and help combat climate change, and before long, the reflected light is making my head ache enough that I risk closing my eyes.

I don't think I fall asleep, but when I open my eyes again, Doug has stopped the tram and opened the door. Since I'm the only person on the tram, he must be waiting for me. But there's nothing outside; it's the literal end of the road. The white pavement we'd been following ends abruptly; ahead it's scrubby bushes, tall bleached-out grasses, and low hills in the distance.

"End of the road," Doug says to make sure I understand he's not going any farther, then chuckles at his joke. I grab my duffel bag and backpack and exit the tram.

"So, Butternut Flats Road?" I ask.

"It's down that little dirt path. Less than a mile. That's what the internet says. Had to switch to that since the New Gault mapping system doesn't work outside city limits."

"And this is the end of the city?"

"Yup, end of the road," he repeats, and now it sounds ominous. *Here's the part of the movie where our idiot hero is gonna get murdered*, I think.

"Listen," Doug says, shifting on his seat so he can look me in the eye. "If you get lost or need help, come back to this tram stop, or any tram stop. As soon as you approach it, we'll know you're here and come get you."

"That's creepy."

"What? No, that's safety. You don't want to have to rely on a schedule when you really have to get somewhere, right?"

"I don't want to rely on anything."

Doug shakes his head sadly. "That's not the community spirit."

"I'm not part of the community. I'm just visiting."

"Well, when you're here, you're family." Doug smiles, closes the door to the tram, and pulls away, circling back toward the city.

When you're here, you're family? Did he just spit out a slogan from a pasta restaurant chain?

I slip the shoulder strap of the duffel over my head so it's firmly across my back, then put the backpack over it—como un camello, Abuela would say, a camel with two humps—and start walking down the dirt track.

After a few minutes, the road widens and I see buildings in the far distance, the remnants of a trailer park, maybe. At least there's a fifty-fifty chance my mother is in one of those. If she's there, I'll have to figure out what to say. I've put off thinking about it long enough. *Of course she's there,* I think. *She asked for you.*

Mom never asks for anything, especially not from me or Dad. To Mom, we're at best an afterthought, at worst an embarrassment. But she called Dad. She asked for me, me *specifically*. She said I was the only one who could help her. She said she needed me. I guess I am that stupid. If this *were* a horror movie, I would probably be the first virgin to die.

I'm soaked with sweat. I've draped my hoodie over my head because the sun was baking my brain and making me want to turn around, find Doug, and beg him to take me back to the bus station. I'm a drama queen, I know. Anaïs and Hudson always tease me about it. I just say, *Yeah, that's how come I'm gonna be a famous filmmaker: I bleed, sweat, and cry drama.*

Eventually, the dirt track dumps me out into a clearing that reveals a tiny house the color of mud.

The house has a little porch, sunken in, but out of the sun, and there's another house—a trailer—not too far down Butternut Flats Road. If Mom doesn't come out, if this was all some elaborate scheme to make me feel like crap, well, would I be surprised?

I should have written a script. I should have storyboarded how this would go, what I would say, how she would look. If I'd done that, maybe I wouldn't feel like my heart was gonna abandon all hope and jump out of my chest. Hudson would tell me to think positive, but that's because his dad is a yoga instructor. I don't know how to be positive about Mom anymore.

I ring the doorbell, then realize there's no chance the bell works. I knock hard on the door. No answer.

I check my phone, the phone that has been acting up, getting no signal, and generally disappointing me. Sometime during the walk, three bars have reappeared. I text:

> **I'm here at 84 Butternut Flats Road.**
> **Where are you.**

After some painfully slow pulsating dots, Mom responds:

> **Chemo went long. I'm too tired to get up**
> **and open the damn door. Let yourself in.**
> **Key under the plant.**

I'm guessing by *plant* she means the faded orange pot filled with dust and a plant corpse. I grab the key and let myself in.

The house is clean, except for pervasive dust that makes the air soupy. A kitchen, table and chairs, dishes washed and stacked, the humming of the fridge. A worn shit-brown couch declares the space to the left of the kitchen as the living room. *Maybe the TV is humming too,* I think. Maybe all the appliances in this place are trying to hum me a message, like, *Leave while you can . . .*

I wonder if I should call out. I don't want to jump-scare Mom into the next life by shouting. But maybe she went back to sleep? She did say chemo went long, and that sounds bad. *Of course it's bad,* my brain yells at me. Stage III cancer is the definition of bad.

I creep to the door on the other side of the kitchen and open it. Thankfully, an empty bedroom, tidy and bland. Must be mine. I put my duffel on the bed and take off my shoes, remembering too late that Mom hates shoes worn inside. This whole experience is going to be one crappy memory train after the other, isn't it?

I text Mom again.

> I'm here! Can I get you anything?
> I don't want to wake you up if you're resting. Want food?

I'm assuming there's food or drink in the house that I could get for her. Or medicine? I wait for her to respond to my text, but it sits there, unread. I plug my phone in and take out the bottle of water I refilled at the bus terminal's water station. Honestly, this water tastes like money. It's clean and cold and it doesn't have any funky aftertaste. You need money to get water to taste like that.

I dig around in my backpack and pull out the neat little box I've handled so often. I tie my hair back with one of the many black hair bands that have migrated to my wrists and open the box of cards. The case is worn and slightly fuzzed from years of hands touching it. The original illustrations—coins, cups, swords, and clubs—are faded away. This baraja española belonged to Abuela's great-grandmother; when it was new, the family lived in a part of Mexico that became Texas. The scent from all those hands spills out, oldest to most recent, like flipping through a photo album of Abuela's life, and I can smell her, a combination of sweat and sugar and hierbas, like falling asleep in an herb garden. My stomach hurts with missing her.

I shuffle and deal: The as de copas is the past card. That makes sense—the ace of cups is stability and home—definitely in the past. I turn over another card and place it to the right of the first. El cuatro de espadas. I can't remember what the four means in this suit, but swords are generally sucky. I'll have to ask Abuela. I place a third card to the right of the four of swords to represent the future, and sigh. It's the same card Abuela pulled for me before I left home.

"El siete de copas, Sebastián. Do you remember what that means?" she'd asked me from her bed as I waited, packed and ready, for Papi to drive me to the bus station.

"Something kinda good?" I'd guessed. Cups were often related to love or good luck, but it didn't matter much. The point of getting Abuela to read the Spanish cards was to spend more time with her and, if I could, make her smile.

"Happy things, yes," she'd said. "After a difficult beginning." She stabbed a swollen brown finger at the seven of cups. "Yo sé that it won't be easy, mijo. But in the end, it will be a good thing."

I scoop the three cards up, shuffle them back into the box, and stash them under my pillow. A deck of antiquated cards is about as effective a tool for guessing the future as a flipped coin or a fortune cookie. I know that. But if the cards are good enough for Abuela, they're good enough for me. Besides, no one can know my future now that I'm—temporarily—living with Mom. It doesn't matter. Mom asked me to come and help her. Abuela wanted me to do this, so this is what I'll do. No matter how much Mom hates me.

2

Lu

I'm asleep and the next second I'm awake, like I was never asleep at all, blinking away the image of the dream I was stuck in until the alarm rescued me.

I pull my phone out from under my pillow, turn off the alarm, and open the Notes app.

People made of dust
In a building made of memories
Single file, lining up to speak—on a jade phone
Connecting them to no one

Ugh. The dream was so vivid, so immersive, and my words just *aren't*. I've been writing poetry for years, but I still have to remind myself to let new words be new—and imperfect.

I promised Mamá I wouldn't sleep with my phone under my pillow, and routinely break that promise, though I feel bad about it. She worries about the experimental phones. *What if they start a fire? If the glass cracks, splinters?* She's heard, from one of her cousins in Colonia, that the chemicals in the phones that make them so fast, so responsive, are corrosive to human tissue.

But the phone doesn't look like trouble in my hand. It looks like it belongs there. I'd never admit it to Diego or Kenzie, but if I can't sleep, if I'm teetering on the edge of an anxiety—*episode, Lu, call them episodes*—I'll skim my fingers across the surface of the phone. It feels glossy, and surprisingly warm for glass. Just touching it makes me feel better, and that—plus two trazodones a night—means I can sleep.

I haven't had a curl-up-and-die panic attack since middle school. When thirteen-year-old me sat across from my therapist for the first time, I didn't know how to talk about the full-body paralysis that took me over when I reached peak anxiety. I didn't think she'd believe me when I said I couldn't physically move my arms or legs, no matter what my brain said. But Dr. Allyson did believe me. She told me to imagine what my anxiety looked like, to give it a name. Nerdy, D&D-loving kid that I was, I described a dragon living in my stomach, whiplike tail with barbed spikes, and claws that razored their way through my insides. I called my dragon Nightmare—no originality points when you're thirteen. I've left that pudgy, bespectacled eighth grader far behind. That's entirely due to meds, therapy, and TECH.

My phone pings with the usual reminder to take my meds, and my calendar updates with school news—assignments, ambassador duties, the lunch menu. In the bathroom, I pee, brush my teeth and my Invisalign, and wet my hair so the curls can bounce back to life. Only then do I allow myself to check texts.

Müthafocker, u op?

Diego's a master at creative spelling since his cheap AF data plan means he has to be careful with his words, or he'll be back on cafeteria duty to work off his word debt.

Cannot help teasing him as I type: **Yes I Am. Alive, AWAKE ALERT ENTHUSIASTIC! Yours truly, Lu Williams Hernandez, ESQ.**

Diego responds with a photo of himself wearing an eye-watering yellow hoodie with an Águilas Cibaeñas logo. He's rebleached the ends of his tight curls so they almost match the color of the hoodie.

Do U think K will like?

I could explain that no amount of new clothes, no hair color change, is going to make Kenzie like him more than as a friend. Instead, I give his photo a thumbs-up emoji. Even at the beginning of the month, I'm not gonna waste that many words explaining something so obvious.

At the bottom of my phone screen, the indicator shows a full word-data bank. Reality will kick me en el culo come the end of the month, like it always does, when I'll barely have enough word data left to utter **OK**. But I don't care. First of the month always feels . . . *plush*. I open Notes, then add *plush* to my Poetry Words dump file before going back to messages and composing a text for Kenzie. Only, she sends one first.

You know I don't care about your massive . . .

I crack a smile in the blue-green light of the phone, waiting.

. . . Data plan . . . we having breakfast today or wha?

I thumb a response, not bothering to tease Kenzie with expensive words.

There's a New Student ☺

Ohhh! Details porfa!

Nothing yet, will keep you informed, Ma'am. Cn you pick me up? Mamá is driving church ppl somewhere boring.

Sure. 45min. Gonna get beautiful first.

Not possible, I send—then panic: Would Kenzie think I'm saying it's not possible for her to be beautiful? I rub my face. I meant that Kenzie was already beautiful. *Fuck,* I think, and I'm so glad that, at least in my own brain, words are free.

I stand in front of the sink, typing, erasing, typing, trying to explain, when another text from Kenzie pops up.

Stop overthinking—45min.

I text Diego that Kenzie's taking us to school today and walk back to my room to get dressed. It's habit now to slide the phone back under my pillow before changing. I don't know for sure that TECH can activate the camera on the phone remotely. That's another thing Mamá is always muttering about. Diego says it too, but Diego watches right-wing news with his dad sometimes. I've heard a few kids at school say it, but I don't believe it. Still, the phone stays under the pillow for this part of the morning. *When in doubt, hedge your bets* is the Williams Hernandez family motto.

I open the closet doors wide to show the entirety of available choices, everything from basic jeans to a shirtdress I bought in a fit of genderfluid optimism, but that hasn't felt right to wear yet. First school day of the month, and I've gotten a message that a new student starts today. That means I'm on ambassador duty. Diego calls it asshat or dork duty, depending on how much of his word data he's used up. I can easily ignore being called an asshat or dork—I've been called much worse. And if wanting to look extra nice as the representative of everything TECH means I'm being an *asshat*, so be it.

The button-down navy shirt with tiny rainbow ice cream cones—a Pride gift from Dad from a few years back—seems welcoming, and I pair it with chinos, cuffs rolled up just once, no-show socks, and ochre checked Vans. That leaves the last ten minutes I've allotted to the morning routine to make the bed and tidy up.

I grab my phone and check the time: two minutes ahead of schedule—I'm that good. I put my hand on my bedroom door and reach for the gold-plated ambassador pin that sits in a glass candy dish with an assortment of buttons, earring studs, and tiny batteries—but it's not there.

I know I put it there on Friday after school. I always put it there. It can't be anywhere else because I always put it there. The first wave of panic—a sharp jolt that feels like stepping into nothing—hits me hard because my brain can't get out of the loop—*I always put it there; it's not there; I always put it there.*

I know I'm supposed to move on to logic—where was the last place I saw it? What are the steps I need to take? But I've never been able to grab on to logic that way.

I press my hands into the dresser, feeling the painted wood grain, waiting for the dizziness to pass. I breathe because my stupid brain can remember that, at least. Longer breaths calm a racing heart. *Why am I like this?*

Ask Mamá, my drowning brain finally spits out. It's an idea I can hold on to. Maybe she found the gold pin in the wash and put it somewhere safe. I open the bedroom door like it's costing me word data—only to find Ofelia three inches from my chest.

"Personal space, Felia," I breathe out. I'm not wasting words on my little nemesis.

"Good morning, goon squad," Felia says, bowing elaborately.

Curiosity distracts my anxiety for a second—it works like that sometimes—and I tumble out more words.

"What the hell's a goon squad?"

"I don't know." She shrugs. "I read it in one of Dad's books. I read some of the book, too, out loud. To Gato." Ofelia peeks through her tangle of dark hair, waiting to see if she's managed to annoy me.

I keep my mouth shut, something Ofelia doesn't know how to do.

"Then I talked to the plants in the garden. You know, scientists say that talking to plants makes them thrive. You can talk to them, and they'll actually grow bigger. Well, *you* can't talk to them. Mami said you have to be more careful with your word budget this month, since you overspent. Again."

"Eavesdropper," I say curtly.

"Not my fault you guys are so loud."

You're a twerp, a pest, you're the best argument for birth control—just some of the words I wish I could say. But there's no point engaging with the little grub, so I shrug and toss the hair from my eyes. Then I see the gold ambassador pin, ludicrously stuck to the middle of Ofelia's T-shirt. The dragon claws release my insides, and relief floods through me.

"Hey! Personal space, pendeje!" Ofelia shrieks as I grab at the pin, undo the backing, and pin it onto my shirt.

"Ladrona," I say quietly, knowing that Ofelia won't understand the Spanish word for thief.

"*Mamá*," Ofelia shouts, a torrent of accusation and embellished wrongdoing rushing out behind her as she runs down the hallway.

Now I'm late to meet Kenzie in the driveway, but I take a minute to check everything is where I need it—then one more look in the mirror to make sure I'm ready. Last time I saw Dr. Allyson in her office, she told me that I treated my appearance like armor. She said it like it was a bad thing.

Downstairs, Felia is complaining to Mamá, who sits on the living room floor packing boxes with donated items for the food pantry.

"Está lloriqueando," I say, moving around Felia to kiss Mamá good morning.

"STOP!" Felia screams, crocodile tears in her eyes.

"Basta," Mamá echoes, "don't tease her with words she doesn't understand."

I hold up my hands. "Just trying to save my word data. Lo siento," I say, completely *un*sorry to have called out her whining. I can talk to Mamá in Spanish all day long and my data won't budge. TECH keeps saying it will start charging for words in foreign languages in the next update, but it hasn't happened yet.

"You never believe me," Felia croaks, stamping her foot. "Lu grabbed me, look, it's all red." She points to three faint marks on her neck. I bet the little actress scratched herself to prove a point—I wouldn't put it past her.

"God help you, Felia, when you turn twelve and actually have to think about what you say before you say it." I pick up an apple from the bowl on the counter and take a bite, more so Mamá sees me eating than because I'm hungry.

"When I get TECH, I'm gonna get the newest biosensor and I'm gonna get *more* words than you do and then you won't be able to boss me around and be so mean!"

"Calma, amores," Mamá says, closing and taping the last box of food. "When you get your phone, menina, you'll have the same restrictions Lu has."

"But I'll get free food and go to the movies and I can go bowling and hang out with all my friends whenever I want!"

What friends? The sarcastic words sit on my tongue, begging to come out. But that's just a knee-jerk reaction. I can save my words for better use.

3

Sebas

I'm wearing my emergency shirt. The dark gray one Papá gave me two years ago for Christmas. It was giant then, now the cuffs are a little short. It doesn't wrinkle, repels smoke and stains, and can get me through everything from funerals to quinceañeras (if I borrow one of Papi's ironic bolo ties) to, today, an eagle-eyed inspection from Mom.

But she isn't up yet, so I put on my favorite movie podcast, *Unspooled*, and make coffee. This episode is about *Men in Black*, which honestly is an all right movie, for all the crap I give Papi about it. I mean, it's his favorite because of the talking pug, so not for any good reason. The scent of coffee fills the little kitchen, and I retain my title of cafecito king because I am able to make a decent cup of coffee with dried-up beans I found in the cupboard and a Mr. Coffee bought in the 1970s.

I check the time on my phone and get sidetracked—a message from Abuela, two texts from Papá worried about me, and an AI video of bunnies eating strawberries from Hudson, which he says is guaranteed to make me laugh. It doesn't. I answer Abuela y Pa with emojis because it's easier, and anyway, how can I tell them that I expect to be Status: Fucked for the foreseeable future? I told them I could do this, and I can.

Two cups down and Mom still isn't up. I stand outside Mom's bedroom door, then nudge it open, expecting her to shout at me any minute. But there's only the sound of a fan. Blackout curtains hung over the window by strips of silver electric tape blot out all daylight. The shape under the covers on the bed is tiny, like a little kid.

"Mom?"

There's no answer. I have to move closer. I'm not a neat person; bouncing around the country these last few years meant I learned it's faster not to bother putting things away. But Mom used to be fanatical about cleanliness—not now. Clothing sits in piles on the floor, and the room smells like weed and sweat.

I stand next to the fan that's blowing directly onto the huddled figure on the bed. Mom doesn't move. I can't tell if she's still breathing, and it's a terrifying thought that almost sends me running.

As I washed dishes the night before I left home, I strained to hear Papi y Abuela arguing—again.

She's too sick for a seventeen-year-old kid to help—it's only going to scare him.

He's stronger than you think, Hernán. What else does he have to do, other than be there and hold her hand? She is alone.

She's alone because she pushed everyone else away.

Sea razonable, mijo. If she wants to make amends with her son, we should help her do that.

Is that what she wants, Mami? Or does she just want to treat her kid like a servant?

No sé, mijo. But even if that were so, she asked for help. Let him do what he can. She is his mamá, no matter what...

What if I've come all this way and Mom is already gone? What if I'm too late?

I turn off the fan, and a second later, Mom's eyes pop open.

"What the hell, Sebastian?"

As a greeting, it's pretty on the money.

"Ma. I thought—" What am I supposed to say? *I thought you were dead*? That isn't the kind of thing you say to someone with cancer.

"I thought I should wake you. Make sure you ate something."

Mom burrows deeper into the covers. "Not hungry."

"But, Ma..."

"Not hungry, dammit. The guy from holy meddlers keeps bringing me Mexican food instead of real, healthy food I can stomach. Then he sits here and makes me talk to him, tries to get me to eat like I'm an imbecile. That's not the kind of help I need, you get me?"

"Yeah. So what do you need?"

"Turn on the damn fan, for one. My face is on fire." I switch the fan back on, full force, and wait.

"Get yourself to that fancy school and sign up for all the things you're supposed to sign up for. That's all the help I need from you, *chico*."

When Mom says *chico,* or any other Spanish word, she makes it sound like a curse.

I turn to leave.

"Wait," Mom croaks. I stop. "You need food for you. Get

yourself something from the dollar store. There's ten bucks taped under the drawer near the fridge." She turns back to face the fan. Those are all the words I'm getting from her.

It wasn't Doug driving the violet tram today. Same hipster shirt-shorts one-piece, same first-name tag (BRENDA), same cheesy greeting. At least it was a quick drive, and only a few people were on the tram with me. Also, Brenda dropped me directly in front of the school and pointed to the signs that would get me to the office, where I'm sitting now, waiting for, I don't know, judgment? A hall pass? Boredom to kill me? My phone is acting like a total bastard, no bars, endlessly loading. I wish I had a book. I wish I had internet so I could text Anaïs that I just thought, *I wish I had a book.* She's constantly trying to get me to read, and I'm constantly dodging her efforts. Film: It's the superior art form.

Next to me is a brown, sullen-looking girl with long black hair wearing a Selena T-shirt. She's got a working phone, at least, but her leg tapping is getting on my nerves.

"Sebastian?"

I look up and my eyes track immediately to the gold name tag—twenty-four hours, and this city's got me trained so goddamn well.

LU HERNANDEZ
(THEY/THEM/THEIRS)

Lu Hernandez is tall, white, kinda angular, with curly gold

hair that's buzzed on the sides, longer in front, the tips a faded green. I stand up.

"Sebas is fine."

"Oh, cool. I'm Lu. I'm the TECH High ambassador, you know, like your kindergarten school buddy, but less embarrassing and with better manners." They point to their name tag. "My pronouns are they/them/theirs."

"Yeah, right. My pronouns are he/him, uh—"

"His?" Lu supplies.

"Right. His. Okay. So, what do we do now?" Jesus. I sound stoned.

"Now I introduce you to the magic of TECH. You will be amazed, astounded, and the envy of all the kids back home."

"You sound like you sell used cars in Florida," I say. Which they do. Exactly like Darius, who used to play bass in Dad's old punk band but now fast-talks people out of their cash.

"What an extremely specific observation." Lu holds open the glass door. "After you."

Next to the school office is another office. Lu angles their phone over a scanner and the door pops open.

"Is this security?" I ask. Maybe I need to take a drug test or a background check before being allowed to start school. I'm brown enough that I usually do get asked my citizenship.

"No, it's TECH."

"I thought this whole school was called TECH?"

"This is TECH High School, but TECH is the company that founded the high school."

Lu smiles at the receptionist, who waves cheerfully back.

"A company owns the school?"

"A company owns the town."

I'm halfway through nodding when I stop. "That's not—Wait, what?"

Lu stops outside of what looks like a storage closet.

"This will go a lot faster if you save your questions for the end."

Lu lets the reader on the lock scan their phone again. Inside, it looks like the caged area of a wholesale club I worked at once.

Behind the wire lockup are rows and rows of matte black boxes, all identical. Lu pulls open the cage door and picks one up, using their phone to scan a barely perceptible QR code on the side. Lu hands me the box like they're doing me a favor.

"Welcome to your future," they say, amping up their perfect smile impossibly, all the way to eleven.

We take the elevator to the top of the building, and now we're walking down a sort of spirally wraparound ramp.

Everyone, and I mean every kid, teacher, janitor, and random person we pass, takes a minute to smile, wave, or fistbump Lu Hernandez. The kid is crazy popular and manages to acknowledge everyone's greetings while continuing to yammer on about this TECH nonsense.

"We have a really successful internship program with Pixar—do you like animation?" Lu asks.

"I'm more of a Studio Ghibli kind of guy," I mutter.

"Oh, cool, yeah, well, we'd like to do some kind of exchange program with Japan, like, you know, a knowledge share with their students and ours, but it's kind of hard to work with other animation studios when you've already built a relationship with Pixar, like, we don't want to offend anyone."

"No, definitely not," I say, completely and blissfully zoning out, with a sprinkling of mumbles and head nods to keep things smooth. At one point, while Lu is showing me the gymnasium and explaining "mixed-use maximization," I just watch their hands. When Lu talks, they use their whole body, shoulders arching, hands moving through the air in front of them, like they're trying to fold their words into logic.

"It's modeled on the Guggenheim," Lu says a few minutes later, when they notice me looking down the spiral ramp back to where this trip to nowhere started. I'm getting hungry, so I nearly go down on bended knee to praise Jesus when I smell pizza.

"Next stop is the gourmet cafeteria," Lu says perkily. All their words have been sunny or knowing or jolly. For a pretty cute individual, they are just *cheesy*.

"Good, I'm starving," I say, and move to walk toward the doors at the end of the open gallery that I realize, now that I've been all over this place, is on the other side of the school office. Gourmet or whatnot, I don't care. I see food and people eating the food. That's good enough for me. Silence would be good too, but that's not going to happen with Lu Hernandez.

They put an arm out in front of me, blocking me like they're saving me from accidentally falling down a well.

"Before we go eat, I just want to make sure you don't have any questions."

"About?"

A little exasperation crosses their face, and actually? It's the first honest expression I've seen on this kid's face.

"You know—TECH, the way it works, the system. I mean, if you have questions after today, no worries, I got you, you can text me and ask away. And there are a ton of explainer videos on the school intranet if anything is tricky, but I know the system inside and out, so, um, that might be, like, easier?"

It's like watching a windup toy—like the ones Pa used to put in my Easter basket, little plastic chicks or bunnies—slow down and finally stop. Gracias a Dios, Lu Hernandez has run out of words to throw at me.

"Not gonna use it, so I'm good."

I move around their outstretched arm toward, hopefully, cheese fries.

4

Lu

Today was supposed to be a good day. But Felia stealing my ambassador pin this morning set everything to wrong. I've got the right words ready to go, I'm smiling, I'm making jokes, I'm pointing out all the amazing things about TECH—the animation studio, the Olympic-sized pool complex, the student lounge. Nothing is making an impact. I haven't hooked the new kid yet.

"Is sighing free?" Sebastian—no, Sebas—asks.

"What? Yeah. Um. All noises and onomatopoeia-type sounds are free. Why?"

"Because you keep doing that sighing thing, and I feel like I'm costing you a lot of money. But if it's free, like, go ahead. Groan if you're feeling it."

I pull at my hair, then push the curls behind my ear. I don't want him to think I'm stressed, but I freaking *am*. I've walked him around the school all morning—nothing makes a dent in this boy. He's not a theater kid—the outdoor amphitheater doesn't impress him at all. Neither do the gender-neutral bathrooms or the multicultural lab. I'm missing some important information about him, the thing that will make his eyes light up.

I love that moment, when a new student sees the part of TECH that speaks to them. Sometimes it's a perk; sometimes it's the realization that words really do matter here. Sometimes it's just me being kind to them, letting them know I get it. I love to see it dawn on them that at TECH, they'll be safe.

I hate it when it doesn't work.

I mentally give myself a shake—I just need to get him to the cafeteria, where the burden of talking to him can fall on someone else for a while. I'm smiling so aggressively, my cheeks hurt. This has never been so hard. At least my word count is frozen—explaining the TECH system is word-heavy. That's the only positive thing about today.

"So if I send, like, a cat meme with words on it to a friend, do those words count?" Sebas asks.

"Words that are incorporated into an image aren't yet tracked, as they're seen as pictures, but they're working on changing that." I'm pretty sure I answered this question already, or one like it. Maybe the fact that he has so many questions is a good thing? But Sebas hasn't put on the biosensor yet or even taken the phone out of the box—even though I've tried to give it to him a couple of times, somehow I ended up carrying it again.

"Huh," he says, then shoots me an inquiring look.

"Doesn't count. It's a sound, not a word."

"But you can read *huh* in a book—doesn't that make it a word?"

I shrug. "You can read *AAARRRRGGGG!* in a book too. Still makes it a sound. Look, I know this system must seem a little much at first, but you'll get the hang of it."

"No doubt."

We're outside the doors to the cafeteria, and I have to put my arm out to stop him from barreling past me.

"Before we go eat, I just want to make sure you don't have any questions."

"About?"

Is he for real? I'm really glad I'm wearing this dark navy shirt—my pits are definitely sweat-stained. Maybe this is a kind of ambassador pop quiz, to see if I know my stuff?

"You know—TECH, the way it works, the system. I mean, if you have questions after today, no worries, I got you, you can text me and ask away. And there are a ton of explainer videos on the school intranet if anything is tricky, but I know the system inside and out, so, um, that might be, like, easier?"

He looks at me. Just looks. The few seconds of silence seem endless. Is there something else I need to say? Something I forgot to mention?

"Not gonna use it, so I'm good," he says, moving around me to get into the cafeteria.

I know I must look ridiculous, standing there como idiota, mouth half-open. I've never had anyone say no. People complain, sure. And I get asked what the most expensive word is, or if Elvish words count (they don't; any made-up language, even made up by Tolkien, doesn't count). When Diego transferred to TECH last year, he pestered me with stupid questions until I nearly screamed.

But I've never had anyone turn TECH, turn *me*, down.

I enter the cafeteria like nothing's happened, because nothing *has* happened.

He turned you down, a voice says in my head. It's ridiculous. He didn't turn *me* down, he turned TECH down. That's not the same thing. But I can't get past the idea that it must have been because of me.

I scan the line looking for Kenzie. Unlike me, she likes to be "surprised" by her lunch, so no ordering ahead for her.

She finds me first. "You're six seconds off your schedule, amor. You good?" Kenzie says, balancing her tray of zucchini fries and a vegan panini.

"New student made me late," I say, still trying to process the thought of someone at TECH not having word restrictions. What's that even like?

"Do you like my new haircut?" she asks.

"It's nice," I say, barely looking at her.

"I haven't cut my hair; that was a test. You failed."

I make myself look at my best friend. Same shoulder-length black hair, same razor-sharp bangs.

"You did cut your bangs a little," I guess.

She nods. "Nice save. So, what's their deal?" Kenzie asks.

"¿Qué?"

Kenzie cocks her head. "New student. Nice, weird, cool, unbalanced, boring, or other?"

"Definitely other. He/him pronouns."

"¿Y?" Diego says, coming up behind Kenzie. He's trying to learn Spanish from Kenzie, who also speaks Korean and can read a little Portuguese. She has a gift for languages, while Diego has a gift for getting into trouble. He complains that his Latino blood is failing him—right out of Spanish II.

We find seats at a table that Isobel and her boyfriend, Micah, are just vacating. Kenzie kicks me under the table, for old times' sake, in a move I interpret as meaning *she's still hot* and *the one that got away* and *ha ha, girls, amirite?* Kenzie knows all my crushes, big and small. We even dated a little freshman year. When Kenzie broke up with me because she liked someone else, I was happy to still be her friend.

A sophomore wearing an apron with the TECH logo on it brings me my lunch. I never feel like eating, but Mamá insists on ordering. I don't really feel hunger, except on the weekends when I don't have to take my ADHD medicine. But I eat because it's what I'm supposed to do. I thank the sophomore and tap the happy face on my phone for good service. I don't want her to get in trouble. She's working at the cafeteria to either make up for a word infraction or save up more word data. Diego's done it before when he's burned through his data and his parents wouldn't pay for more words. Kenzie is too careful for that to happen to her. And I rely heavily on the Spanish Mamá taught me the year I was homeschooled. Still, kitchen duty is always one expletive-laden tirade away.

"The new kid didn't take the TECH," I say as casually as I can.

The silence from Kenzie and Diego would be deafening, but it's already pretty quiet in the cafeteria.

"¿Qué?" Diego manages to choke out.

I unwrap my lunch: chicken katsu with rice, spicy mayo sauce, and bonito flakes, all the things I like on a good day. Not today. My anxiety spins.

"Can he say no?" Kenzie asks.

I try to shrug it off. "I mean, he can do what he wants, but I don't think it's gonna stick."

"Maybe you didn't explain it right?" Diego says, giving

voice to the exact worry that's burning through my stomach. I push my lunch away.

"Shut up, pendejo," Kenzie says.

"Hey!" Diego yelps.

"Both of you, cállense, just, don't make a big deal about it," I say. The cafeteria has huge windows that look out over the compact green lawns, laid out like a New England college quad. I happen to know that the lush green grass is watered with reclaimed wastewater and that the amphitheater that Sebas barely looked at was modeled after a famous Roman ruin in Wales. I stare at it because it's beautiful and soothing, and the whole TECH campus, and everyone on it, is connected to each other and to TECH. Except Sebastian Ascencio.

"You peeping for Callan?" Diego says, mentioning an Asian boy I think I said had cute hair once. Diego can't stand silence. It's one of the reasons he's always maxing out his word data. If it's quiet for too long, he has to open his mouth, pour out syllables, choosing words he hopes will confuse the word tracker.

"Yeah, man, always peeping, you know the vibes," I say. After school today, at the pep rally, we get to scream our lungs out and watch center forward Callan, the rest of the basketball team, the cheer squad, and anyone else. *It will be fun,* I tell myself sternly so I'll believe it. But I can't stop thinking of Sebas saying no, walking away, unconcerned.

5

Sebas

"Do you know where the dollar store is?" I ask the driver at a yellow tram stop.

Lu told me I could get to the discount store if I took the yellow tram. But what if they're punking me because I turned down the tech? The look on their face when I said no was nearly satisfying, except I could tell they were hurt too. Like I'd turned *them* down, not this stupid school. My deeply patchy phone reception—not a single bar, like permanent airplane mode—meant I stood outside school forever trying to figure out directions. Lu asked me if I needed help, which was them being kind, or them being a Stepford kid, doing what was required of them. I don't know. I'm an asshole sometimes.

"I think the yellow tram will take you nearest, but you could ask any tram driver. They're all really nice," Lu had said, as if being nice was what I was looking for.

The tram driver nods. "Yup. I can take you there." And it's such a relief that he's just normal nice, not saccharine sweet, that I genuinely smile. "Since you're the only one here, it'll take about ten minutes," he says.

I sit and put my backpack on the floor between my feet, like I always do on public transportation. Which is ridiculous, trying to protect my junk on a spotless, empty tram in a town where everyone has more money than me.

The tram driver, name-tagged JAMES, puts on some music. Classical, the kind that people who don't know anything about classical music play. Vivaldi. It reminds me of a commercial for a plastic surgeon that used to be on repeat when I was little, watching telenovelas with Abuela, waiting for hours for Mom to come pick me up. Most of the time, she just forgot. I'd sleep in Abuela's bed, tucked under her arm, surrounded by the smell of the herbs she grew and then turned into stews, medicines, and magic.

I touch the baraja española in my bag, just for the comfort, then pull out my phone to watch the short video I made of Abuela doing una tirada de cartas. It's just her hands moving deftly through the meanings of each card, what they represent for most people, and what they meant for *me*. I want to turn it into something eventually, something creative that will make other people feel the way I do when I see her, when I hear her gravel-and-honey voice, sometimes with a cough, sometimes with a laugh.

"Here you go," James says, stopping the tram and opening the door. "This is the New Gault city limit. No other tram stops further out."

I see the blinding yellow sign of the dollar store a few blocks away—and not much else.

"Thank you," I say, getting off the tram.

"No problem. I'll be here when you come out. Doubt anyone else will need the tram."

I turn back to him. "No one uses it?"

James shrugs. "Well, let's just say that it's not as useful as TECH thought it would be."

Twenty-four hours in this real-life Stepford has confirmed my worst suspicions: New Gault is a glittering bubble, protecting its immaculate self from the grubby presence of discount chain stores and people like me and Mom. It isn't being subtle about it.

The dollar store is almost like being home with Papá y Abuela. Not that Abuela would ever let me buy any actual food at a discount store. That's what the outdoor mercado is for. But the off-brand shampoos and batteries are just as good as the fancy ones.

I hunt up and down the aisles looking for things that might tempt Mom. I can't remember what Mom used to eat. Even when Mom took me out for a special treat, I'd eat; Mom would smoke.

What do cancer patients eat? I pull out my phone again to do a search before remembering that it's a useless piece of crap—and then realize that it's working now. Eight messages pop up—from Anaïs, Pa, and Hudson. I send quick replies to all messages, letting them know I'm fine, somewhat annoyed, and safe, and in a weird place with sucky cell service. I send the last message to Anaïs, including a photo I take of a dented can of SPAM, literally because it's right in front of me, then start to fill my basket.

Memorial Sloan Kettering has a list of foods that can help cancer patients experiencing mouth sores. Is that Mom? What about constipation? The lists are categorized by symptoms, and other than knowing she's exhausted and in pain, I don't know what her symptoms are like.

An article about eating while on chemo is the best I can do. I pick knockoff fruity gelatin cups in green apple and blackberry, applesauce with cinnamon, beef stew with carrots and baby onions in a little tin with a pull tab. There's no fresh fruit or veg anywhere, but at least this food is cheap, and there's a chance Mom will eat some of it.

I buy lemon-scented shampoo and conditioner, and a cool notebook with flamingos on the cover. It reminds me of being in Florida for the summer while Papi worked on a hotel building site four years ago. I saw flamingos on cars, on lawns, on signs, and on clothes. Not one real flamingo in three months.

Mom watches me as I take the groceries out of the bags. I can't tell if it's because she doesn't trust me or because she's hungry—or maybe something else entirely that I can't even guess. I ball up the plastic bags and shove them under the sink.

"Okay, Ma. What looks good?"

For a second, I think she's gonna laugh. Nothing looks good. On the kitchen table is a collection of mismatched cans—some needing a can opener, which I hope to God Mom has—some with pull tabs. At least Mom has a working microwave.

I watch her skin-and-bones arm reach out over the can collection and tap once on a can of beef stew before turning her face away, as if it makes her sick.

I pick up the other cans and put them away. Then, with exaggerated care because Mom is watching, I open the beef stew, pour the contents into a glass bowl, and add a little water to the mess. It smells like salt and aluminum and maybe carrots? I guess I'm just spoiled. Until Abuela's stroke, every great meal I've ever had came from her hands. Eating out isn't that much of a treat for me and Papá when, as Abuela likes to remind us, there is comida en casa.

"How was school?" Mom croaks, clears her throat, then repeats herself. I turn on the microwave.

"Good. Fine. You know. First-day stuff."

Mom pulls out her vape pen and sets it on the table, then readjusts the soft purple hat that envelops her head.

"Did you get everything you were supposed to get?"

I think about the day I had. First with the phone Lu tried to pawn off on me, then with the e-signs in the hallways flashing daily affirmations and upcoming events, like goat yoga and conflict resolution classes and meditation in the nondenominational chapel. Then there was the slightly creepy silence. Most kids I saw had their faces in their phones, but almost no one talked unless it was about school, a subject they were learning, or something completely boring like "How are you?" or "Need help finding your classes?" Lots of people went out of their way to say hello to me, followed by "This school is eco-certified by the state of California as a green zone," or "Have you visited the sleep lab?" What kind of bullshit is a sleep lab?

When I asked about class assignments or readings, or literally anything else that might clue me in to what I actually need to know (i.e., not goat yoga), I was told that I'd get all that with my TECH suite of tools, whatever the hell that means.

"Yeah," I say, remembering to answer Mom. "I got everything I needed. It's a really nice school," I add, knowing she wants to hear my appreciation.

"It's the best damn school in the country," she wheezes. The wheezing leads to her taking a hit from her vape pen. Thin vapor balloons out, so unlike cigarette smoke, smelling like every gig Papi has ever dragged me to. There's no way vaping is good for a cancer patient. But catch me telling Ma that? No fear.

The microwave beeps, and I take out the glass bowl, giving it a stir and testing the temp against my wrist, something I learned from babysitting my primo Marcelo.

I add some saltines to the plate next to the soup, then put it on the table in front of Mom. She rolls her shoulders as if her zip-up sweatshirt is too tight on her, but it hangs off her like it belongs to someone bigger, healthier.

"What about you?" Mom asks, laying a paper napkin on her lap.

"I'll eat some of what God's Love We Deliver dropped off. You know, the Mexican shit you hate," I say, hoping it comes off as funny, not sharp. But she doesn't notice. She spoons stew into her mouth.

"How's your grandma?" she asks.

"She's better. Dad says she'll be back on her feet, cooking up a storm, by summertime."

"Your grandma is a good woman," Mom says like it's costing her to compliment Abuela.

I just nod.

"She'd make sure to switch to English when I was in the room, unlike the rest of your family. They'd just yap, yap, yap away in Spanish, talking shit about me." She eats another spoonful of stew.

"She even tried to teach me to cook once. Was real decent to me when no one else bothered." I keep quiet. "You're a real conversationalist, huh?"

"When does God's Love We Deliver usually come?" I ask, changing the subject. If I can get them to deliver some American-type food, Mom would be 10 percent less bitchy.

She eats another spoonful, then pushes the bowl away.

"Unfortunately, they come when you're at school, or else I'd make *you* talk to them."

"They don't just drop the food off?"

"Oh, I wish. I have to sit here and talk to them. Be nice."

I snort, then try to turn it into a cough.

"You think I can't be nice?"

"I didn't say that."

"I can be nice. I used to be nice for a fucking living."

I don't ask what she means, she's gonna tell me anyway.

"When I worked at the Marriott at the marina, remember? Had to be nice to everyone, especially the assholes." She eats a saltine. "Remember?"

I dimly remember being little, visiting her at work, standing behind a desk I couldn't see over, and playing with a plastic bin filled with tiny bottles of shampoo and body wash. I used them like blocks to build houses. I don't remember her being that nice. At least not to me.

"Yeah. I remember."

Mom eats one more saltine, and maybe we're both remembering, but very different things.

"Okay. I'm going to sleep," she says suddenly, dragging herself up from the chair and leaving the nearly full bowl of cold stew on the table. I wait until Mom's shut her bedroom door before I toss the stew in the trash. Abuela would say it's a sin to throw out food. She'd also say that this isn't what she'd call food.

I wash the bowl, then take out one of Mom's charity meals—chicken enchiladas—and heat that up. I eat as slowly as I can, in a sort of fog. It's only seven o'clock. Connectivity is better on this side of the bubble, but still patchy, so no streaming movies. I download as many podcasts as I can, even though download speeds are throttled to a crawl. This is some bullshit here. Obviously New Gault has the best of everything—but one mile out of New Gault, it's a wasteland.

I check to make sure the door to Mom's bedroom is still closed, then take out the cartas españolas. Might as well ask the universe what straight-up fuckery awaits me tomorrow. And if Lu Hernandez, with the green-tipped curls and constantly moving hands, will be leading me around like they did today. Weirdly, I wouldn't hate that.

6

Lu

I stand in front of Sebastian's desk before first period as Mrs. Marseglia looks on. Teachers don't technically have to come in this early—there's an educational package that plays every morning for thirty minutes instead—but Mrs. Marseglia always does. I think it's because she's new and not yet used to how TECH does things differently. I don't really want her to watch me work, but I can't say that, so I push back my hair and square my shoulders. I messed up yesterday, I know that. But today is a new chance. I *have* to get Sebastian—Sebas—to see all the benefits of TECH. I have to get him to say yes.

Sebas is doodling on the cover of a magazine, *Digital Filmmaker*, a chaotic jumble of equipment glamour shots. He draws stars over the words LOCATION MAGIC. I fake-cough to get his attention.

"I know you're there," he says without looking up. "I'm just waiting for you to say something."

"And I'm waiting for you to acknowledge me." It comes out prim and annoyed, but I can't help that.

"I'm just playing with you." He smiles up through a curtain of black hair. It's the kind of smile that you don't see coming. The kind with a hook in it, catching my attention even when I don't want to be caught. Better just get it over with. I put the TECH box on Sebas's desk and watch his smile evaporate. It's almost eight. I've got minutes to close the deal.

"I guess I didn't do it right yesterday," he says.

"Do what right?"

"Say no to you. Sometimes that happens, so let me try again." He looks at me, not breaking eye contact for a full thirty seconds, even as people start to walk into the classroom, and my stomach flutters.

"I don't want the thing you're trying to give me. I won't take it, and I won't count words. I am super grateful—not really, but I figure it doesn't hurt to be polite—for the offer. But really and truly. No."

I blink. "You didn't even hear what I have to say."

"There was more than what you said yesterday?" He looks genuinely curious.

I exhale. "Not more, but, like, I should say it better. I don't think you totally got the picture of how great the whole system is."

The kids walking into class stop to stare, standing close together. They would whisper about us if they could spare the words. I ignore them.

"I think I do," Sebas says.

I run through the benefits of TECH, looking for an approach. "Have you seen the art wing?"

"Yup. Nice," he says, sounding politely bored.

"You know you can talk to anyone in the world, for any amount of time, for free."

"I can already do that with WhatsUp."

"You get access to all this cool technology. The download times are ridiculous. You can stream anything, huge movies, no lag time, no glitches. This whole system is on a real 5G platform, like they have in Europe and China, and like they don't have in the US."

"Uh-huh."

"You know who has the fastest internet speeds—for download and upload *and* mobile—in the world?"

"Nope."

"Taiwan . . . and New Gault," I say. I know my smile is getting dangerously close to manic, but I can't tone it down mid-smile.

Sebas tilts his head. "How do you know?"

"What?"

"Have you been to Taiwan? Maybe tried to download every episode of *Legacy of the Water Dragon* while holding an antique stopwatch?"

I almost say "What?" again, but I'm too smart to repeat words. I wait for him to make his point. It's killing me a little bit.

"Because," Sebas continues, "unless you did that—and I'd applaud you on your taste in animated TV shows of the early 2000s—you don't know."

"I've read about it, okay? And that's not my point. My point is—" Dammit, repetition again. Why am I so flustered?

"*My* point is that I already said no. But also, I really like things to be true. So while I'm happy to talk about all sorts of shit . . ." Sebas doesn't say it loud, but puts a little extra emphasis on the expensive word, and I can't help but cringe. Kyle and Teagan are standing near me. I see them stiffen.

Sebas keeps going like he doesn't know or care. "When someone tries to sell me something, I'm not gonna believe all sorts of shit, right?"

I check my phone. One minute. Anxiety is beating a pulse against my ear. Now's the time to say something clever, to be charming.

"It's totally free!" I say desperately.

Sebas frowns. "You said words cost money with that thing."

I have seconds. "I don't think I did a great job of explaining. Can you have lunch with me?" Ugh, I sound like an ashhat.

"I can," Sebas says, pulling a pink notebook covered in flamingos out of his bag. "And I even will. But can we leave school for it? This place is already getting on my nerves."

The whiteboard screen that covers nearly the entire front wall of the classroom turns on. The TECH logo, animated in friendly colors, buzzes very slightly, the signal for students to get into their seats. I watch Sebas look around as kids silently take out their laptops.

The morning message comes on. A celebrity from a TV show Ofelia adores explains, like she does every morning, that we're engaging in an important social experiment and becoming better people.

How can I text Sebas the address for the lunch place when he doesn't have a TECH phone? I take the pen he was doodling with and write on the back cover of his notebook: *Sound Café, corner of Concept and Conflict, 12:45.* I leave Sebas watching the morning announcements like he's watching a car crash, and I know I have to do better. I have to get him to say yes.

7

Sebas

So far, and no one has asked my opinion, TECH High School is a joke. The morning announcements are a series of short videos delivered with cringey enthusiasm by people who are supposed to be celebrities, but I've never heard of them. Then there was a message from the TECH CEO, Dan Chin, an Asian guy who looks like he belongs on the cover of one of the money magazines Papi sometimes gets but never reads.

"TECH is different," the CEO says warmly, then the video cuts to a clip of a kid trying to teach a dog to skateboard, which is mildly funny, since the dog is only interested in licking faces. "We want you to feel safe to be yourself, whatever that self is. When all of us think before we speak, before we text, we care about the person receiving our words." A quick shot of cupped hands opening to release a monarch butterfly, then the hands dissolve into a mass of butterflies. Decent effects; corny as hell. "That makes all of us better and makes the world a better place," the CEO continues against an even cornier clip of a ton of butterflies landing on the exterior of TECH High School. "And we can have some fun too." Dan Chin smiles direct to camera, before cutting back to the skateboarding video, dog and kid gliding down the street on a longboard into the actual sunset. As a piece of propaganda, it's okay.

What isn't okay is the next five minutes, when Mrs. Marseglia asks everyone to rate the morning announcement video on a scale of one to five. Maybe answering a teacher's question doesn't cost words (I can't remember what Lu said was free and what wasn't), but everyone is super eager to share their thoughts in a way that should be unheard-of this early in the morning. There's a long, boring discussion on how this week's skateboarding video was much cuter than last week's hot air balloon video. One girl in the back of the classroom shouts out that she's allergic to dogs, so she can't relate to this week's video. People argue like this is important, like they're all back in kindergarten. Everyone is *that* desperate to say something.

Mrs. Marseglia, damn her, chooses this moment to call on me. Of course she does.

"Sebastian, I'd love to hear your thoughts on the video, since you're new to TECH."

Shitshitshitshit. "It was cool. Good," I hedge. Everyone's quiet now, looking at me. Permission to gawk at the new kid? *Granted*.

"Uh, the swarm of butterflies in the video reminds me of a movie my tío Floro made me watch, his favorite horror movie, when I was way too young. *Them*—it's about killer ants that get irradiated by an atomic blast and become giant and start killing people, and there's an FBI agent that has to find the queen ant's nest and destroy it, and there's a little girl for the cuteness factor and obviously for sympathy and as something the main character has to protect, oh, and she's mute, so she can't say what's happened, that way it can sustain the mystery, which makes sense. It's really about the horror of atomic power. People think it's just a fifties B movie, but it's actually good. Was nominated for an Oscar." The silence in the room is *thick*, and I keep wanting to add more explanations, but that seems like a bad idea. Still, I'm not really finished—I can't just end like that. I turn to the blond girl in the back. "I'm allergic to cats, so, um, I feel you." And that's just my first class.

"Okay, let's take out our laptops and log in to the classroom," Mr. Silva says in Anatomy. I have to decide if I can get away with pretending my flamingo notebook is a laptop or if I should raise my hand and tell Mr. Silva that I don't have a laptop. My hand goes up.

"Uh, Mr. Silva, I don't have a laptop."

He frowns at me like this is a moral failing of mine. "Did you forget it?"

"No."

"Where's your TECH one?"

"I didn't get one."

"You didn't get your TECH suite of tools?" I just shake my head. I'm learning my lesson. Keeping my mouth shut.

"I'll log you out a temporary laptop. But you can't take it home. You have to return it to the TECH office at the end of the day. Okay?"

I nod. This all takes so long, and then I'm finally able to log in to the classroom platform and see that there's a red hourglass flashing next to my name when I try to click on anything. It says NO PHONE CONNECTED; CHECK WITH YOUR AMBASSADOR. And that's it. I can't do anything. I can't log in to any of the materials, I can't take the icebreaker quiz, I can't see my schedule. The laptop is useless to me except to shield the fact that I'm sketching storyboards for my cartas documentary in my notebook. I already took a lot of footage of Abuela explaining the cartas, sure, but also just of her telling me about her life, showing me las plantas in her garden. I want to turn it into something incredible that will help me get into film school, but I can't stay focused.

I keep thinking about Mom. I don't want to think about her. I don't even want to let her flash across my brain. But the way she looks. I used to think she looked like a Barbie—like those videos me and my primos would watch, Barbie Mermaid, Barbie Princess, Barbie Princess Mermaid with Magical Dolphin, etc. Mom used to look like that, with honey-gold hair, blue eyes, and perfect clothes. And she was *my* mom. Somehow that made me really proud, ignorant pendejo that I was. I still remember the Barbie-doll look she gave me the last time I saw her in person, at my Anglo grandparents' house. Polite and cold, with an automatic, plastic smile. Like I didn't belong to her; like she didn't know me.

The cancer seems to have taken her apart and put her back together with fewer pieces, like there are chunks missing. When Papi called this morning, on my walk to the tram, and asked how she was, the first word out of my mouth was *smaller*. Does cancer do that to you, make you actually have less volume?

I know Abuela is shorter than she used to be. She says she is, but she's almost always been shorter than me. Okay, yeah, I wasn't some kind of giant baby, but even in middle school, I towered over her. "Tall for a Mexican" is some of the crap I get a lot, like a Mexican is one type of way.

My stomach makes hungry sounds, and I get looks from a kid next to me wearing an X-Arcane hoodie. What had Lu said? Is snorting a word or is it just a sound? What about sneezing? Not that it matters. I'll meet Lu for lunch because I'm curious about what else they could possibly say. They're good at talking, I'll give them that. But you won't catch me getting into some Big Brother foolishness, the kind of shit that routinely happens in the Bay Area that the rest of the world finds cuckoo bananas, but that people at this latitude think is perfectly normal. Maybe Lu is right. Maybe this TECH system has some good things about it. But I won't be in New Gault long enough to find out.

8

Lu

Anxiety meds are supposed to calm me down. ADHD meds are supposed to rev me—or at least my brain—up. It's supposed to mix together in my bloodstream and equal out, make sense, make me act and feel normal. It usually does. Not the way I felt before I was diagnosed, but sort of the way cold medicine makes me feel better, but not normal. Better is what I want. Normal is for other people. Which is why waiting for Sebas outside the Sound Café makes me feel *off*, like someone's picked up the ground I'm standing on and shaken it.

But once I get Sebas to say yes to TECH, I'll feel better *and* normal again. It will be a relief to go back to the worries I understand.

Dr. Allyson thinks this is part of my negative thought pattern, but I argued with her that it's my coping mechanism. She's not the only one who can read *Psychology Today* and the *DSM*.

When Sebas finally gets to the café ten minutes late, I feel a flutter and a loosening in my stomach. I tell myself that it's just my parasympathetic nervous system hiccupping.

"Sorry," he says, "I got lost."

"How did you get lost? This place is only a ten-minute walk from campus." I push the café door open.

"Because the campus map was confusing. It looked like you could get from the exit near Lab Five straight to Concept, but there's a stupid building in the way, so I asked my nearest tram driver. I think I've met them all now. Or they're clones of each other."

"There's a campus map?"

"How else would I find anything?" Sebas says, waving a printed pamphlet in front of me.

That's my cue to go full salesperson. "If you were in the TECH program, you could have just asked your biosensor to direct you. It's got a GPS, but, like, it knows the second you've taken a wrong step and will tell you the right way to go."

"Yeah, but I didn't have to sign up for anything to get this," he says. "Mrs. Jackson gave it to me for nothing." He grins like he's won an argument, his smile like a fox, a hook, an open door.

I press down on my own answering smile to cover just how much I liked his and try to focus. I lead Sebas to a table by the window, the best table to people-watch, the one with the best light too. Many social media photo shoots take place at this table. Behind us on the wall, there's a neon-pink sign that says NOTHING IS IMPOSSIBLE. I turn back to smile at Sebas, but he's still lingering by the door.

"Shouldn't we order food before sitting? I'm super hungry, and I have Film next period."

"We have time. Sit. We order from the table."

He sits, looking uncomfortable with his hunched shoulders,

hair falling into his eyes. Does he ever pull it back into a ponytail, or is it always swinging around his face, half hiding, half revealing? I made sure to take my extended-release focus meds, even though I don't have to take them every day if I don't feel like I need them. Somehow, they're no match for the distraction that is Sebastian Ascencio.

I take my TECH phone out and open the app. "Are you a vegetarian or vegan or allergic to anything?"

"Allergic to cats, but not any food."

"Oh." I can't hide my disappointment. It's one of the most popular features of TECH.

"Did you want me to be allergic to something? I could probably eat something and sneeze, if it makes you feel better."

"No, it's just that it's cool— Let me— Let's pretend that you're allergic to something. What don't you like?"

"Lima beans."

"Okay." I type *allergic to lima beans*.

A list of menu suggestions fills the screen, and I pass the phone to Sebas.

"Not a lima bean in sight." I smile, only a little deflated.

"Making the world safe from lima beans. I like it." He smiles.

"Yeah, well, if you were deathly allergic to lima beans, it would be amazing, you have to admit. Just tap what you want to order." I look out the window and wave to another TECH student whose name I should remember—I was their ambassador, after all—but I don't, and that bothers me for some reason. Am I just having a really off couple of days, or is it something else?

Sebas hands me back my phone. He's ordered a grilled cheese with chipotle sauce and tomatoes, a lime soda, and a bag of kettle chips, all good choices. I order a salad and half a ham-and-cheese sandwich because Mamá checks my meal selections. Lucky for me, the biosensor only reports that I order food, not—yet—how much of it I eat. I don't know how she expects me to eat with so much anxiety living rent-free in my stomach.

"Okay, it'll be out in a few minutes."

"What about paying? I can pay for my own lunch," Sebas says.

"That's why I wanted to come here. It's one of twenty places in New Gault where students don't have to pay."

"Like, at all?" Sebas's face holds the first signs of interest I've seen in him since I met him. *Don't blow it,* I think.

"If you're part of the TECH program, you don't have to pay for food."

I watch him carefully. I need to figure out what to say, what to emphasize, and what to gloss over. Every student is different—everyone has their own reasons for why TECH is life-changing. I just have to figure out what Sebas needs.

"See, it's just one of the ways that it's worth it to be in the program," I say, finally, *finally* feeling like I'm getting it right. Relief makes me loose, relaxed, and I smile for real.

9

Sebas

The Sound Café is basically a white box with chairs. Muzak plays, and little potted cacti sit on each table, the only spots of color in the room except for a cringey neon sign on the wall. There's no smell of food, no clatter of silverware. I'm gonna starve.

Lu is talking, smiling. They have perfect teeth, a gorgeous smile. I don't want to like it, since they're hell-bent on selling me garbage, but I'm man enough to admit their smile is attractive. *They're* attractive—the way all the best salespeople have to be. *Ugly doesn't move merchandise*—what's that a quote from? If my phone had any bars, I'd look it up; it sounds like a movie quote. Anyway, it must be awkward to love to talk so much and to be charged for all those words. Honestly, if it wasn't for being so bored and lonely, I'd eat the saltines that I swiped from Mom's and call it a day.

Mom woke up in the middle of the night coughing so hard that I thought I'd have to call an ambulance. It sounded like end-times coughing. When I went into Mom's room, phone in hand, the nine and the one already tapped out, Mom was hunched over, spitting into a bowl and crying. When she saw me, she told me to piss off and go back to bed. I figured if she could be that mean, she couldn't be dying. I propped the pillows up high behind her, like Abuela does for me when I'm sick, and wished I had some Vicks, though I doubt Mom would use it. She turned on her side, ignoring me completely. I stood in the dark until I heard Mom's slight snore and went back to bed. It was an hour before I fell asleep again.

"Are you listening?" Lu says, when it's clear that I'm not.

"Yeah. I mean, no? Something about integrated contact trace capability? I'm sorry. I didn't get a lot of sleep last night."

"Why?"

"What?"

"Why didn't you get any sleep?"

I shrug and smile, which is usually enough to get people to stop asking me questions. But Lu just looks at me. I like their shirt. It's dark green, sort of military, and it looks like it might be made of the same kind of material as my emergency shirt— able to withstand anything. But it's got two orange stripes down one sleeve. Like it's unbalanced on purpose.

"I like your shirt," I say.

Lu looks down, possibly just realizing they're wearing a shirt from their surprised expression, then sort of blushes a bit. It's cute. Maybe I'm delirious from hunger and that's why my thoughts are going sideways.

"Sorry, go ahead," I say, trying to look interested. Lu's words wash over me like a stream of background noise from a late-night infomercial. Free food is cool, no doubt, but most of the perks of being part of the program involve things I'm not gonna be around for, like tax deductions and college money.

It takes me a second, then two, to realize that the flow of words has stopped, and I look up. Lu looks pissed. I turn to see two girls walking into the café.

"What are you doing here, Ofelia?" they say when the two girls—they're maybe twelve?—stop by the table.

"You're sitting at our table, pendeje," says the one with the curls held back with a butterfly clip. The other one, a Black girl with long black braids, giggles. They're both wearing shirts for K-pop bands I've never heard of.

"Go away, pulga. We were here first."

The one with the butterfly clip glares at Lu, then looks at me and smiles. That's when I know this kid is Lu's sister. Same thousand-watt smile. "Are you new here? Welcome to New Gault! Have you seen the Olympic swimming pool?"

I bust out laughing, I can't help it. She sounds like a mini-Lu. I don't know if the sibling rivalry would turn to actual bloodshed. I'm an only child, so I assume all siblings want to murder each other—that's what cinema has taught me—but I don't get a chance to find out because the food finally arrives. By drone.

Honest to Jesucristo *drone*. I watch it dip unsteadily in its flight from a serving door that opens in the back wall, a white takeout box in its basket. The drone lands at our table and sits like a dog waiting to be told it's a good boy.

The two girls sit down at the next booth. Lu is trying to ignore their sister's presence by removing the takeout box from the drone's basket.

"Great, huh?" they say, a little distracted. "Plus, guaranteed, no lima beans." They push the white box over to me. The drone whirs next to Lu until they say, "Um, thanks," then it bounces into the air and back toward the serving hatch, where another two drones are starting toward our table.

We both start eating in silence, which is fine with me, but probably annoys Lu no end. I wonder if it's that they have so much to say that they're bursting to get it all out before their word data runs out, or if they're just naturally like that.

"So," Lu says, shifting their fork through their salad, "what do you think about it?"

"It's actually a fucking delicious sandwich," I say. They wince at the f-bomb. I kinda knew they would.

Lu takes a steadying breath, and I feel a little bad for messing with them.

"I mean about TECH, about the whole thing."

I wipe my mouth and start in on my chips. "I have some questions."

"Okay."

"Do you get paid for everybody you sign up to TECH?"

"Of course not!"

"Because you're spending your time hanging out with me and trying to get me to do this thing, so I have to ask. What's in it for you?"

Lu looks so offended, I've got to believe it's genuine. Maybe I went too far.

"Never mind," I say, trying to smooth things out. "I get it. Words *cost* money, but a lot of other things don't cost money, I could see how that would be interesting for some people."

Lu exhales. I'm sorry I'm about to disappoint them. "But not for me. I'm only here for a little while. To help my mom out while my dad stays with my abuela, who's recovering from a stroke. I won't be in New Gault this summer, and I won't be back for senior year, so there's no point, right?"

Lu is quiet for a minute, and I'm worried that I've upset them. Which I didn't care about yesterday, but today, I just don't want to. Once again, I keep going, because I'm in it now, no other way to dig out.

"Also, I'm not great with civil liberties being plundered, and cursing is one of my favorite pastimes." *End with a joke,* Papá would say. *Boys, girls, everyone likes funny people. Makes you more attractive.* That only seems to work in movies.

"I'm sorry about your abuelita. Is she doing okay?" Lu asks.

Not what I expected to come out of their mouth.

"Yeah, she's doing a lot better. She says her brain is sharper now because she can't remember any of the bad times from before 1985."

"What? Is that true?" Lu asks.

"Doubt it, but Abuela is always playing. She couldn't remember some things right after the stroke, but now she's almost back to normal." I think about taking out the baraja española, showing Lu the latest tirada Abuela taught me. It's a simple one: a card for the problem, a card for the challenge, and then a card that offers the solution.

"You speak Spanish with your family, right?" Lu finally says.

"Yeah?"

"You can speak Spanish all you want with TECH. There's no charge for words in another language. You can even curse and it won't make a dent."

I laugh, shaking my head. "Yeah, almost had me there. But I can already do that, as long as Abuela doesn't hear me. Gracias, pero no, gracias." Honestly, does Lu think about anything other than TECH? I wonder if their bedroom is draped in TECH merch. Like, TECH throw pillows and TECH mugs and TECH bath towels.

"What's so funny?" they ask.

"You are. You take this shit way too serious." I bring my tray to the composting bin, even though I'm sure there's some robot minion that's meant to do it, and return to the table to find the two little girls huddled up on either side of Lu, making them watch a viral video.

"Listen, I think there's some things you still don't understand about TECH," Lu begins for the millionth time.

The girls lean in to them, one pulling on their shoulder, the other growling, "Watch, it's funny!" I'm not gonna have a better chance to escape.

"Thanks for lunch! And for explaining things. I got it now, okay, but no thanks!" I shout, and I'm out the door.

10

Lu

"Remind me again why we're out in shitsville on a Tuesday night?"

"Just because you can curse, Diego, doesn't mean you need to," Kenzie says, swiping a hand at Diego and narrowly missing him. Diego knows Kenzie well enough to move his seat way back out of her range.

"Yo, I'm excited to give my tongue free rein, you feel me?"

"There's just so much wrong with all the words you choose." Kenzie rubs the space between her eyebrows.

The side road dwindles to a track, then gravel, before I pull Mamá's minivan into the tall yellow grass, right in the shadow of a two-hundred-foot-high cell tower. I stare out the windshield at the land beyond the bolted iron legs of the tower. Evidence of the wildfire that destroyed Gault five years ago persists out here. On the New Gault side, oak and pine trees thrive. On the sliver of land that's left of old Gault, the pine trees are gone, the ground too deeply scorched to regrow trees, so the shallow grasses took over. They move like water in the breeze. I know fire is a natural part of the ecosystem, but I can't help seeing the ghost shapes of trees against the night sky.

When we first moved here, this still-scorched strip of land seemed like proof of the world we were leaving: razed to the ground, consumed by fire and carelessness. Inside the circle of New Gault, I felt like I could finally breathe. But more than three years on, I'm still hung up on this barren space. Like, I need to listen to it, to find out what it has to say. Lately, I've been trying to write poems about it. Only, I haven't been able to come up with the right words for how it makes me feel.

"Don't you guys think it's ironic that we can get the best Wi-Fi, and no restrictions, far away from TECH here under this rusty-ass, janky-ass—"

"I know you aren't paying for it, Diego, but I don't think you really needed that second *ass*," I say.

"—cell tower?"

Kenzie lolls her head from side to side, making her neck crack in a way that makes me a tiny bit nauseous. "What I want to know is why we couldn't go to Dry Town instead. And hang out with friends?"

I engage the brake and turn to face her.

"Have I ever, in the history of us, agreed to go to Dry Town with you?"

"Nope."

"And have I explained, clearly and concisely, practically with accompanying graphics, why I won't go to Dry Town?"

Kenzie lobs a lazy smile at me. "You know you sound all sexy when you get pedantic, right?"

"And *you* know I won't go to Dry Town."

"I'll go," Diego says, butting into the conversation.

Kenzie shrugs. I'm her occasional pet project, the human she'd most like to fix, and I love her for it. Most of the time.

"No one ever wants to go to Dry Town with me," Diego whines.

"Porque you're whiny, hermano," Kenzie says.

"I whine because you don't go with me," Diego huffs, leaning back, and I just don't want to deal with their bickering.

"Fine, I'll drive you to Dry Town, but I'm not hanging out in the parking lot like last time. I don't want to see anyone."

"Which one of your exes are we avoiding this week?" Kenzie says.

If only this were an ex-sized problem. "No. Just. I'm freaking out, okay?"

"Not because of the pulga's thievery, right? I mean, your sister is gonna keep doing that. It's not something to worry about."

Kenzie tries to tune the car's satellite radio to a station that isn't the Acoustic Coffee Hour program Mamá usually listens to. My parents are abnormally obsessed with acoustic versions of mediocre songs.

"Give me that aux, man," Diego says, gesturing at Kenzie. She ignores his request for access to the stereo's Bluetooth.

"I'm not avoiding exes. I don't like Dry Town, I don't want to give up my phone, and I— Wait, are you saying I date too much?"

Kenzie and Diego exchange a look.

"No," Kenzie says.

"Maybe?" Diego shrugs.

"No, of course not too much," Kenzie says smoothly. "It's just that you tend to fall in like with a lot of people."

"So. Many. People," Diego agrees.

"Not that many people," I protest.

"Amigue, the list is real long," Diego says.

"Are you saying I have a loose character?"

"I'm saying you spread your . . . smiles around pretty freely. Remember Isobel? And Charles, not Charlie?"

"Yeah, what was up with Charles? He was, like, the last person I would have thought you'd be into. Because he was definitely not, like, a *you* kind of person," Kenzie interjects.

"What does that mean?"

"I don't know. Like, he didn't like anything you like."

Kenzie leans in and peers at me closely. I let this happen. I invite my friends to talk about things and that's how I end up under Kenzie's searchlight stare, twenty miles outside of the city limits, in a car with boxes of Jollibee on a school night.

"Look. I don't know the real reason you're freaking out. It's not an ex. Or maybe it is an ex, but it's, like, the *idea* of your exes, not an actual person."

"You do remember that you're one of my exes?" I say to Kenzie. Her grin is wide and wild.

"The best ex you'll ever have, friend," she says, and tugs at the ear where I'm wearing the little topaz stud she gave me as a breakup gift. "Besides, we were little baby freshmen. It barely counts." She waves our dating history away.

"Is it that Sebas kid?" Diego says from the back seat. He isn't even looking at me or Kenzie. He's scrolling through some app that ranks favorite anime characters. *Even the clueless sometimes hit the mark,* I think.

"Yeah, what's up with Sebas?" Kenzie says. "You went to Sound Café with him, right?"

I steal a fry from Kenzie's stash, to buy more time to think. "It was so . . . ugh."

"I just don't understand why he won't use TECH. Like, who wouldn't?" Diego asks.

"Well," Kenzie says, taking the discarded onions from my sandwich wrapper, "I can think of someone who wouldn't want their words tracked. Someone who wasn't gonna stay here and get any of the benefits that make being here worth it."

"Yeah," I concede, "but even for the short term, who wouldn't want to get all that technology, free food, free transport—I mean, like, you cannot live like this in any other city in California—in the world!"

"Someone with Tourette's," Diego says.

We turn to stare at him in horror.

"That's someone who wouldn't want to do the TECH program. You know, because maybe they wouldn't be able to, like, control the cursing, so they'd rack up the costs. Be a nightmare."

"You're a nightmare," Kenzie says. "That's a stereotype, and Sebas doesn't have Tourette's."

"Never said he did," Diego says, trying to sound dignified.

"We're here to talk about why Lu is spiraling, Diego. Try to focus."

"I'm not spiraling," I say.

"You're always spiraling," he says. "I just like to come along for the ride so I can say some nasty shit."

Kenzie leans her head on my shoulder. "You did your best. Sebas won't do the TECH thing. It's not your problem."

"Becker will make it my problem."

Diego leans back in his seat. "What if you just explained to Sebas that you need him to say yes so that you can live your best life, and would he do you a solid and be a . . . you know, like, someone who's always doing shit for others."

"A nice person?" I say at the same time that Kenzie says, "A martyr?"

Diego and Kenzie bump fists and laugh.

"We want him to fall on his metaphorical sword and take the L for Lu," Kenzie says.

"What? Wait, I lost you, I mean, you lost me."

"Diego, I love you, you utter tool," Kenzie says, so casually that I know she's forgotten her words before they've left her mouth. But if she could see Diego's face in the rearview mirror, like I can, she'd know he's latched on to the first part of her sentence and not the last.

"Okay, you think I should ask him to do this for me, a stranger he cares nothing about? Kenzie, what do you think I should do?"

She's quiet for a second.

"I know you see this as your responsibility, Lu, but it's not. You're not letting anyone down if this guy decides he doesn't want to play by their rules. That's on him, not you."

"I hate when you're right," I say, pulling her into a hug, despite the choking sounds Diego makes from the back seat. He's got to learn that Kenzie and I are just friends, and his jealous shit will never get her to see him as anything other than a bro. And I have to learn to listen to her.

"You're smart," I tell her.

"And pretty."

I laugh. "And pretty."

"And good at life," she adds, settling back into her seat.

"Agreed."

"Anyone got any more fries?" Diego says plaintively.

"I have cold lumpia," I say, passing back the Jollibee carton.

"I'll take it. Dry Town food is too expensive."

I take the hint and put the minivan into reverse, piloting out of this side track and back to the county road, toward Dry Town.

"I'm going home after this, so get your own sasses back from Dry Town," I mumble.

"Will do," Kenzie says.

Dry Town is a stand-alone building a few miles from where old Gault used to be. How it escaped the last big wildfire is a mystery. It used to be a drive-through liquor store back when the surrounding towns, including Gault, were dry—as in, no alcohol sold in the city limits. Since those laws were rolled back in the '70s, the building has been everything from a carpet showroom to a strip joint. Only the giant neon sign with its cartoonish lettering and depiction of a bottle of moonshine, a cactus, and an arrow survived. I've driven here dozens of times; I've never gone in.

"Is this the magic night when we get Lu to come inside and see how awesome Dry Town is?" Kenzie teases.

"Nah, they ain't going in. They hate people," Diego says.

"I do not hate people. I just don't like being without my phone."

Dry Town is bring-your-own-everything, play board games in the corner, listen to music and hang out with your friends, sing karaoke, make out with whoever, buy their expensive fried dough balls, but under no circumstances are you allowed to have any phones inside. There's a phone check where you have to leave your device—but I hear you do get a coupon for three dollars off the fried dough balls and a token for one use of the photo booth. It makes me itchy just thinking about not being able to have my phone. It's one thing to drive out to the cell phone tower, where the TECH phones' reception is so patchy they can't properly track your words; it's another thing to leave your phone in some random locker. No one has phones, so I guess that means no one is posting evil crap on Snap or Stories, but what's stopping them from saying that same crap to my face?

TECH kids go to Dry Town, but other kids from farther out do, too, because the Dry Town owners are cool, and they somehow never get busted. And anyway, the drinking, the vaping, the lighting up, that's all happening in the cars, off premises. What else are they gonna be busted for? Playing D&D without a license?

Diego bounces from the car like a dog let out of his crate, like he's already forgotten I exist. Kenzie gets out of the car, then turns back, ducking her head in with the wry little smile she has that says, *Come on, don't you want to have fun?* I could, with a shove and a pull, be talked into loving her like I used to—like we used to—but it would be useless. We're so much better as friends.

"Come on, Lu. One time? For me? Just to see what it's like?"

"Nena, did you put glitter in your hair?"

"Hair fragrance, has shimmer—smells like honey, see?" She wafts her hair toward me.

"*C'mon*, Kenzie!" Diego yelps from the door.

"Go on, your puppy calls."

"He isn't my anything, and you know it." She closes the

door but reaches through the open window to touch my face with her fingertips. "One day, you're gonna feel brave enough to take a chance, ¿sí?"

"Un día," I say.

I watch her catch up to Diego and pass through the doors of Dry Town. The neon lights shine down in stained-glass-window colors. I hear the beat of music and surprised laughter popping off like rockets. I feel how heavy it is to keep myself outside, how stupid I am to make myself follow rules I know I can break, that everyone else breaks.

But I can't. The risk is too high for me. My memories keep me safe. My anxiety keeps me safe. I drive back to New Gault at exactly the speed limit.

11

Sebas

Sure, I was all "civil liberties" and shit when I told Lu no, then no thank you, this week, but do you know how much a breakfast sandwich costs in New Gault?

"That'll be $19.57." The girl behind the counter smiles at me like she's not stabbing me right in the wallet. I thought this unassuming coffee place would be cheap and decent. It looks like a thousand other city coffee shops that just want to fill contractors and tired gente full of carbs and café con leche. But I've been deceived. I ordered coffee, light and sweet, and a bacon, egg, and cheese on a roll. That should be a fiver, ten with inflation.

I hold open my wallet, searching for a twenty I think I have somewhere, and my TECH ID shows for a second.

"Oh, I'm sorry!" The girl flushes, looking guilty. "I didn't realize you were a student. If you just scan your phone, I can get that right for you."

"My phone is dead," I lie. "I'm new here and totally forgot to charge it last night." I shrug like this is real cute instead of painful.

She can't be more than twenty and probably went to TECH

in the recent past. She glances behind her to see if anyone is looking, then smiles. "It's fine! Just show me next time you come in."

"You sure?" I give her what I hope is a flirty look, the kind I've seen Pa hand around to everyone he wants to charm. She just ducks her head under her Coffee Joint baseball cap, gives me an encouraging smile, and says she'll see me next time. But of course, I can't ever come back in here.

The sandwich, which went from nearly twenty bucks to free, tastes amazing. I wonder if that's why. Still, I scarf it down, trying to not burn myself with the café, and make it to my classes on time. Students get all sorts of notifications on their phones—of room changes, assignment reminders, even which bathrooms are out of order. Kids move through the school like they're a living part of it, and I'm out here like un menso trying to find someone to tell me where they moved Anatomy.

That's how Lu finds me, my flamingo notebook open to the page where I wrote down room numbers in one hand and the map Mrs. Jackson gave me of each floor in the other.

"Hey," they say with a wave. I notice they don't bound up to me with ridiculous amounts of energy and a sales pitch on their lips. They hang back. This must be a new strategy.

"Hey. You good?" I ask. They look good—like, *sharp*. Pale blue jeans, golden sweatshirt, and gray high tops with a little red heart on one. Pretty sure the heart has googly eyes. And a wide leather cuff on their wrist. Like I said, sharp.

"I'm fine. I thought you might not know where Anatomy lab moved to, so"—they shrug—"I can show you."

I hesitate. Despite scoring a free and delicious breakfast

sandwich off New Gault, I don't feel like being badgered with its virtues.

Lu puts up their hands. "Will not try to sell you on TECH—even though it's life-changing! I'm too tired for that," they promise.

I follow Lu up the ramp and make small talk about how Mrs. Jackson is the nicest school office lady I've ever met.

"How many have you met?" they ask.

"Four. That's just the high school ones. I don't count the middle school and elementary school ones, since they have to be nice."

On the second floor, one stream of students moves in one direction, a second stream in another. I follow Lu as they nod, wave, and easily fit themselves into the stream. I'll admit, this shit is easier when you know where you're going. Or if you follow someone who does.

"How did you end up at four different high schools?" Lu asks.

"You know, family shit," I say. It's not exactly a record-scratch screech, but everyone around us looks up with shocked faces, then moves a tiny bit away from us, like my swear will get them dirty.

"Sorry," I hate myself for saying.

"It's fine. We're just not used to it."

We arrive at a large lab room with floor-to-ceiling windows overlooking the quad. All the other students are already sitting, murmuring quietly. I wonder if volume matters at all, like, is a whispered *fuuuuuck* less offensive than if I shout it? *Doesn't matter, pendejo. You're not doing this foolishness.* The biosensor on Lu's wrist flashes a blue light.

"That means it's two minutes until class starts."

"I wondered how everyone knew when to do shi—" I stop myself just in time, and Lu smiles at me.

"You'll get used to it," they say.

No doubt.

That amazing freebie breakfast sandwich is a distant memory. I'm trying to work up the nerve to ask Lu to take me to that Sound Café again so I can eat good instead of the PB&J on saltines I made myself this morning. It's not like I can't cook. I just need to get myself to a real supermarket somewhere. I'd kill for a BLT, honestly.

I'm loitering near the front entrance when Lu and their friends come up to me. I've seen them in classes before and I know their names, but it's nice that they want to actually say hi to me—especially since they've probably already been talking about me.

"Hey, Sebas. This is Kenzie and Diego."

"Hey," I say, and Kenzie waves lilac-tipped nails at me. Pretty Asian girl with multiple piercings in only one ear—there's a story there. The dude is brown, like me, and has tight curls dark at the root, then orange, then bleached blond at the ends.

"Where you from?" Diego asks.

"San Marcos."

"Nah, man, like, what's your cultura?"

Kenzie and Lu exchange a look.

"We're Mexican," I say, erasing Mom's whole side of the

family in a way that would infuriate her if she knew.

"Niiiice," he says, coming in for a complicated fist bump. "I'm Dominican. Most of my family is out in New York, but Mami y Papi moved us out here for some fruiting reason."

That makes me bust out laughing, and Kenzie and Lu grin, but Diego looks embarrassed.

Lu saves the awkward situation by saying those magic words. "You guys hungry?"

When we walk right past Sound Café, my stomach almost leaps out of my body and makes for the door. A block later, they turn in to a burrito place called Los Hermanos, and I'm not mad at this choice. When we sit and they all take out their phones, there's a moment where I'm wondering if I will have to actually eat off their plates. I decide I'm not too proud.

Lu passes me their phone with the menu pulled up. "Pick whatever you want. I'm just getting fries."

"Is that, like, cool? I don't want to take your food," I say.

"TECH can't tell who's eating what—not yet anyway. Besides, I'm never hungry during the day. It's my ADHD medicine. I'll eat like a beast tonight, don't worry. The tortas are really good, or the quesadillas."

"I'm getting the carne asada fries," Diego says.

"Yes, love, you always get the carne asada fries, we know," Kenzie says.

"Sebas doesn't know. And anyway, they're dope."

I order a carnitas burrito and a tamarind Jarrito and hand the phone back to Lu.

It's almost a shame I don't have the TECH phone, because the way these three talk, weaving in stories, people, and places I never heard of, I'm the one keeping my words to myself.

Finally, the food comes—not delivered by drones but by a lady who looks like my tía Margarita back home, with her long silver-streaked black braid down her back, and her hands full of delicious food.

"Buen provecho, chicos," she says after handing us our bottles of Jarritos.

"Gracias, Carmen," Lu says, and taps their phone screen for the tip.

"Por lo menos las palabras en español son gratis," I say, unwrapping my burrito.

Kenzie answers, "Spanish words are free, but not everyone speaks Spanish." She gives Diego a look, and his blushing face must match mine, because I know better.

"Sorry, man," I say, "I didn't mean to assume."

"No hay de qué," he says a little awkwardly. "My parents never wanted to teach us kids, so I'm constantly being talked to in Spanish by random people who think I understand. I'm learning, though. My girl Kenzie is gonna teach me." Diego tries to put his arm around Kenzie in an overly friendly way. She stops him by smacking it away. I see his face flame again, and I know he's going to explode.

"Why you gotta be such a fucking tease?" Diego shouts, pushing his chair out and standing. His biosensor flashes red like this is an emergency, and I just stare at it for a minute. In movies there's a whole setup that happens when you're introduced to the thing—I don't know, like a ring of power or a gauntlet with stones. Doesn't matter what it is, you know it's there for a reason, and you can expect that shit to glow with Elvish writing or blow up. I stare at Diego's flashing biosensor like that.

Lu is out of their chair and next to Diego in a second, just whispering and trying to get him to calm down. The look on Diego's face is like he crashed his mamá's car. Lu puts their arm around him and leads him away.

Kenzie scrolls through her phone, unfazed.

"That was, um, something," I say.

"Oh, yeah, sorry." She puts her phone down. "You're not used to his shirt, so you don't know that's a common freaking occurrence. Like weekly. By Friday, Diego will be working his word debt off at the cafeteria if he's not careful."

I want to ask why she's friends with him. He gives off angry dude vibes a mile away.

"He obviously likes you and has a temper," I say.

"Ya think?"

Okay, so that really is obvious.

I look around the little restaurant. There's a glass counter that sells fresh-baked pastries and Mexican candies. Lu and Diego are huddled there. Carmen is talking to them.

"Hey, can I ask you a non-angry-dude question?"

Kenzie smiles and smooths back her hair. "Is it about TECH? Lu will be so pissed if I'm the one who converts you after barely trying."

"Yeah, no. It's about Lu."

"What about them?" she asks.

I'm not sure how to ask what I've been wondering. "Are they always so . . ." *Sales-y? Pushy? Annoying?* "Serious about TECH? Like, why do they go so hard on it?"

Kenzie gives me a look, all her attention focused on me—I can almost understand why Diego is so into her.

"You know we used to date, right?"

"No. How would I know that?"

She waves her hand dismissively. "I forget you aren't on TECH. Nothing dies on our socials—words, pictures, every bad haircut, every terrible crush—kept forever on the TECH archives, part of the record, easy to find." She grabs my phone, takes a selfie, and enters her number into my contacts. "There. Now you can ask me anything you want about TECH or Lu or anything else."

"*Was* Lu a terrible crush?"

"No way," she says perkily. "They are amazing. So amazing that I'd much rather be friends with them. Lasts longer." Then she finishes her mandarin Jarrito in one swig. "I just forgot that you don't know about them."

"Okay. So what don't I know?"

Kenzie darts her eyes to where Lu and Diego are picking up a huge white box from the bakery counter.

"How much it means to them. The way they see it, TECH saves lives."

Before I can ask what she means, Diego places the box on the table and opens it; four rainbow conchas are nestled inside.

"Apology conchas. I'm sorry I'm such a d-bag sometimes," Diego says.

I wait to see what Kenzie does—this is her apology, really. She just takes out a concha and starts eating it. Lu and Diego sit down and start eating too. I take the last concha, and it's so good, crunchy sugar topping, pillowy soft inside. Maybe eating apology conchas is how I get initiated into this group. Do I even want to be? I don't have time for anything but dealing with Mom. But I keep thinking of Lu, wondering whose life needed saving.

12

Lu

Friday morning, I get a text from the ambassador program, and instead of feeling excited about a new student, I feel ill. I still have Sebas's TECH box in my locker. I thought I'd take a day or two, have a new plan, new words to convince him, something. But I can't think of anything. I just sort of watch him in the hallways, in the cafeteria. I see him leaving late because he's not getting any of the notifications on his phone of changing class periods. He looks lost all the time.

There's no new student waiting for me at the office. When I finally get Mrs. Jackson's attention at the front desk, she waves me through, behind her massive desk and down a hallway. It's so different from my Palo Alto middle school, where anyone meeting with the principal had to be buzzed in through bulletproof doors. Dad likes to say the difference is that all of New Gault is bulletproof.

When I get to Becker's office, he's at his standing desk, jogging in place. He's a white guy, about the same age as Dad, but not as pleasantly fuzzy. Assistant Principal Becker is a collection of hard triangles overlaid with a struggling tan. When he sees me hovering at the door, he turns on his smile.

"Hey! Come in, Lu, come right on *in!*" Adults and their empty word usage. SMH.

I trade hovering outside his door with hovering just inside his door.

Becker places a TECH box on his standing desk, and at first I think it's for a new student. But then I realize it's the one I tried to give to Sebas. The one that I left in my locker.

"Sebastian Ascencio," Becker says.

I try not to freak at the thought of Becker going into my locker. It's clear in all our messaging that lockers are not private, that TECH can go into them at any time. And it's not like I have anything to hide there. But it feels—alarming.

"Yeah. He didn't want it." I shrug, hoping I seem unbothered by the appearance of my box of failure.

Becker raises an eyebrow while turning down a corner of his mouth, like a comic book villain.

"You're a great asset to this school, to the TECH program. Someone like you, thriving in this experimental environment."

Someone like me. That could mean so many things. Someone queer. Someone Latinx with the added bonus of being comfortingly white-presenting. I'm someone that TECH can put on their website to show how progressive they are. I hate being a failure at this.

"The problem, Lu, is that we need to have one hundred percent participation in the program for the school to work. You get that, right? We won't tolerate bullying."

"What bullying?" Did I miss something? Has Sebas done something during his first week at TECH that caused someone else pain? And now it's not theoretical failure, but actual failure that spreads anxiety goosebumps across my skin.

Becker gestures lazily in the air. "Bullying is everywhere. Its *potential* is everywhere. That's why we use TECH. That's why we need to make sure everyone is using the same system. Level playing field."

When I don't answer him right away, he continues. "So, if you can meet with him again—"

"He was pretty firm about not being interested in the program."

"We can't let anyone into TECH who might be a threat," Becker says, his voice clipped. "And the only way to make sure everyone is as good as they should be is for them to be in the program." He gives me a lipless smile, which is worse than his disapproving face. "You're the best TECH ambassador we have. So, can I count on you?"

I let silence fill Becker's office, a futile couple of seconds of rebellion. "Absolutely, sir," I finally say, because what else can I say?

13

Sebas

You can't buy food at the TECH cafeteria. You can't get on the school-wide intranet. You can't access your class schedule or a map of the school or even figure out where the health suite is without the motherfucking TECH phone. Correction, *I* can't do any of those things. It's Monday again in Stepford, the start of another week of maddening frustration. I'm having fantasies about burning down the whole campus, I won't lie. Not like *I've made plans and bought an accelerant* kind of fantasies, I'm not a monster. But, like, wouldn't it be great if all this just sort of developed itself into ashes so I could get on with my life?

The answer is no. I ask classmates and teachers for help and printouts, loaner laptops. I get a lot of pitying looks and a lot of adults telling me to just sign up for TECH so all these problems disappear.

I tell Mrs. Jackson that my mom has religious reasons for not wanting me to use technology. In fact, I tell her that Mom is Amish, hoping that settles the matter and that people stop looking at me and treating me like a leopard.

On my walk home from the tram, my phone bars finally coming back to existence, I text Hudson that I'm being treated like a leopard. He responds, **that's leper, you fuckwit,** and I laugh because I kind of knew that, but also didn't, and now I'm going to tell everyone that I'm being treated like a wild cat and not someone with an infectious disease.

Anaïs, who is also on this thread, informs both of us that this is ableist language and that we are clearly *both* fuckwits. I can't really argue with that.

At home, I check the fridge, seeing that God's Love has dropped off more food that Mom won't eat. I leave her the one labeled pork loin with baby carrots and applesauce, then put two cheese-and-bean enchilada dinners into the microwave on high for seven minutes.

"Where the hell have you been?"

Immediately, I feel guilty, though I haven't done anything wrong. It's Mom's tone that has always made me feel like an explosion is only a few words away.

"At school. Then looking around."

"And now you're sneaking around my house."

"I'm not sneaking. I'm making food. Want some? There's pork and applesauce." Deflection used to work with Mom. It used to be a way to distract her from a near-constant anger. But she's not into food anymore, or much of anything else.

She pulls the kitchen chair out and sits. I haven't really seen her much this week, and almost never out of her bed. In the mornings, I check to make sure she hasn't died—grim but true. After school, I travel on the trams, talking to the rotation of tram drivers, who seem to be the only staff the sparsely used transport has. Twice, I've gone back to the dollar store to buy the things that Mom seemed to like—the applesauce and the rice pudding.

"You need money. For school stuff," she says. I can't tell if she's asking me or telling me.

"I'm good." I pour myself some cranberry juice into a chipped Snoopy mug.

She looks at me like she can see through my pockets into my wallet.

"Really, Mom. I've got everything I need."

"Must be nice to have so much cash, Mr. Moneybags," she sniffs.

"I didn't say that. I just said I'm okay."

"I wish I were okay," she mutters, then coughs hard. She's wearing a scarf around her head, a pretty yellow one with white roses. She touches it gently, like she's making sure it's where it's supposed to be. "I'll be okay. Soon, we'll both be better than okay." She smiles. Again, not sure if this is a question or a statement, so I give her a small smile back. Then there's silence and the sound of the microwave tray rotating with a squeak. Because I'm stupid, I have a sudden urge to laugh. I pretend to be really interested in my juice. I don't even like cranberry juice, but Mom said the chemo killed her taste buds, so she can only taste really tart, bitter, or sour things.

"That was your favorite mug, you remember?"

She says this while I'm mid-sip, so I almost dribble juice on myself.

"Oh yeah. I forgot," I say, because I did. I look at the mug, trying to juggle my memory, but nothing happens. It's Snoopy kicking a soccer ball and smiling. Bright green in a red circle, and Snoopy in the middle looking, honestly, like he has no idea how to play soccer.

"You don't remember?" Mom asks. I shrug, which I hope is noncommittal.

"We put you in the peewee soccer team in town. You loved your uniform so much, you barely took it off. Then I saw this cup, the same green as your uniform, and I had to have it for you. You drank your chocolate milk out of it every day."

I nod like I remember, but I don't. Mom takes a long drag on her vape, exhales. Two minutes until my food is done.

Mom laughs suddenly. "And then, when the first practice comes along, and they blow the whistle to start playing, you stand there, in your green uniform, cleats—those were expensive, too, but your dad insisted we do it right—and what do you do?"

This, I do remember. It's legendary in our family.

"I walk off the field."

"You walk off the field!" She cackles. I mean, I'm glad she's enjoying herself. "You walked over to the other kids' parents on the sidelines and started talking to them, you walked over to the snack table and talked to the parents there, you even asked the assistant coach if he liked Snoopy too!"

"I was, like, five, Ma."

"You were four. So damn cute in that uniform. Never could get you to play any sports. Not that I cared. It wasn't your thing."

The microwave finally, mercifully, dings. I pull out my food and ask Mom if she wants the pork loin.

"Yeah, okay. Sure. You eating out here with me?" It is the last thing I want to do. I have to check in with Abuela and I need to try to do some school stuff—I'm so fucking behind.

"Yeah. Sounds good," I say, and she smiles bright at me. I turn to get the saltines, the napkins, and anything else I can think of, just so I don't have to look at her when she's like this, when she's acting like the mom I had before she left.

I'm exactly stupid enough to fall for it.

14

Lu

"Mamá!" I screech, knowing I sound like what Diego would call a *lil beyotch*. But I'm beyond annoyed. Ofelia, acting like the shady cartoon fox in *Dora*, has swiped my biosensor. Again.

"Ma!"

"What's up, Lu?" Dad answers from the kitchen. *Crap.* Mom must be doing churchy things, and Dad is covering morning parent duty.

"Felia stole my biosensor." I hook my backpack onto the back of the barstool and sit at the kitchen island.

"Did not!" Felia pouts, not pausing the game she's playing on her device.

"Yes, you did, ladrona."

"Papá, make them say it in English."

"¿Por qué? Porque you don't speak español, tonta?"

"*Dad!* They—they called me a name!"

"Lu, did you call your sister a name?"

I consider lying: He probably doesn't know the word for *thief* or for *idiot*. But he might. I'm so freaking tired. I just want the stupid biosensor back.

"I'm sorry, Felia," I say without turning to look at her, but making it sound convincingly sincere.

Dad raises an eyebrow at Ofelia, and she sighs, digging into her back pocket. She slides the biosensor across the counter and shrugs.

"Dad. Tell her she can't take my stuff." I know it's pointless. Talking won't change anything.

"I didn't take it. You left it on the table."

"*Dad.*"

"Ofelia," he begins sternly, "don't touch your sibling's stuff. No matter where it is, it's not your business to touch it." He slides two banana chocolate chip pancakes onto her plate. "And, honey, stop using words to taunt Lu."

Ofelia, her mouth full of pancake, moves her hand to indicate talking. Then, because she can afford unlimited words, she adds, "Blah blah blah," through her food.

"Qué asco," I say, disgusted. I strap the biosensor to my wrist and tap the screen to make the word meter appear. It's still comfortingly high.

"Lu, have you seen the brochures I left for you?" Dad asks.

I go full deer-in-headlights for a couple of seconds before responding in a way that I hope doesn't sound panicky. "The college fair ones?"

"Yeah. That's coming up pretty soon. Your mom and I thought we could all go down to the one in San Bernardino next month."

"Sure. I mean, I've got time." I shrug. I feel Felia's eyes on me, Dad's eyes, everyone's eyes. I scroll through messages on my phone, not seeing a word. *Breathe.*

"Gap year, remember?" With Dr. Allyson's help, I got my parents to agree to a gap year, another year of living at home, of not having to think about moving out of New Gault. Dad looks like he wants to argue.

"I have a question," Felia says as Dad gives her two more pancakes to replace the ones she's already inhaled. Mine sit on my plate like they're disappointed in me.

I turn toward my sister with an ambassador-worthy smile. If it can distract Dad from asking about college, whatever Ofelia has to say will be worth it.

"What's your question?" I smile.

"Who's Sebas?" she says in a singsong voice.

"You need to have an actual conversation, why?" Kenzie asks when she answers her phone on the seventh ring.

"Because I'm freaking out! The pulga stole my biosensor—"

"Again?" Kenzie asks. She's driving her sib to school, so I have to drive myself.

"Yes, again—and she saw Sebas's name on the biosensor—then blurted it out to Dad." I pace my room, picking up lint from the carpet, reorganizing the things on top of my dresser.

"Oh yeah, the last word you use on your phone shows up on your biosensor," Kenzie says.

"What is the fruiting point of words showing up on the biosensor? It's supposed to check my vitals and make sure I'm not having a heart attack or a seizure—not embarrass me in front of my family!" I've moved on from organizing things in my room to tugging on my hair. If I move to biting my nails, my day is totally effed.

"Dios, you must be real upset if you're using one of Diego's made-up curse words. What's next? Clock-pucker?"

I fight against the laugh that rises in my chest, then give in. Kenzie always knows how to make a space for my frustration to leak out.

"Better?" Kenzie asks.

"Mildly," I admit.

"So, what was the embarrassing part—did your dad do anything goofy?"

I flop onto the bed. "Not really. He told Felia to get her shoes on so she wouldn't be late for the tram. Then he asked me if Sebas was my new crush."

"Ah."

I sit right back up again. "What's that supposed to mean?"

"Well, it's a fair question. Is he?"

"Please, do not. I'm just trying to get the guy to agree to TECH, and then I can stop worrying about it. It's been more than a week."

"And yet you keep talking about him."

This weird idea flashes across my mind: What if TECH has been counting my words like normal, but somewhere, someone is looking through the heaps of words I spend and has figured out that a whole lot of them are about Sebastian Ascencio?

"Only because he won't say yes to me! What is taking so long?"

"I have no idea. I can ask him if you want. I'm seeing him for lunch today."

My mouth drops open, and I have to force out my next word.

"¿Qué?"

"Yeah, he called me last night, wants to ask me some questions about New Gault. Wouldn't it be hilarious if I got him to say yes to TECH?" She laughs, tinny and faraway. I can't think of anything I'd find less funny.

"Plus, he's cuuuute," Kenzie continues, and I hear her sibling, Jet, making throwing up sounds in the background. "Shut the front door, Jet, or I'll make you listen to my Japanese City Pop playlist," Kenzie shouts right into the phone.

"He's so not your type," I say, sounding more confident than I feel.

"He really isn't," she agrees. "But boredom is real, and I hate to feel it."

I bury my face in my comforter and take a second to make my voice sound fine.

"See you at school, K," I say, wanting this conversation to end.

15

Sebas

While I stuff my face with pancakes and home fries, Kenzie stares at me like I'm an egg she expects to hatch any minute. It takes me a while to convince her that I don't need her to help me get TECH—*how many times do I have to say no to that TECH crap?*—and that I don't want to ask her about Lu, though I sort of do.

"I need to find a job, and I'm not sure where to start," I say.

"Why?" Her face makes having to find a job seem like a foreign concept, and I guess to these kids it sort of is.

"The usual reasons. Money. Wanting to be a productive member of society. No, actually, just money."

"Okay," she says, expression growing pensive. "I won't repeat all the stuff Lu has already told you—about the perks and benefits of taking the TECH stuff."

"Appreciate you," I say.

"You can get a job out at the Grandview Mall. That's ten miles away, though, not in New Gault."

"What about a place like this? I've worked in restaurants before."

Kenzie shrugs. "I don't think high school kids get jobs in

New Gault. The only youngish people I see working in restaurants around here are college kids living with their parents while going to Valley Community. I mean, kids don't really need money here."

"Speak for yourself."

At least Kenzie looks a little embarrassed by this.

"You could get a job at Dry Town," she says, leaning forward excitedly.

"What's Dry Town?"

"It's outside of New Gault too."

"No car. If the tram doesn't go there, I don't go there."

"Maybe Lu could drive you. Or I could sometimes. Diego's on probation for speeding, so no ride from him for a while. But we could do it. We go all the time."

"Um," I hedge, because relying on other people to drive me around sounds hellish. "Maybe. But what is Dry Town, exactly?"

"It's a hangout. Lots of kids go there, not just from New Gault, but a lot of the surrounding school districts, thank God. TECH is so small still. It's stifling with just the sad hundred."

"There are only a hundred students at TECH?" That can't be right.

"No, there's actually close to six hundred. But that's in all grades, and still pretty small. My middle school had two thousand kids in it. This feels like a fishbowl." She waves her hands around to indicate all this.

"I know they pay cash under the table at Dry Town," Kenzie adds, and that seals it for me. Mom's clearly strapped for cash, as well as needing me to help take care of her. I know Papá would send me money if I needed it, and I have savings, but not the kind of money to keep a family afloat. I can do that, or at least help.

Last night, I kept waiting for Mom to revert back to Mommie Dearest. It's what I'm used to. But we kept it to happy memories, nothing about her parents, my cousins, or anything else. I've got a mental map of the safe topics to cover. Snoopy, Abuela, and how Mom still manages to remember so many Pokémon characters—all good. Papi, politics, or anything past me in second grade—definitely not. She went to bed happy last night, and I felt like I'd run a marathon. When I told Abuela how it went, she was so happy. "Maybe she can come here, mijo, and we can take care of her," she said. That's a ridiculous idea, but Abuela is a hardcore optimist. "And where else could she go, amor? Her own family won't speak to her." When I say Mom is like Faye Dunaway in *Mommie Dearest*, I mean she burned *all* her bridges down.

It's almost five and I'm waiting for Lu outside the same retro diner where Kenzie took me to lunch earlier.

When Lu pulls up, they look confused.

"You still have time to take me to Dry Town?" I ask. Kenzie told me she'd arranged everything, but now I'm not sure.

"Yeah, um, sure, get in."

I do and buckle my seat belt. Lu still hasn't said anything or pulled away from the curb.

"Kenzie did ask you to drive me, right?"

"Yeah, but I thought I was driving both of you. And she didn't explain why we're going so early. Dry Town doesn't open until seven."

"I'm looking for a job." The surprise on these New Gault kids' faces when I say *job*, jeez. "So. This is cool?" I ask.

"Yeah, sure. I don't mind," Lu says.

Only, they clearly do mind. They're gripping the wheel of their car and frowning like the devil.

"Next time, I'll ask someone else," I say.

"I can take you."

"Because you're so relentlessly nice, right?"

"Because I can do it. I'm not busy." They pull away from the front of the diner and head out of New Gault.

"What do you do with your time?" I ask, after there's been a long, awkward silence.

"Huh?"

"You don't have to have a job and you do all your ambassador shit"—Lu winces—"sorry, *stuff* at school. Do you, like, do sports or anything?" Maybe they have a terrible soccer story we can bond over.

"My life is brimming with extracurricular activities, don't worry," Lu replies pointedly.

"Shit," I say, this time on purpose. "I'm just trying to be human."

"I'm sorry," Lu says, looking at me fleetingly as they drive down the empty road. I mean *empty*. We're a mile outside of New Gault, and there's nothing around, no towns, no buildings, no rest stops, nada.

"I'm just kind of a nervous driver, and I don't really like Dry Town, so I'm—I'm coming off like a d-bag."

"No harm," I say, resigning myself to silence with this kid. Which is hilarious, because they had all these fucking words for me when they were trying to lure me to the dark side. I glance at the display. They're driving a painful thirty miles an hour. On a highway. It's a good thing there aren't any other cars.

"I write poetry," Lu says quietly.

"Oh," I say, then realize that sounds shitty. "Oh, that's really cool," I add.

Lu gives me a wry look. "You don't like poetry?"

"I don't know anything about it. But it's cool. Like, do you publish anything?"

I expect them to say, *No, of course not, I'm a freaking teen.*

"Yeah, I've been published in a couple of journals. I send out a lot of poems—they mostly get rejected. But I do that every Sunday—send out poems to at least five places."

Honestly did not know there were five places to send poetry to. I'm out of my depth, but these are the most words they've said to me that were not about TECH in the little time I've known them.

"What do you write about?"

"Myself. Not in, like, an egotistical way, but, like, what happens to me when I get nervous."

"What happens to you?"

"Out-of-body experience."

"Like in *Body Snatchers*?"

"Like what?" They almost turn to look at me, but then their eyes snap back to the road.

"*Invasion of the Body Snatchers*?" Lu shakes their head, and I explain. "The movie? From the 1950s? And then a remake in the seventies, which is the superior version, with Donald Sutherland?" I don't mention the 2000s re-remake because it doesn't deserve a mention.

"Never saw it," Lu says, then makes a left down a small county road. In just a few minutes we pass from nothing on the horizon to a honking big parking lot with a square building in the center. A multicolored neon sign, in letters that have to be six feet tall, spells out DRY TOWN. There's a neon bottle complete with three *X*'s, and a green cactus.

I get out of the car, tug at my shirt. My indestructible, get-me-through-anything shirt has been doing all the work lately. I hope it can get me this job.

Lu stays in the car.

"You're not coming in?"

"Can't."

"You been banned?"

"What? No! I just don't like being without my phone, and you have to surrender your phone in there."

I look at them like they must be lying. "Kenzie didn't tell me that."

"She loves not having her words counted. That's why she comes to Dry Town all the time. And anyway, what does it matter to you? You don't have a phone."

I do have a phone, but not a TECH phone, so I guess that doesn't matter. "So I go in there, and I'm not the oddball without a TECH phone anymore? I get to be normal?"

Lu gives me a sardonic look.

"Okay, you know what I mean. But what about you?"

"I'll hang out here. Take your time."

"But what if it takes a while?"

"I'm not gonna abandon you amongst the tumbleweeds. I'll read. And write. Don't worry about me."

Feels weird to leave them in the parking lot. They parked right under one of three parking lot lights—it's just gotten dark enough for those lights to come on.

I walk to the door, wondering if I'm ready for this, and look back to see Lu watching me. They give me a thumbs-up and I nod. I open the door into Dry Town.

It looks like my tío Roberto's rec room when we visited him in Omaha two summers ago. Everything is wood paneled, there's a green-and-white checked lino floor, and the walls glow with more neon signage than Vegas. All beer and liquor brands—PBR, Stoli, Tecate, just to name a few. Right over the entrance is a painted banner that says YOU SHALL NOT PASS (WITH YOUR PHONE), with an arrow pointing to a set of lockers—the kind they have at community pools, the keys attached to curly bands. No one's there, or in the main room where tables are scattered with abandoned board games. There's a Skee-Ball machine in the corner, and way in the back, a counter with stools. Swing doors behind the counter are propped open, and "Dancing Queen" pumps from a back room.

"Hello?" I call out when I get to the counter. A large woman with a high blond ponytail comes out, dragging a huge box of glassware across the floor.

"Can I help you with that?" I ask.

"I don't know, can you?" she says, peering up at me and wiping her forehead with her arm. She's a pretty white woman, wearing a T-shirt that says VISIT BUTTZVILLE, NEW

JERSEY and has a cartoon of a dancing hot dog. I walk around the counter and pick up the box of glassware—carajo, it's heavy—and ask where she wants it.

"Strong guy, huh? Okay, well, we all have our gifts. The end of the counter is fine. I need to replace all the glasses that broke last weekend."

I put the box at the end of the counter, and she thanks me before starting to unpack it.

"What can I do for you?" she asks.

"I was wondering if you're hiring?"

"How old are you?"

"Seventeen."

"Where do you live?" She's not even looking at me as she stacks glass after glass on the counter.

"New Gault. Well, sort of."

She glances up at me, then shakes her head regretfully. "Nope."

"Wait, you're only hiring if I'm not living in New Gault?"

"Yup."

"Come on."

"Look, I'm not sure why you want to work here—I don't remember seeing you before, but I'm not here most nights now that we've got a kid—but I'm telling you, we don't hire TECH kids. They never stay, their work ethic sucks, no offense, and they're more trouble than they're worth."

"I'm not a TECH kid."

She stops stacking glassware to turn to me. "Explain?"

"I live there with my mom, but only for a little while, until she gets better. Um, she's sick. And I didn't take the TECH phone." I hold up my crappy phone for inspection. Her pale blond eyebrows arch up. "Besides, just because I live in New Gault doesn't mean I can't work hard."

"Thing is, I don't need someone to do the grunt work. I do that just fine. And my wife, Ana, does all the selling and schmoozy stuff. What I really need is entertainment." She puts her hands on her hips, and her face is serious. Which is hard to take with the dancing hot dog on her T-shirt.

I look at the Skee-Ball in the corner, the Ms. Pac-Man arcade game next to it, all the board games on the tables. "Don't you have enough entertaining stuff?" I ask.

"There are no phones allowed in here, so kids get bored fast. And despite all the signage, we don't serve alcohol. It's hard to keep anyone's attention, never mind the gnat-sized focus you all have. Can you sing?"

"Not at all."

"Are you funny?"

"Only when I'm not trying," I say, and I get a snort from her.

"I'm sorry, I'd like to help, but there's really nothing you can do here."

I thank her and walk away slowly because I'm racking my brain for something I can do that someone, anyone, would find entertaining. I can't show any movies I've made because I've yet to finish one that's longer than fifteen minutes, and anyway, how do you get paid for that kind of thing at a local hangout? Maybe if I'd finished the documentary on Abuela and las cartas...

I turn abruptly and walk back.

"I'm Sebastian, and I can tell the future," I say in a movie-trailer voice.

A slow smile spreads across her face. "Okay..."

"I can read tarot cards; my abuela taught me. She's from the old country." The old country of Texas, but who has to know that?

"Hmm. That sounds promising." She taps her fingers on the counter.

"I can read palms too," I say, which is a total lie that I instantly regret, because she could just reach out a hand to have me read her palm now, and I have no idea how to do that. I just opened my mouth and lies came out.

The woman looks at her hands, dusty from hauling boxes. "I'm Sheila. I can offer you two nights a week to start, and you can read your tarot cards, do your palmistry stuff. I'll pay you ten dollars an hour for helping me clean up and stuff, off the books. You give us ten percent of whatever you make with the woo-woo stuff. Tips are all yours. Yes?"

"Yes! Thank you, Sheila. When can I start?"

"You can start by helping me schlep the rest of these glasses out from the back. Then, come by tomorrow night and help me bus the tables until Ana clocks in. For that, you get ten bucks, too, no tips. Then you can read my palm."

Twenty-four hours to learn how to read palms. How hard can that be?

16

Lu

I made myself stop chewing pen caps in fourth grade when Emmy Shepherd noticed and said I was gross. I don't blame her for that. It's gross getting your saliva all over things that other people might borrow. But I *had* to chew something, so I graduated to my fingers—or rather, my cuticles. Mamá can tell when I'm in a bad way just by looking at how many Band-Aids I've got around my fingertips. Two weeks ago, at the end of March, my fingers were almost healed. Now, as I wait for Sebas to come out of Dry Town, I'm pulling at a cuticle like it's a thread I've got to unravel.

I pause to add a voice memo to my poetry file: "Cuticle like a thread to unravel." I don't know if it makes sense for any poem I'm writing, but it sounds kind of good. When I look up, Sebas is walking toward the car. I take a tissue from the glove box and wrap it around my bleeding thumb.

"Hey," he says when he gets into the car. "I wasn't sure if you'd still be here."

I roll my eyes. "I told you I'd wait. You didn't believe me?"

"I didn't *not* believe you." He shrugs, then buckles his seat belt.

"So? Did they have a job?"

"Not exactly. She said she didn't hire TECH kids."

"You aren't technically a TECH kid."

"That's what I said. But she said she didn't really need a busboy or anything like that." He's smiling like there's more. It's that hooky smile again. I feel it tugging against me, pulling all my attention to him.

"But . . . ?" I encourage.

"But she's gonna hire me anyway as . . . wait for it . . ."

"Drama queen," I say, smiling despite myself.

"A tarot card reader."

My confused face must strike him as funny, because he busts out laughing.

"Can you read tarot cards?" I didn't take him for an astrology person, but then again, I can't ever read him right. That's why I failed with him.

"Well, I've been learning how to do a tirada with Spanish cards, the ones with clubs and coins and cups, you know?"

I shake my head. "I only know the ones with the hanged man or death or the creepy lady."

"I think a lot of the meanings are similar." Sebas scrolls through his camera roll, then shows me a photo of an adorable old lady, wrapped in a crochet blanket, smiling down at a spread of cards. The cards are in primary colors: a knight on a horse holding up a club, another card of crossed swords. They look vaguely familiar.

"That looks like the deck my abuelo in Montevideo uses to play truco."

"All the old folks use these cards—and they get competitive as fu—fruit," Sebas says, glancing down at my biosensor. I laugh.

"You don't have to watch *your* words, remember?"

"Yeah, but if everyone looks at you like a leopard when you say the wrong thing, it makes it awkward."

"Leopard?"

"I mean *leper*—never mind, I always get that one wrong," Sebas says. He pulls off his elastic band and shakes out his hair. It moves like a nightfall of silky threads. I make a voice recording so I don't forget: "Silky threads."

"Silky threads?" Sebas asks with a raised eyebrow.

"Sorry." I'm sure flames are busting out from my cheeks. "When I think of some phrase or description I like, I have to get it down before I forget."

"Where did 'silky threads' come from?" He smiles and pushes his hair off his shoulders and— Is this flirting? It can't be.

"I was thinking of the night sky. Like, poetry stuff." I shrug.

"Okay. I don't know any poetry. Can I hear some?"

"Like, mine?" I squeak.

"Or, I don't know, other people's?" He reaches up, putting his palms against the roof of the car, and leans into a long stretch that turns his body into a bow.

My mind goes blank.

"Do you want to get something to eat?" I blurt out. He shakes out his arms, looking at me with a question in his eyes. I scramble. "You know, so you can get, like, free food or whatever. I don't mind. We could go anywhere you want. If you're hungry."

"Thanks. But I've got to go home."

"Oh." Maybe he's offended I'm treating him like a charity case. Or maybe he just isn't hungry. Or maybe he thinks I'm an ashhole because I get to have free food and he doesn't.

My thoughts chase each other as I drive him home. It takes me a while to find the dirt road that leads down to his mom's house.

"Thanks for driving me," Sebas says, getting out of the car. "Now that I potentially have a job, I have to practice reading cards. Oh, and learn to read palms. Two hours online and I'll be golden."

"If you need help, um, let me know."

"Sure," he says with a wave, and walks to the door of the dingy brown house.

I wonder if he really will.

17

Sebas

I'm on a high from lying my way into a job, and I definitely didn't want to go home. I would have loved to hang out with Lu, maybe get them to read me some poetry. But I have to make sure Mom is okay. I already feel guilty for not helping more, but once I start getting cash, that will change. I gently push open her bedroom door and look in—she's in her usual small lump, the fan on her face. Her TV is on without the volume. It's on that network that only plays reruns from the '70s and '80s. Her eyes are closed, and her chest moves up and down. I'm relieved—then I ping-pong back to guilt, because I didn't talk to her at all today.

I call Abuela, who is happy to hear from me. She always is, but as lonely as I am, it's so fucking welcome.

"¿Cómo estás, mijo?"

"Bien, Abue. How are you? Really, I mean?"

"I'm good, mijo. You know I don't lie to you. I am much better and taking it easy."

"No pillerías in the middle of the night? I know you like to cause trouble." Papi said he was worried about how much she got up at night, in case she had another stroke or fell. He's put a baby monitor in her room so he can hear her.

The reception on my phone glitches, lags, and her tiny image freezes, mouth wide open in a laugh. I grab a screenshot of it because it's so beautiful seeing her laugh. "Not too much getting up, amor. I miss my partner in crime," she says over the frozen image.

"I miss you too." When she doesn't answer, and I still can't see a live image, I ask, "Can you hear me, Abuela?"

"Sí, amor." Her image speeds up, showing me, in triple time, the small movements she made while the image was stuck.

"Oh, you were frozen."

"Better now?"

"Sí."

"Okay, well, tell me about you, amor."

"I got a job doing tiradas de cartas for people."

She claps her hands, delighted. "¡Qué bueno! And you want to talk about it?"

I angle my phone so it's showing the cards I've laid out on the bed.

"Is this right, Abue?"

She puts on her glasses and peers at her screen. "Well, it's a start. But don't forget the cliente has to shuffle the cards first. They should hold their question, or questions, in their mind as they do. Then you lay out las cartas, ¿sí?"

"Okay, let's pretend I did that." She laughs again.

We end up talking for more than an hour—halfway through, I have to move the phone and all the cards because I've run down the battery and I need to plug it in. She freezes up again, then calls me back on audio, so I have to describe the cards that come up and what I think they mean. Finally, she says she's tired and will go lie down for her "first sleep."

"If you're up a las tres, call me, mijito. You know I'll be making myself un tecito!"

"Okay, Abuela. Gracias por todo."

"Te quiero mucho, amor," she says.

Why does it make me want to cry, hearing her say she loves me, when she always ends our conversations that way? "I love you too, Abuela," I say, and hang up.

I should try to sleep, or try to catch up on schoolwork, but I can't relax. So, instead, I binge-watch videos on palmistry. I make notes in my flamingo notebook until my neck hurts from being bent over. Even lying in bed, waiting for sleep, I wonder if I can pull this off, if I'm fooling myself thinking any of this helps Mom at all. If Lu will agree to drive me back to Dry Town. Shit. I forgot to ask them. I type out the question, even though it's late and they probably are already asleep. But right away, I see the three dots that they're replying.

Of course I'll take you. Already planned on it.

I like their message, then respond with what I hope is a cheerful

TY!

Like a dork, I fall asleep with my crappy phone in my hand, in case Lu texts again.

School is a repetitive nightmare. The only difference is that today, I asked Mrs. Jackson to print out my grades from the virtual classroom and a list of all the assignments I haven't turned in... because I didn't know I had them. Lu and Kenzie ask me to join them for lunch, but instead I go to the library, where there's a laptop connected to the school-wide system where I can do all my work. I rush through the bullshit assignments like the icebreaker quiz and the persuasive essay for AP English—here's where going to so many different schools is a blessing; I repurpose an old essay—and watch my grade jump up from 0 to a 53 percent. I'm going to have to spend every morning, lunch, and afternoon working this hard just to pass.

"Hungry?"

Lu stands in front of me with a little paper bag.

"Always."

"I figured. We went back to Sound Café, and I got you that grilled cheese you like. It's a little cold and congealed, but it's probably still good." They hold the bag out to me.

"*Congealed* and *cheese* are two words that just go together. Thanks." I unpack the bag and start to unwrap the sandwich.

"You can't eat in here!"

Lu looks scandalized. Even though there's no one, not even a librarian, around.

I put the sandwich to my mouth real slow, while watching them, like I'm daring them to stop me.

Lu looks away, blushing. I don't know why I'm messing with them; they did just bring me food. But there's something really adorable about the way their cheeks go pink.

"Okay, where should we go so I can eat the congealed protein package without breaking the rules?"

A slight smile plays on Lu's mouth. "Let's go sit outside. We've got about twenty minutes before the next class."

I follow them out of the library doors to the quad, where a path cuts the square into triangles. We sit on a bench, and I eat my delicious sandwich, even though it's awkward having Lu watch me.

"Want some?" I say through a mouthful of cheese.

"You're like my sister, Ofelia."

"Who you don't like, clearly."

"She talks with her mouth full too."

I freeze mid-chew. Honestly, I don't get them. Do they want to be friends or don't they? I can't tell if they like me or can't stand me.

"Okay. Well, thanks for the sandwich," I say, getting up.

"I'm sorry!" Lu says, getting up, too, and putting a hand on my arm so I don't leave.

I sit back down.

"You don't have to babysit me anymore, you know."

"I'm not," they say, surprised.

"I mean, I'm not gonna do the TECH thing."

"Okay."

"I can't read you at all, you know that?"

They lift their chin. "There's nothing to read."

"You bring me food. You look at me like I'm a science project. And I remind you of your sister, who you don't like. So. Why are you here?"

They look so pained, their green-tipped curls in disarray around their forehead and their eyes darting side to side, like I asked them an impossible question.

"Because you're my failure," Lu blurts out.

If this were a movie, I'd set up a medium shot of us sitting on this bench, me still holding the crust of a sandwich and Lu's words hanging between us. I'd stage the scene with graffiti or falling trash or something, a visual clue to how shitty calling me a failure is.

"Well, fuck," I say, and leave before they can say anything else stupid.

18

Lu

Because you're my failure. That's what I said to him two days ago, and it's still ringing in my ears. I'm such a pendeje sometimes.

I drove Sebas to and from Dry Town on Wednesday night and sat in my car trying to write, but everything I wrote was garbage.

I apologized to Sebas right away, and he said it was fine, but I can tell it isn't. I mean, I called him a failure—*my* failure. But that's how I feel. Like this is a problem I have to carry around with me, work on, try to solve until I get frustrated and put it away again. Oh God. I'm essentially describing one of Dad's vintage Rubik's Cubes.

Even with me, Diego, and Kenzie hanging out with Sebas, he's like a ghost roaming the school: always standing a little outside of everyone, outside of what everyone knows. And I'm just watching it happen. When Mr. Becker called me back into his office today, I told him there were special circumstances and I was working on it. He told me to try a different strategy, he'd be working on the problem too, and we'd see where we were in a week. Now both of us are trying to solve this Rubik's Cube. It makes me queasy.

The only bright spot is that Sebas is making bank at Dry Town.

"Sorry I'm so late," he says at midnight Friday night as I unlock the car doors to let him in. He's wearing a tight black T-shirt with DRY TOWN on it, and his skin is glowy with sweat, pieces of hair stuck to his heated face. Warmth radiates from him. It's kinda mesmerizing, watching as he reaches up to release his long hair from its ponytail, slipping the black elastic band onto his wrist. Did I know he had arms like that?

"You okay?" he asks.

"Absolutely. How did it go?"

He laughs. "It actually went incredible. I made five hundred dollars!"

"What? How?"

"I don't know! Sheila and Ana were surprised and fucking pleased as anything. I started charging twenty bucks for a short reading—ten minutes—but everyone wanted more, so I added a deluxe reading—twenty minutes—and then tonight, I made up a 'Mercury in Retrograde Is Coming for Your Ass' reading—for fifty bucks you get thirty minutes for las cartas, a palm reading, *and* an aura cleansing with crystals."

"Do you know how to do that?"

"How can I know how to do that? I just made it up! Ana had some chunks of crystals in a box on the game shelf, and I just used those."

He leans the passenger seat back until it's almost horizontal. His black hair pools over the leather seat, looking so smooth and touchable.

"You've got that look on your face, so before you start lecturing me on the evils of lying to people, know that (A) I did learn a lot about palmistry from online videos, and (B) most of astronomy is bullshit anyway."

"Astrology."

"What?"

"Astrology is the star signs, the 'Mercury in retrograde' stuff. Astronomy is an actual science, like the positions of planets and the stars."

"Oh. I always get those confused." He grins.

His smile is so easy and inviting, even when I'm telling him he's wrong about something. I don't know what to do with him—his warmth, the smell of him, deodorant over sweat.

"You okay?" Sebas repeats.

"I'm just super tired," I say.

"Hey, I'm sorry I keep asking you to drive me."

"No, I want to," I say, turning on the engine.

"But it's so boring for you. Are you sure you won't come in next time?"

"I can't. Thanks, though."

"Have you written lots of good poems?"

"So many." I think I wrote three words. If I were to write anything down now, the way my brain has locked in on Sebas's arms and sweaty face, it would be the kind of erotica Mamá doesn't know I know she reads.

"Would you ever show me?"

"What?"

"Your poetry. I mean, you're published, so you must be good."

"That's not at all how it works," I say.

"Of course it is. No one's gonna publish trash poetry."

I laugh. "I kind of wish 'trash poetry' were its own category. Just the word vomit of a late night."

"Word vomit," Sebas repeats while smiling. "Very vivid. Bet we could write trash poetry right now."

"Damn, you are so keyed up," I say, a little jealous of his energy.

"I can't help it. People hype me up. I feel better when I'm around them. It's a weird thing. And I've been a little lonely."

"It's got to be miserable for you to have to travel so much from school to school."

"It really messed me up for a while. We're pretty settled now. Papá doesn't do the traveling for construction jobs like he used to, not now that he's got his own business."

"I had to be homeschooled for a while, so I know it can suck. But all that time with Mamá meant I learned Spanish."

"It's not so bad—at least I have Abuela. And I have new friends, now that we're hopefully staying in San Marcos for a while."

"But they're there and you're here," I say, pointing out the obvious.

He raises his seat back and digs through his backpack for his phone. "It's fine. I won't be here long. Help my mom; go home. Simple."

My stomach drops a little at the thought of Sebas leaving. Of not seeing him every day and now nearly every night. I don't like the idea. And whatever else this is, it's *not* simple.

Sebas connects his phone to the stereo. A dancy pop tune from a Mexican indie band starts to play. He turns up the volume, then leans his head against the window and sings along, grinning wildly. His hair whips back in the spring air.

"They'll tell tales about you down the generations, the boy who said no!" I say, slightly giddy from the air or the pheromones, the contact high from Sebas's extrovert vibes. Can you get drunk off someone else's good time?

"Kenzie says she can drive me tomorrow night, if you want a break from me," he says.

Hell no, I almost say, the way I do when Mamá suggests thinking about college or leaving New Gault, even for vacation. Absolutely not gonna let Kenzie drive Sebas.

I shrug. "It's fine. I like to drive you." *My beautiful failure.*

19

Sebas

I guess I expected something to go right, and that was my first mistake. Or I was just not thinking at all. That's how I find myself in the kitchen staring at Mom, her face full of rage at one in the morning.

"You sack of shit," she says as a greeting. I freeze and my stomach twists. Just like when I was little, I don't know what I've done wrong, but I know it's gonna hurt. I swallow my confusion and stay quiet.

"I tried to make my appointment for the new oncologist, the one working exclusively for New Gault Medical. The one leading the clinical trials that everyone with my kind of cancer is literally dying to get into. Know what they said?" She wheezes. "She informed me that only residents of New Gault were allowed to see Dr. Webber. I explained that my son here was at the TECH school, and we'd be moving into New Gault any day now. Everyone was so helpful, like there would be no problem at all, when we figured out what the problem was. Eventually, we figured it out. It's you. You're the fucking problem."

She sits at the kitchen table, dressed in warm clothes and a thick robe like it's the middle of winter. She doesn't have her soft hat on, so I can see the wispy long blond threads of hair clinging to her head. It's so *wrong*, but it makes me think of *Ghost Rider*, another terrible movie that my dad loves. The strands of hair like flames shooting from a demon skull. My mom.

"Why would you say no to the fucking phone, Sebastian?"

I feel like that time I was in a car accident with my cousin in Laguna Beach. Everything was fine and then it wasn't. I got out while Javier talked to the driver who'd crashed into us. I stood next to the crunched car, shaking like a wet dog, trying to make sense of what had happened. I grab the back of the kitchen chair like it's gonna keep me from shaking.

"Because it, uh, sounded like a drag. And an invasion of privacy." I try to inject disinterest into my voice.

"You are some waste of space, you know that?"

I wait. It's better to hear it all from her before deciding how to respond. But it's so hard to be still.

"Didn't your piece of shit father tell you why you were coming? Or are you just too stupid to do what you're here to do?"

I wonder how much money all Mom's curse words would have cost if Mom had to keep clean. *She'd be bankrupt in a week,* I think.

"Did you hear me, *chico*?"

"Papi told me you needed help. He told me you wouldn't take the help from anyone else, just me."

"Well, then, it's that asshat's fault, I guess," Mom wheezes. "And don't call him *Papi* like you're some ignorant wet—"

"Stop." Just like that, I'm *pissed*. Honestly, I want to punch something. I'm not going to. But I want to. "You want me here, you don't get to say racist shit to me."

"Oh really? I don't *get* to, huh?"

"I'll just leave. And whatever messed-up reason you want me to be here, too bad."

"Sebastian." Mom takes a long, rattling breath. "Listen. Honey." The endearment sounds wrong, a badly dubbed audio track. "The reason you're here, the reason it had to be you, is so you could be part of the TECH program."

"What?"

"Yes. That's why it had to be you. I thought your . . . father . . . had explained it. I explained it to him really clearly, but I guess that was just too—" She stops herself from insulting her ex-husband. "If you're registered as a student at the school *and* you participate in the program, we get a whole lot of benefits."

"A fancy phone and a fitness monitor?"

"That's not all it is! I'd get to live in the city itself, in a fancy building, not this crap-ass place outside town. And I'd be able to go to the Cancer Institute, not that shitty county hospital, for *free*. We'd get payments that double my disability. We'd get a car."

"They'd give you a car just for that?"

Mom nods eagerly, as if the mention of a car will be the thing that changes my mind. She doesn't even know that I can't drive.

"You'd get to drive it sometimes, too, as long as you take me to my appointments. And you could buy yourself more clothing and music, books and things. There'd be money for all that."

When was the last time Mom knew a single, specific thing about me, about what I might want and like? Third grade, maybe.

"Why don't *you* just sign up?" I interrupt. "Why does it have to be me?"

"Because it has to be a kid between twelve and eighteen—didn't they explain it to you at school?"

Maybe Lu did say something about that, but they said so much, it's hard to remember it all.

"So you'll do it, hon? You'll get the phone and biosensor, right? That will be so good, and you'll have all this—this technology and gadgets and crap, ha, more than any other kid in America. You'll do it, right, Sebby?"

Mom's nickname for me, one I haven't heard in years, hovers between us. I used to hate when she called me Sebby because I thought it sounded like *baby*. But she was the only one who ever called me that and it hurts to hear it now. This time was supposed to be different. She asked for me, needed *me*. I thought it meant she finally wanted me around, that she had changed or I was enough or *something*. But it's just more of the same bullshit. If I can be what she needs, then I can be around. As soon as she doesn't need me anymore, she'll leave.

"No."

When she goes for me, the fury on her face making her look like chalk, I duck, not because she can really hurt me, but more because she might hurt herself.

I grab the duffel bag from my room—to hell with anything I've left behind. Then I'm out the door, running for all I'm worth, toward the lights of New Gault.

20

Lu

I can't go home after dropping Sebas off. I'm electricity and exclamation points and hormonal confusion. All because of Sebas. I drive around the city, knowing there's a chance Mamá, half asleep, is watching me move through New Gault, a blip on her screen. I come home when I'm tired, and as long as I get enough sleep—since Mamá gets an alert if my biosensor dips below eight hours of sleep—she doesn't complain.

I'm finally ravenously hungry, so I drive toward the twenty-four-hour Scooter's Shakes inside the bus terminal, hoping they're not out of frozen custard. The later it is, the more my ADHD meds have worn off, and the more I feel like eating. I park under the huge sign that runs down the side of the terminal, E-A-T-S picked out in individual bulbs like it came straight from Broadway.

The streets are predictably empty, except for a man who's marching away from the terminal like he's missed his bus. And then I recognize him. It's Sebas.

"Hey," I say, getting out of the car and walking toward him. He spins around, looking wild-eyed.

"What the fuck do you want?"

I stop. "Whoa. Nothing. Sorry. I thought you needed help." I take a step back.

"Wait," Sebas says, putting down his bag and pushing the hair from his eyes. "I'm sorry. I'm just so done."

"Okay."

"I am." Sebas heaves a huge breath and lets it out, shuddering slightly. He's *crying*.

"I'm done," he says again.

I hate seeing him cry like this, like it's being wrung out of him. I want to ask, what happened, who hurt you? But I don't know how.

"I wanted to catch the bus home, but they stop running at midnight, even though this place is supposed to be open twenty-four hours."

"I think only the restaurants and bowling alley stay open."

"Who," Sebas laughs bitterly, "wants to bowl in the middle of the night?"

"I can drive you home, if you want."

"All the way to San Marcos?" Sebas growls through his gritted teeth, and the tears keep coming.

"Do you want to just sit in the car? So you're not, like, in the street?"

"Not that it matters," Sebas says. "These are the cleanest goddamn streets I've ever seen. There's not even gum stuck to them."

"Spitting out your gum onto the street is a violation. Thousand-dollar fine," I say automatically.

Sebas howls with laughter, and that's much more disturbing

than his crying. It's like the same anger that drove his tears now fuels his unhinged laughter.

He climbs into the car, cradling his bag in his lap. I tap my fingers against the steering wheel like a song caught on repeat.

After a few minutes of silence, he sniffs. "Are you gonna drive?"

"I don't know where to take you."

"You know where I live," he says dully.

"But you don't want to go home, right? I mean, you were trying to get on a bus."

Sebas buries his face in his hands, rubbing at his eyes. "I don't even know what I'm trying to do."

Something catastrophic must have happened between the time I left him at home and now. I recognize the shape of it.

"Do you want to stay at my house? My parents have a guesthouse—well, like a room that's all on its own. My friends sometimes stay there if they need a place to crash."

"Are we friends?" Sebas asks, his tone flat.

It feels weird to say yes and weird to say no. I don't know what we are. I know that I have to be the one to drive Sebas to Dry Town, that I make excuses so I can talk to him at school. I know I've binge-watched his favorite TV show, watched *Invasion of the Body Snatchers* (1978)—even though I hate sci-fi—so that I could, maybe, understand him a little more than I do.

I didn't realize how long I've been in my head, until Sebas laughs sarcastically. "I guess we're not friends, and that tracks. You called me a failure, and you're not wrong."

"Hey," I say, turning to face him. "I didn't say you were a failure. I said you were *my* failure. I'm the one who messed up, who couldn't get you to say yes to me." I shake my head. I don't want to talk about TECH. I don't care about that right now. "We are friends. I want to be."

He closes his eyes, tipping his head against the headrest like it's too heavy to hold up.

"Me too," he sighs.

I pull the car out into the empty streets, the anxiety beast in my stomach doing weird fluttering things as I think about how much I want to be more than friends.

21

Sebas

I stand in the dimly lit kitchen of Lu's house, unsure how I got here. I remember everything from Lu calling out to me at the bus terminal to arriving here, a house with red-orange tiles on the roof. I remember that we're officially friends now, and that before settling in San Marcos, I didn't have a great track record of keeping friends. When we'd move to a new place, I'd leave the friends I made behind. Simple. Or it was simple. Being friends with Lu doesn't feel simple.

"Ma, this is Sebas. He's new at TECH. Missed the last bus to San Marcos, so is it okay for him to stay in the shed?"

"Hola, Señora Hernandez," I say. Lu's mom must be where Lu gets their curls, but not their height; she's kinda short with lots of light brown hair, big and wild, though that might be because it's so late. She's looking at me with sharp, dark eyes. I'm probably about to witness Lu's mother yell at them.

"Hola, Sebas. Bienvenid—" She stops for a second before continuing in English, "You're very welcome here."

"He uses he/him pronouns, Ma," Lu says. "So you can use *bienvenido*."

"Is it really okay that I stay?" I ask.

"Of course, it's no trouble."

I follow Lu out sliding glass doors to a paved stone backyard. A small in-ground pool, kidney-shaped like one of the plastic bowls Mom has in her room, glows with underwater lights. To the left of the pool is a tiny house. Lu keys the code into the lock, opens the door, and turns on the lights. Framed posters of Paris cityscapes cover the walls, and a basket of healthy snacks sits next to a mini fridge. Christmas lights hang over a bed, and a huge TV is crammed into a corner. Frilled cotton curtains cover the two small windows. Another curtain hides a toilet, tiny shower, and sink.

Lu flops down on the bed. The only other place to sit is a dainty padded stool.

"Aren't you gonna sit?"

I sit, keeping my bag at my feet, again like I'm on public transport. Even knowing I'm ridiculous doesn't make me act any different.

Lu reaches over to the mini fridge and pulls out a bottle of soda with a picture of a bull on it.

"Want one?"

"What is it?"

"It's pomelo. Like grapefruit soda. My cousin in Montevideo shipped it to me for my birthday. There's grapefruit soda you can get here, but it's not as good as the Uruguayan one, Paso de los Toros," Lu says, passing me a bottle.

"Bull Crossing? Bull Passage?" I translate.

"Something like that."

It's good—not too sweet, and I'm thirsty, so I glug some down. And then I have to burp.

"Salud," Lu says. "Easy, amigue."

"Amigue?"

They shrug. "I'm trying to use gender-neutral Spanish when I can. It's hard to remember."

"I've never tried, but it's got to be hard to avoid gender in Spanish."

Lu smirks. "Especially when not everyone agrees it should happen. One of my tutors, before Mamá took over teaching me Spanish, basically tortured me about it, refused to even acknowledge that there was a need for inclusive language."

I make the universal *tsk* sound for disgust and burp again, which makes Lu laugh. "What does that pendejo know?"

"Ha! That's my favorite curse word! Pendeja/pendejo/pendeje—so versatile, perfect for so many situations, a solid four out of five on the offensiveness scale."

"And not trackable by TECH," I say, then burp again, getting a noseful of grapefruit-scented air for my trouble.

"You're learning!" Lu says, lying across the bed on their back, propped up on a multitude of pillows.

We sip soda in silence for a few minutes, and it's not uncomfortable, at least not to me. I don't feel tired anymore. I don't feel anything exactly, except okay. Reading the cards, making up crystal aura cleanings, the bounce I got from making so much cash—all of that was hours, days, years ago. Now I'm in stasis, hoping time stands still.

Because tomorrow will bring a world of hurt. But the night, which is already the next day, seems to have so much room in it, like I can sit in this night and just be.

"Do you want to talk about it?" Lu asks. They're tapping their rings against the glass soda bottle, looking up at the ceiling.

"I want to ask a question," I say.

"Yeah, of course."

"Why do you love it here so much? I mean, what does all this New Gault stuff do for you?" I remember Kenzie saying that Lu thought New Gault could save lives, and after what Mom told me tonight, that being here could maybe save *her* life, I just want to understand.

Lu lets out a huge sigh. "I don't always love it here. Sometimes I feel so stuck in the same pattern, the same restaurants, the same—everything."

I'm so surprised, I turn to look right at them. But they keep their eyes on the ceiling.

"If it works—" They start, pause, then begin again. "If New Gault works like it's supposed to work, it means no bullying. No hate speech. No trolls, no death threats. People wouldn't be so desperate they don't know how to keep living."

Not nameless, random people wouldn't be desperate. *They* wouldn't be desperate. Is that what Lu means?

"There was a time, when I was younger, that me, my friends, we weren't safe. Because people could say whatever they wanted. Because even if it was against the rules, those rules didn't apply to them. Words can be weaponized, you know?"

I nod, remembering Mom's face as I stormed out of her house. The words she spewed at me were so fucking sharp, I still feel them digging under my skin.

"My mom says that if I do the TECH thing, she'll get better health care. Is that true?" I ask.

Lu sits up, crossing their legs. "It's one of the reasons we're here. The neurotherapy I did when we first moved here wasn't covered by insurance. It would have been way too much for my folks to afford. But here, it was free."

More silence. This time, not so comfortable.

"Hey, sorry, it's so late," I say. "You want to get to bed, right? And I, um, have to get going pretty early."

"How sick is your mom, Sebas?"

I blow out my breath, exasperated. *Well, what else are they gonna think?* I feel like a trash-fire drama queen who has cried, screamed, and burped the night away. In a handful of hours, I'll be on my way home. Abuela and Papi will understand. Won't they?

"She's got cancer. That's why I came. I thought I was helping her, like making food and that kind of thing. I didn't realize—you probably told me—that saying no to TECH meant she wouldn't get the medical stuff she needs. Today, she found out I'd said no to TECH, and she just—she lost it. And I should not make a person with cancer upset, right? I mean, that makes me a terrible person, right?" I'm not even asking Lu this question, I know the answer. The guilt crashes over me and I can't stop the tears. What does Lu think of me? A son who turned down brand-new technology and a thousand other amazing things—not to mention lifesaving medical stuff—for his mother, and then abandoned her?

The ugliest voice in my head screams to be heard: *Because she abandoned you first! Because she did everything she could to make you feel small, make you feel like you weren't good enough—and she's still fucking doing it.*

"I'm really sorry," Lu says.

"It's all good," I say, lying to them and to myself. It takes me a minute to notice their hand holding mine, the cold sensation of metal rings registering on my skin. There's so much, I don't know, *kindness* in their touch that it makes me feel hot, or angry, or something.

I take my hand back like it's on fire. "Hey, you don't have any toothpaste, do you? I forgot to grab some on my way out." I use my T-shirt to wipe my eyes.

Lu squints up at me like they might say something, be kind to me again, and I just *can't*. I'd 1,000 percent rather hear their TECH bullshit right now.

"There's a ton of stuff here in this hospitality basket."

"Hospitality in a basket," I snort. "We live in a beautiful world."

"We really do," Lu says, then stands, stretching. "If you need anything, just text me. I tend to sleep with my phone in my hand—not in a creepy way."

"When I think of you, Lu, it will always be in a totally noncreepy way. Palabra."

"Palabra," Lu agrees, letting themselves out of the shed.

I lock the door behind them. *Now what?*

22

Lu

I get up before my alarm, before Mamá, despite being as tired as I have ever been. I get dressed and heat up Dad's French toast stuffed with dulce de leche in the microwave and make instant coffee. Mamá is just out of the shower when I open the sliding door to the backyard, balancing the French toast, coffee, and a carton of milk. I can't remember if there is any milk or creamer in the shed's mini fridge.

I rehearsed what to say to Sebas from the second I opened my eyes, maybe even while I was asleep. *The dulce de leche is from Uruguay. Same primo that sends me the Paso de los Toros sends us this case of Conaprole. It was started in a place called Punta Ballena, which is, like—* God, I'm so rambly. How can I talk about dulce de leche when all I can think about is Sebas crying, his mom fighting cancer? How can I talk about anything else?

I stop in front of the shed, having no free hand to knock. *Why am I so nervous? I'm just bringing him breakfast.* I slept so badly. I'd nod off, only to wake up thinking my phone had vibrated with a text from Sebas. But there was nothing. Mamá is gonna murder me when she sees how little sleep I've gotten.

I put the plate of French toast on the patio and knock. The

sky is lightening in the east with a line of orange on the horizon that seems to undo the gray-clouded sky. A fragment of a poem forms in my head: *A fire horizon unzips the sky / take yesterday, unlight the fire, unsay the words.* I take a picture of the sky and add the poem fragment to my Notes app, wondering why the sky and the fragment make me feel breathless. Then I knock again. No answer. When I try the door, it opens. Inside, the shed is pristine, the bed made. And Sebas is gone.

23

Sebas

Luckily, I forgot to leave the spare key, because there's a good chance Mom might not let me back in. That would be the fucking capper. After coming back, ready to swallow my pride and act apologetic, Mom kicking me out would be all I need. Abuela made me come back—well, not made—Abuela doesn't make anyone do anything.

Four words—that's all she had to say when I called her at three a.m. I told her everything, how horrible Mom had been, how lonely I feel, how this town wants to make me pay for the words I use.

"Then come home, mijo." Four words. And as soon as she said that, as soon as I knew she'd support me going home, I knew I wouldn't.

I open the front door. The first thing I notice is the smell. It reminds me of the time Papá lost a container of milk in the van. He thought he'd forgotten to buy the milk, but it had been there, sitting under the window in the space where the spare tire used to be, going rancid. After a few days, the goo in the bottle built up some milky gasses and exploded, raining chunks of wannabe yogurt all over the back of the van. Papá gave me twenty bucks to clean it out with bleach. It was not enough.

"Mom?"

The house is silent. I don't even hear the steady white noise of Mom's fan going full blast on her flushed skin.

I thought I'd never be back.

I slip my phone out of my pocket and dial the nine and the one. *She's gonna be fine and scream at me for waking her up. She's gonna be fine, and she's gonna be pissed.* The door to her room is open, another bad sign. It takes everything I have in me to stay, not to run all the way to the New Gault bus station, as if I'd never changed my mind.

The sheets are pulled off the bed, and Mom sits glassy-eyed on the floor, propped up against the bed.

"I need to go—" She coughs, turns her head, and vomits on the floor—only a little, a thin stream of watery liquid. I see it far away, through a frame, a viewfinder, so the horror doesn't touch me.

"Need to go to the ER," Mom finishes, wiping her mouth with the edge of the sheet. She has her shoes on, and her purse nearby, her phone in her hand. "No goddamn Ubers around."

"I'll call an ambulance," I say, surprisingly calm.

"Wait."

She pulls a card from her pocket and holds it out to me.

"This ambulance," she pants, unable to catch a breath. "They know me. Will go to the county hospital, not New Gault Medical Center."

"Mom, we should go to the nearest hospital, the one here. They can't refuse you."

"Oh yeah, they won't refuse me. They'll charge me a fucking arm and a leg, and I can't do that. Call this service. Tell them we're in Lower Gault Township, and we want—we want—" She struggles, wheezing. "Want to go to Sierra General. They know me," she repeats, closing her eyes.

I step back into the kitchen and dial the number. They ask me a lot of questions, some answers I know, some that I guess. She's a cancer patient; she's undergoing chemo; she's been vomiting; she might have a fever, I don't know. They said they'd be right here, but what does that mean? And what do I do now? I can't go back into Mom's room, not yet.

I text Pa what's going on, and he immediately calls, but I decline it. If I'm texting you, it means I can't handle talking to you right now, you know? I text him that I'm fine and the ambulance will be here soon, and he writes a long message about how well I'm doing and what a good son I am—it's the last thing I want to hear, because I know it's not true. I just like his message, then tell him I'll keep him posted.

A message from Lu pops up with a photo of breakfast.

You missed out on my (dad's) dulce de leche
French toast! LOL. Just wanted to say bye and
I hope you are okay. And suerte. Maybe see
you sometime, if you come back to visit your
mom. Okay. Bye!

I imagine Lu typing out this message, like, a thousand times before hitting send.

I tap out, **Looks amazing. I'm sorry I left without saying goodbye. But things are happening. I don't know what to do. I'll text you later. Thanks for everything.**

Then I delete most of it and send, **I'm sorry I left without saying goodbye.**

There's a knock on the door, and I don't have time to think about how inadequate my words are. I let the EMTs in, take them to Mom, answer their questions. I pick up her purse, collect all the bottles of medication from her bedside table, comply with every one of Mom's raspy demands. They have her on a stretcher and out the door in minutes. I hesitate at the door, afraid to leave, afraid to be left behind.

24

Lu

"Like watching the most boring action movie ever," Diego whines as he finishes Kenzie's yogurt and berries. He gestures with his spoon to the matte black TECH box that Kenzie and I have been staring at. "Is it going to explode?"

"Shut up," I say, finishing my coffee. It's early Monday morning, and the cafeteria is starting to fill up. Mostly, it's just staff and students working off their word debt. I'm here so I can return Sebas's phone back to the lockup before classes start. Kenzie and Diego are here for moral support.

I lean my head on the table, inhaling the smell of orange-scented disinfectant. The once-pristine TECH box is dinged at the corners, and there's a scratch across one side. Becker messaged first thing to tell me we couldn't wait any more for Sebas to say yes to the phone and biosensor. As soon as the TECH office opens, I have to hand it in. Then there'll be another painful interaction with Mr. Becker, underscoring how I failed.

"That's mine, right?" A hand snatches the black box from my view. The three of us look up as Sebastian sits across from us.

"Hey" is all I can think to say.

The silence lengthens until Diego breaks it. "Lu said you left town."

"I almost did. Turns out, this place is hard to leave," Sebas says. He smiles at me like we share a secret, and my face floods with heat.

"So, one more time, how do I do this TECH thing?"

After Kenzie and Diego leave, I help Sebas set up the phone and the biosensor band.

"It doesn't tell time?" he says, shocked.

"I know, right? Like, the newer one, the matte black one, does. And does a ton of other stuff, but it's an upgrade."

"An upgrade?"

"Yeah, you need the bigger word data plan."

"Is that what you have? Unlimited word data?"

"No one has unlimited data. There's always a limit. Otherwise, they wouldn't be able to get you to watch what you say. You're starting toward the end of the month, so you'll get a prorated number of words, but the basic package that everyone starts with is two hundred thousand words a month."

"Whoa. That seems like a lot of words. *Is* that a lot of words?"

"Average word usage is about seven thousand words a day—or at least that's what TECH says," I say.

Sebas straps the biosensor on his wrist. He holds his brown wrist with the teal band next to my pale, freckled wrist sporting the same teal band.

"I may need a lot of help figuring out how to do this, okay?"

"I'm your TECH buddy for life," I joke stupidly. "As long as you don't drop any f-bombs or harass anyone, you'll be fine."

"So how do you cope? You take off the biosensor thingy, get into the shower, and sing along to the most explicit playlist you have?" Sebas smiles.

"Yeah, no. You can't take off the biosensor."

"What? Like, not even in the shower?"

"No. And not at night, or while swimming, or anything else. That's the whole point. That you *don't* use words you're not supposed to. The biosensor tracks your vital signs, how much sleep, exercise, oxygen you're getting, and also extends the reach of the phone so all your words are tracked. Both are waterproof, and if either starts to malfunction, you get a replacement, all free."

Sebas looks at me with dawning dread. I *know* I told him all this already. Rules and word meters and restrictions and fines—I explained it. But then, I guess he never thought he'd *do* any of it.

He raises the teal biosensor close to his face, tapping the tiny screen once, and the last words he said appear: *What? Like, not even in the shower?* Another tap brings up the word meter, all green bars, like a full tank of gas.

"What about charging it?"

"The proprietary battery has self-charging technology. Uses moisture collected from the air to charge."

Dread turns to disbelief on his face. "You are shi-irting me," he stammers.

"Not shirting you. You can take it off—it's not like it's hermetically sealed to your wrist or anything. I tend to take it off for about an hour in the morning, just to give my skin a break—but you do rack up some fees the longer you don't have it on, unless you leave New Gault, there aren't any word restrictions outside of the city limits, and I know some people who really take advantage of that, but—" Sebas puts his hand over mine and I shut up.

"It's cool," he says. "Didn't mean to freak out. I've got a lot of, um, stuff going on right now, and some cursing would have been, let's say, convenient?"

"How are things with your mom?" I ask.

"She's, um, she's in the hospital," Sebas says, like he's apologizing for the fact.

"Oh my God." I stand up. Not sure why I'm standing up, like I'm going to jump into action and—do what, exactly?

Sebas tugs at my hand, so I sit down again, this time closer to him. And he doesn't let go.

"She's going to be all right," he says. "I'm going to do this TECH thing, and she's going to get better. Simple."

I can think of a thousand ways none of this is simple, but the words don't come. He keeps hold of my hand, scrolling through his new phone with the other. And I lean into the feeling of Sebas holding my hand, like I'm brave enough to just accept it, to not let my anxiety take over. I stare at the intense blackness of his hair, and I wish I could write a poem about the depth of it, the way it frames his face. But all the words that I come up with are so clichéd and overused. *Inky, liquid, a curtain.* I spent a lot of my weekend trying to think of new words, or at least new combinations of words, that describe Sebas as his hair falls across his brown face. Like *night*. Like *the golden hour before sunset.* Jesus, it's all so cringe. If I'm feeling this unsettled, you'd think I'd get some decent poetry out of it. Words are failing me.

My phone vibrates with a message from the school office.

I unlace my hand from his, and Sebas grins sheepishly, like he forgot he'd left his hand there.

"Message from Assistant Principal Becker—probably wants to congratulate me for finally getting you to open the box. I'll probably get a medal. Or a bronze statue in my likeness."

"You deserve all the good things," he says sincerely. I add his words to the stack of feelings I'm already struggling through today. "And I'm a pinche pendejo," he says, then looks at his phone—all green, no word infractions.

"Told you Spanish would come in handy. Say all the malas palabras you want—but make it foreign." I get up and grab my backpack. I have about fifteen minutes to do my victory lap with Becker before my first class.

"See you later."

"No doubt," he says, still scrolling through his phone, toggling all the apps open. He looks up, his face alight.

"We can go to lunch!"

I laugh. "Anywhere you want in New Gault."

"Ramen?"

"Oh yeah, we got you." I give him a little awkward wave as I leave the cafeteria.

I feel lighter. Not like a weight has been lifted. That's so corny. But more like I couldn't remember something, and now I can.

I type into my poetry file: *Recovered rooms I forgot how to live in*. Then delete every word of that trite sentence. Maybe now that I don't have to worry about Sebas taking TECH, I can work on some better poetry, carajo.

25

Sebas

Four days in, and it's not *that* hard to avoid using words on the "dirty thirty" when I'm at school. No one's gonna call me a little bitch or make lewd comments as a girl walks past. With everyone else being chill, it's not that hard to do the same. Okay, an f-bomb slipped out the first day, but Lu was right; I just got a warning light flashing on my biosensor, and my word count has been pretty damn healthy all week. *The trouble,* I think as I board the tram and nod at the driver, *is Mom.*

The doctor said she'll be released today or tomorrow. The infection that had gotten into the Hickman port—a hole, basically, right into her veins to make getting chemotherapy easier—is finally clearing up. She's been in the hospital for six days. And though I'd deny it under torture if anyone asked me, those days have been amazing.

The TECH phone is ridiculously fast. I stream movies and games, chat with Anaïs and Hudson back in San Marcos for hours, finally using the weirdo crowdsourced app that Anaïs likes for messaging, which is huge, buggy, and used to crash my old phone. I even watch her making her own paper from recycled paper bags, her newest hobby. I video chat with Abuela at three a.m. for our pillería, and we both make toast at opposite ends of the state (hers with cream cheese, mine with Nutella) and talk until we feel sleepy. Abuela is getting better, and we're making plans on what we'll do when I get back.

And at school, there's Lu. We've had lunch together every day this week, then gone out to dinner: one night sushi, another night pizza, another—my favorite so far—an all-night pancake place. Then we do one of the free activities Lu tried so hard to sell me on, like bowling or karaoke. Sometimes Kenzie and Diego join us, but mostly, it's just us.

I'm walking through the grass from the tram stop to Mom's when I notice a moving truck parked outside the house and a woman in a suit standing in front of the open door. My heart speeds up as I race to the house. This can't be good.

"What happened?" I pant, out of breath.

"Hi! Are you Sebastian?"

"Yeah, yes."

"I'm Callie from city hall. Actually, I work for TECH, but it's hard to tell the difference these days, right?" She doesn't pause for a response. "I'm sorry it took us so long to get this going, but we didn't know your mom was in the hospital, and we had to get her the right paperwork and everything. Her social worker was very helpful."

"Is Mom okay?"

"Oh! Yes, she was released from the hospital this morning. TECH provided transportation. Now we're moving her."

"Where?"

"Into New Gault."

"You're moving us into the city?"

"Yes. You'll both be much more comfortable. Your mom is already in the new apartment. You should have a text message from city hall with the address." She frowned. "I probably didn't need this big of a truck. But better safe than sorry, right?"

I feel like I've walked onto a movie set that keeps filming despite the fact that I don't belong in this scene.

"Should I go pack up my stuff?"

"You had the second bedroom, yes?"

I nod.

"Already done! Let me see . . . Yes, this is it."

A cardboard box the size of a mini fridge is stamped BEDROOM #2. My green duffel bag, crammed with semi-clean clothes, fills the box. I dig through the bag until I find Abuela's cartas españolas. I slip them into my pocket, then walk back to the tram to ask CHRISTINE to take me to my new home.

Mom and I are eating takeout from the American Boi diner in town. I ordered a Reuben because I like sauerkraut, and it reminds me of Papá, with his famous love of all things pickled. Mom ordered pork chops with roast potatoes and applesauce. She tried a bite of everything, but only finished the applesauce.

"You did good, kid," she says with a satisfied grin.

I nod, glad I still have sandwich in my mouth.

"Now, you'll see, everything will be better. Look at this place—I mean, have you ever seen anything so fancy?"

I scan Mom's new apartment, trying to see it the way she does. Every surface gleams, everything is new, everything has a place designed for it. The whole apartment is painted a pleasant, soothing yellow. When I made an offhand remark that the color reminded me of a mango, the way it could be both yellow and rosy pink, Mom snapped, "It's sunshine yellow!" As if mango yellow is somehow an insult. I'm back to avoiding minefields.

"The color is supposed to help with my healing. Oh, and the best thing, I start chemo at New Gault Medical on Monday."

"That's great, Mom," I say for the thousandth time. She pushes away her plate, and that's my signal to clean up. I scrape the plates into the automatic garbage can that whirs when I get close to it, the lid lifting like a dog waiting for scraps. I can almost feel my mother smiling behind me, like a helpful garbage can is her doing.

"How are you doing with your grades?" Mom asks.

The words *Since when do you care?* try to climb out my mouth. "Fine."

Mom takes out her vape pen and loads a cartridge. Soon, a cloud of medical cannabis wafts over us. "Are you still doing movie stuff?"

"How do you know about that?" I ask, kinda shocked. I can't imagine Papi talking to Mom, or Mom *asking* about me.

"Your grandma told me, last time I talked to her."

"You talk to Abuela?" My voice squeaks, but I can't help it—I'm, like, disbelieving.

Mom takes a little tube of cream out of her pocket and rubs it into her hands, her arms. The smell of it is so specific, so *Mom*—sweet with vanilla and roses—that it's like traveling back in time.

"I do talk to your grandma sometimes. She calls me, asks me how I am. Tells me that she's praying for me." She scoffs. I tense up, ready to defend Abuela against any negative shit Mom says about her. "Like I deserve her prayers," she mumbles.

I concentrate on washing the dishes, forgetting until I'm halfway through that there's a brand-new dishwasher in this apartment. Doesn't matter. I'm happy to have something to do with my hands.

"So, are you still making movies?" Mom asks.

"Um, yeah," I say without turning around. "I'm actually working on a movie about Abuela."

I hear the crackle of Mom hitting the vape pen, then the exhale of another cloud of vapor. "Would that be, um, popular?" she says carefully.

"Definitely not. But it's not like I'm trying to make a Marvel movie. I just want to make a reel that eventually gets me into USC."

Mom's quiet for a minute. Is she getting ready to tell me that there's no way I could ever get into the University of Southern California?

"Does the fancy phone they gave you help you take good video, or film, or whatever?"

I haven't even tried it for that yet. But between the phone and the TECH laptop, I could get all kinds of editing software that I just couldn't run on my crappy old phone.

"I don't know. I have to figure that out." I shrug. "But I've got so many more possibilities. It's—it's really great, Ma."

Mom relaxes her shoulders, sinking farther into her chair. "That's good, Sebby. I'm glad it's good for both of us."

If this were a movie, this would be the moment where the main character realizes something profound, something important about his mother or himself. What I realize is that I don't know my mom as well as I thought.

"I'm going to bed. You did good, Sebastian," she says,

shuffling her feet down the hall to her bedroom, still in the hospital socks with the slip-proof grips on the soles.

I dry the plates, then put them away. I throw all the compostable takeout containers into a special bin, making the already-spotless kitchen ant-proof. Though honestly, would ants dare?

In my bedroom, there's wallpaper with yellow and gray zigzags. I flop on the bed and prop the TECH phone against the headboard.

When Abuela answers, she's sitting up in bed with her favorite cherry-red scarf tied around her thin shoulders.

"You see me, Abuela?"

"Sí, angelito. ¡Qué clarito te veo, amor!"

"How are you, Abue?"

"Vivian sent me Cuban coffee and pastelitos from that panadería, you know, Azúcar? So you know I'm feeling good," Abuela says. I still can't get over how clearly I can see her, how good it feels to have long face-to-face talks that aren't interrupted by lost sound, freezing visuals, or dropped connections.

"That's because everyone loves you, Abue."

She gives me a dismissive wave of her hand. "How are you, mijo?"

"Good. Mom and I moved into a new apartment in New Gault. See?" I lift the phone and scan it around the room slowly. It's probably just reading as a yellow blur.

"Your papi told me your mother finally got her wish. And she's feeling good?"

I tell Abuela that Mom is much better now she's in New Gault. I *didn't* tell her about Mom's hospital stay. At first because I was too panicked, just trying to figure out what to do.

Then I worried Abuela would tell me to come home again. And I couldn't do it. I couldn't leave Mom in the hospital by herself.

"Y ¿las cartas?" she asks, peering close to her screen. "Do you need help with the card readings?"

"No, I think I'm okay." Sheila and Ana came up with the idea of hosting High Spirits Tea, which means I'm doing more readings, and they're serving little cakes and boba tea. I'm supposed to be communing with ghosts, I guess, going by the spirits part of things, but I guarantee nothing. I just do the tirada, see what's in the cards, and try to figure out what the asker wants to hear. I want people to be happy, hopeful. What's the point if they don't at least get that? Don't tell me las cartas aren't a form of therapy, because I won't believe it.

And Lu drives me both ways, every night I work. They still refuse to enter Dry Town. Even knowing this, I can't help but look up every time the doors open, hoping they've changed their mind. Instead, they sit in their car and write poems they won't show me. The more I ask, the redder their cheeks get, and the more I wish I could hear their words.

"Mijo, ¿estás durmiendo?" Abuela asks, and I realize I've had my eyes closed, my head on my pillow, while Abuela was talking.

"Sorry, Abue. I'm just tired."

"Then we should sleep. Buenas noches, amor," she says with a blown kiss. I blow one back to her and hang up.

I fall asleep practically hugging my new phone, like a complete imbécil.

26

Lu

I push the driver's seat back to give me more room to cross my legs. Waiting for hours in the parking lot of Dry Town should be boring, but it isn't. My brain goes into creative mode once I drop Sebas off, and the words have started to flow. Though, right now, I'm working on a poem that keeps slipping away from me.

> *Trees become ash, then air, then breath*
> *recycled through bodies, lungs, into words that may be*
> *fire, maybe burn, may be consumed, back to ash.*

Sebas opens the car door, dropping onto the passenger seat like a stone.

"You okay?"

"I swear to Jesucristo, if I get one more client asking me for a private aura cleansing, I will not be responsible for my actions."

I snort. "Must be tough being you."

He buckles his seat belt and shakes back his loose hair. "Don't start with me. I'm just reading las cartas, minding my own business." He touches both his wrists, looking for a black elastic band.

I open the glove box, take out a pack of plain bands, and hand it to Sebas.

His face is so delighted, I'm super self-conscious all of a sudden.

"You got these for me?"

"Pues, I didn't get them for myself," I say, gesturing to my own short hair.

"Gracias, amigue. I appreciate you," he says, taking a band out of the packet and tying back his hair.

"Are you tired?" I hope the answer is no. I don't want to drive him home yet.

Sebas gives me a smile that's a question and an invitation. "I'm up for adventure if you are—what've you got in mind?"

"We can do go-karts? Or karaoke. I can call Kenzie and see if she's up for going out?"

"Can we do something chill? And just on our own?" he asks. I'm simultaneously relieved and panicked. My anxiety is a chaotic monster. "Can we go—like, somewhere that isn't New Gault and isn't Dry Town?"

I look at him blankly.

"C'mon," he says at my silence. "I know you don't go into some places, fair, but there's got to be somewhere *else*?"

Without responding, I pull out of the Dry Town parking lot and head back toward New Gault. Before entering the city limits, I turn down the long dirt path that leads to the cell tower.

"You're being mysterious," Sebas says after a few minutes. He connects his phone to the audio to play music. This is the new normal, something we just do now; I drive, Sebas puts on his music, we talk. It makes me smile.

"I'm not trying to be mysterious. I'm taking you somewhere *else*. There isn't a lot of 'else' around here."

The farther down the path we drive, the narrower it gets, the thin grasses brushing the car with a whooshing sound.

"Okay, this seems very horror movie, Mexican kid gets murdered first," Sebas says when I park in the clearing near the base of the cell tower. I turn off the engine but leave the headlights on.

I get out and climb onto the hood. Sebas sits next to me.

"This is 'else.' It's not New Gault, and it's not Gault. When I first moved here, I used to come here to see how far I could go."

"Meaning?" Sebas asks.

"I wanted to know where it started, the place where I'd be safe," I say, pointing to the trees that signal the start of New Gault. "They planted trees there, after the last big wildfire, the one that destroyed the old town. Then built New Gault over the ashes."

We look out in silence, past the metal of the cell tower base, past the yellow grasses, into the covering night. I want him to understand why it matters, and I thought bringing him here would help, but now I just think I sound nuts.

"'Now let the night be dark for all of me. / Let the night be too dark for me to see / Into the future. Let what will be be.'"

Sebas turns his face to me, and the wonder on it makes my stomach drop.

"That's not me; that's Robert Frost," I say.

"Say it again."

I repeat the last line. "'Let what will be be.'"

"The way you say it," Sebas says, shaking his head, "like it's part of you, instead of something you memorized."

"It was one of the poems I sort of grabbed onto in middle school, when I had to leave my old school."

"What happened that you had to leave?" Sebas asks.

I've been trying to figure out what happened, why it happened, for years. And it's all tied up and buried in my own guilt—no matter how many times Dr. Allyson tells me it wasn't my fault. How long will it take for my heart, or whatever stands in for it, to believe that? Dr. Allyson says that's up to me.

"It was at the end of sixth grade. My best friend, Luke, and I were supposed to be in the talent show that year.

"We were both obsessed with this anime about giants terrorizing a walled city—it was an intense phase. We signed up to dance to the theme song, not a little clip, but the whole song—in Japanese—it's, like, six minutes long. My dad even ordered us costumes from Japan." I remember being so purely happy when they arrived, knowing we'd look amazing, knowing the whole thing was the best idea Luke and I had ever had.

"We choreographed it ourselves and practiced every day after school. When we signed up, our friends thought it was a cool idea, but three months later they were sick of us practicing and talking about it—and playing that song. I can get a little, um, fixated on things, you might have noticed."

Sebas gives me a sideways smile. "I am aware."

"The night of the talent show, we were in a classroom, getting ready. There was supposed to be a teacher in there with us to make sure we didn't steal or break things, but there wasn't anyone there."

When Jordan and his friends came in, it was like a scene from that anime; they were giants compared to us, even though they were only a year older. "Which one of you dykes and fruits wants to get pantsed first?" Jordan said. And my brain stuttered.

"These guys came in. We knew them. They sometimes hung out with Luke's brother. They'd been friendly to us before, until they weren't."

I've told this story like it happened to someone else a dozen times or more. I *can* tell it without breaking down. I draw my knees up, hug them with my arms.

"They called us names, homophobic slurs, you know the kind of shizz. It wasn't like we'd never heard that before. I was used to keeping my head down, just ignoring it. But Luke wouldn't be quiet. Which just made him stand out."

"What the hell, Jordan?" Luke said.

"We have a volunteer!" Jordan said, and his friends cheered. Is it weird that I can't remember their names? They should be carved into my memory; instead, they're just a mass of menacing boys, except for Jordan. We knew him. He wasn't someone we were supposed to be afraid of.

"Luke tried to get away, but they grabbed him. One of the girls slipped out the door—to find a teacher, it turned out. Unlike me, she knew what to do."

"You're lucky we didn't do this to you onstage, you twerp. Keep your fucking pedo shit to yourself from now on."

"They stripped off his belt and pulled down his pants, laughing as he turned red and started crying."

"Jesus," Sebas says.

"Yeah." I put my head on my knees. I wish saying this much

was enough. That this was already the hard part. But it's not even close.

"By the time someone came, those guys had gone, and I'd helped Luke get himself together. We called his dad to take us both home. Luke made me promise not to say anything. So I didn't.

"That was only the start of things. The in-school stuff was mostly intimidation, but the online stuff was brutal. They created a private social account, posting pictures of Luke in class that they'd taken—close-ups of the back of his head, his T-shirt, through a bathroom stall—then more homophobic stuff, captions, everything." I squeeze my knees tighter, keeping myself together.

"Posts would go up, gross, threatening, horrible, then disappear, only to be come back later, reposted, shared again and again. It grew so fast, and I didn't even know all of it at the time.

"Six months later, just before the start of seventh grade, Luke died by suicide. It all came out then, the secret accounts, the bullying, the incident at the talent show. The students who were responsible got off with suspension. I think they all went to other schools. I don't know, because I wasn't able to go back into that school building. Mami homeschooled me until we moved to New Gault."

Usually, closing my eyes is enough to center me when I'm feeling a bit wobbly. Like, it's a safe space I can retreat to. But not seeing Sebas, not knowing if his face is disgusted, or disbelieving, or—

"Is a hug okay?" he asks.

I open my eyes. Sebas is so close, his knee touching mine.

I want to make a joke, but I can't reliably use my voice. My chest is full of tears. I nod, and he scoots even closer, hip to hip, and puts his arms around me. I bury my head against his chest and let myself cry.

27

Sebas

Kenzie picks me up after breakfast on Saturday.

"Didn't you just live somewhere else?" she asks.

"Yeah. We're moving on up, as they say."

"Who says?"

"My dad, mostly. It's a TV reference from a thousand years ago. No matter how much he'd like me to, I never ask for details."

"Smart."

"Thanks for the ride," I say.

"It's no trouble, and anyway, I don't want to be alone with Diego yet, so I picked you up first."

"He's still on your shiii—"

"Shhh list, yes, my very shiiizzy shhh list." Kenzie eyeballs the seat belt until I click it into place. "How's the word tracking going?"

"Meh, to be honest. It's not like I can't stop cursing or anything, but I have to sort of think about what I say before I say it. And I'm not as good as you guys are at coming up with replacement words. It's exhausting."

"You get used to it," Kenzie says, turning right onto a street called Fortitude, which looks exactly like all the other streets in the residential ring of New Gault. She parallel parks outside of Diego's place, taking a few tries to get her SUV as close to the curb as she wants it. Once we're parked, she texts Diego. His apartment building looks almost exactly like Mom's new apartment building. I wonder who gets to decide who lives where. If everything is free, how do you get assigned a house? If you hate sunshine yellow—and I'm starting to—can you ask for a paint job? Or to move? How much choice does anyone have? Or are you just supposed to be really grateful for having a place to live? Free is free, right?

"Este pendejo de mierda... ¡me cago en diez!" Kenzie groans.

That's a lot of curse words, even though they're in Spanish. "Everything okay?" I ask.

"No. I mean, it's fine. Diego can't hang out. He burned through his data for April."

"Already? It's, like, mid-April."

"April twenty-first."

"So, now we pick up Lu?"

"No, Lu's not coming either." Kenzie waves her phone at me like I can read the messages. "They have a therapist appointment and anticipate needing a break from humans."

Maybe they're not coming because of last night. I hope I wasn't an insensitive idiota, but I couldn't think of anything to say after they opened up and spilled all their guts to me. They went through hell, and it still hurts. I haven't lost anyone close to me yet, gracias a Dios, but I've been through some shit. Just when it seems like it shouldn't hurt anymore, there it is again, a fresh cut, a new bruise. I don't know. I just held Lu because it seemed like the only thing I could do. I'm not like them; I don't have easy words to make people feel better. I wish I did. Even afterward, when they dropped me off at home and I hugged them again, tight, it wasn't awkward. Not for me. But maybe for them?

"Do you want me to take you home?" Kenzie says, sounding over it.

I don't really feel like hanging out with Kenzie without Lu, but I don't want to go home either.

"No, let's go do something. Let's have fun without those cabrones."

"Um, are you hungry?" Kenzie asks.

"Not even a little. Pancake Haus delivered bright and early. I ate mine and Mom's."

"You ate your mom's food? You monster."

I shrug. "It was going to go to waste. But she's doing better," I say as we pull away from Diego's apartment.

"I'm glad she's doing better. Lu said she was unwell," Kenzie says. "Do you mind if we go to the mall? I need some stuff from the Makeup Bar."

"I don't mind."

"Not too girly a destination for you?"

"I like girly. I like boy-y too, so if you want to go drag racing, I'm here for it."

"Your gendered idea of fun is, um, interesting."

"I want to cast a wide net when it comes to fun. And anyway, I don't get out of New Gault much, so I'm up for anything."

"Three cheers for anything, I guess."

Even though I'm not hungry, there's no way I can pass up a hot dog on a stick.

"You'll pay for it in more ways than one," Kenzie says, frowning at the display. There are pretzel-wrapped hot dogs, corn dogs, a hot dog wrapped in bacon that looks like a burnt offering, and some sad Tater Tots.

"I really like hot dogs. I'm kind of famous for it." I remember the reel Anaïs made of me and Hudson eating taco dogs from a food truck in Sherman Heights. It got over a thousand likes, and I was only up half the night with malestar. If Anaïs was here, she would be daring me to eat the burnt monstrosity from the display case, and Hudson would be ready to speed-dial emergency services. I miss them.

"I know I'll pay for it. Doesn't matter. The heart wants what the heart wants." I order the pretzel dog and a Coke. Kenzie wisely orders only the strawberry lemonade.

The trip to the Makeup Bar was fun, especially helping her pick out lipstick. I pushed hard for a blue-green matte shade called Sea Witch, but she went for something red called Carnation. Both looked good on her. Then she used my arms as perfume testers—she only likes the neutral-gendered ones because, she says, all the others smell like car freshener trees or scented garbage bags. The one that smelled like a fireplace was my favorite. I wondered if Lu would like it. I almost bought a small bottle before I changed my mind.

"How long are you visiting your mom?" Kenzie asks.

"I don't know. Until she doesn't need me anymore."

Kenzie's phone buzzes.

"It's Lu. They want to know what shade I picked." She pouts and takes a selfie to send.

"Want to send them a picture of me eating a mediocre hot dog?" The pretzel dog overpromised, underdelivered. I take a photo of the half of it I won't be eating and send it to Hudson and Anaïs with the caption **Power of the Pretzel Dog? One Star.**

"Let's not threaten them with a good time, right?"

I snort, then take my own selfie to send to Lu. If they're feeling awkward, I want them to know it's all good between us. I add a hot dog emoji, hit send, then wish I hadn't. Well, at least it wasn't an accidental eggplant.

Kenzie drops me off at Mom's, and I have a few hours to kill before Lu picks me up to take me to Dry Town.

Mom is sitting by the sliding door to the one-person-at-a-time balcony off our new kitchen. The door is open a little, letting in air, and she sits in the sun. She reminds me of a lizard on a rock, and that sounds like I'm being a jerk, calling my mom a lizard, but as someone who always wanted to own a whole bunch of reptiles when I was little, it's a compliment. What I mean is, she looks warm and content. I try to sneak past her so I don't ruin the moment.

"Sebby, you're home. Come sit with me."

I pull up a chair and sit, my feet in the sun, watching the blue sky, the white clouds, and the ballooning vapor from Mom's vape.

"We should go on an adventure," Mom says.

"What?"

"We should go somewhere. I've been cooped up in here too

long. I don't even know what this town has to offer. What have you and your friends been doing?"

I try to imagine Mom in her floral pajamas bowling, or doing karaoke, or going to the movies. I can't picture it.

"Uh, what do you feel like doing?"

"I told you, an adventure. Like we used to have, remember?" She smiles at me expectantly.

I panic a little, like I'm staring at a test for a class I never heard of. Then I do remember something: a note under my pillow on the first day of summer, a map that led a few houses away to a tiny swimming hole, Mom and Papi waiting with a picnic and a cooler full of strawberry soda. I remember feeling like I was the luckiest kid alive. I know that was the last summer we were happy together.

"You got a hand-drawn map for me, Ma?"

"Not this time! I've got nothing planned. Cancer teaches you that planning is for people who want to piss off fate. Not me. I feel good today, Sebby. Don't you think we deserve an adventure?"

Zero, absolutely zero amount of hope will go into this, I tell myself. But I smile at her and wait for her to get dressed. We're out the door and standing at the tram stop faster than I thought possible. She's moving better, walking better, and she's holding on to my arm because she doesn't want to have to sit down in the tram stop seats.

"My butt is too flat from all the sitting I've done. Don't you think?"

I avert my eyes. "I'm not looking at your butt, Mom."

"Are you blushing, you cheeky kid?"

"I'm not. Like any kid, I don't want to talk butts with my parents." I try to sound dignified.

"So I shouldn't bring up how much you loved that underpants book when you were in second grade?"

"That's different. That's a classic." It's true. And the movie was even better. I stand by that statement.

The tram arrives and I go to help Mom up the step, but the driver hits a button and the tram lowers to be flush with the sidewalk.

She faces the driver. It's STEVE, a moderately entertaining guy who sometimes moonlights on the blue tram line.

"Good afternoon, dear lady. Where wouldst thou command I convey thee?"

Oh Jesus.

Mom giggles.

"Steve, you're not funny," I say.

"Yeah, but I used to play Shakespeare at the Ren Faire in Hollister, so I know what I'm doing."

I settle Mom in the seat nearest the driver so she can chat with Steve all she wants. Her face lights up as they talk about the merits of *As You Like It* versus *A Midsummer Night's Dream*—the latter being overrated, the former underrated, or maybe I got that wrong. I feel like I'm watching one of those shows where the character you've known forever turns out to be a sleeper Russian agent, or an alien, or, I don't know, a charming mom who has opinions on Shakespeare?

I surreptitiously record a little bit of it—it's too good not to. I send it to Lu, and text, **So, how's your day going?**

I get the three dots for a good while, but a response never

materializes. Maybe getting your guts dragged out of you by your therapist is just as bad as it sounds.

You okay?

No response.

Want me to ask Kenzie to drive me tonight? I text after a full minute.

No.

Then:

Sorry. Just cleaning my closet. I'm good.
See you at 7

"Seb, look at this, have you seen this?" Mom says.

We're outside the bus station next to the Scooter's Shakes sign, the same place Lu picked me up when I was a raging mess.

Mom's face is all excitement. I hope she doesn't faint.

"They have bowling!"

28

Lu

There's always fallout from falling apart.

That's one thing I've learned from years of therapy. It felt good to tell Sebas about Luke and what happened. It felt amazing to have him hold me as I cried. Better than I imagined. But once I got home, tried to fall asleep, my anxiety became a storm.

You're such a mess. How could he be interested in you after you cried all over him? Now he just feels sorry for you.

I give up trying to sleep and go downstairs to make myself a cup of manzanilla tea, quietly, so I don't wake Mami. She used to joke that she's such a light sleeper, she'd hear us when we turned over in our sleep. It's kind of true, but I manage to get back to my room with tea and some homemade alfajores. If I can't sleep, I will write.

The poem that's been running through my brain becomes elusive as soon as I try to pin it down with concrete words. I start with images and feelings. Then I need to find the words that fit together, turn my tangled feelings into something truer. Not just for others, for me. Poetry is how I try to understand myself.

The first poem I ever wrote was about velvet-horned deer,

and it was awful. I used the word *mist* four separate times, and not on purpose. But writing that poem loosened something in my chest and made me feel like I could float instead of feeling like I was drowning.

I scroll through Notes to find inspiration.

A gray skirt of ash drags against the ground where nothing will grow again
The silent space between the world and safety

I find the fragment I wrote on the morning I brought Sebas French toast.

A fire horizon unzips the sky.

I like it, but I don't know how the pieces could work together.

I tap my rings against my phone and try to focus on one thing that made me feel safe.

It's Sebas. His arms around me and the smell of his skin, salt and sweat and something soft, like powder. It's him, coming closer instead of pulling away.

I write a list poem, thinking of him. It's kind of cringey, but I feel like that about a lot of my poems at first. It's too late to take another sleeping pill, so I take half a melatonin and try to rest, the words that I wrote swirling in my head.

Elsewhere
How to hug in a place between safety and the world:
A boy with nightfall hair

Salt skin
Arms that speak, sigh
Ancient tears
Foreheads touch
Knees next to knees
Safety isn't always a place.

I get up late on Saturday, but when I do, I don't feel awful, which is ... surprising, but I'll take it.

Mami y Dad took Felia to some event in Sacramento, so I'm free for the day until I take Sebas to work.

When he texts me, I don't know how to respond at first. I spent a lot of time with him in my head last night, and now he's sending me videos of his mom on the tram.

You okay?

I type a response, then erase it, then type again, but don't hit send.

Want me to ask Kenzie to drive me tonight? he texts after a full minute.

No. Definitely don't want that to happen.

Sorry. Just cleaning my closet.
I'm good. See you at 7

He sends a couple of emojis, including the crystal ball, which is, like, his signature now.

I decide to really clean out my closet, because it's a mess.

The secret to my tidy room is to put things I don't want to deal with in the closet. Maybe it's time to deal with some of those things.

I sit cross-legged in front of my closet and set a timer. I can definitely get lost in something like this. Two hours until I have to shower and get ready for tonight—with plenty of time to change my outfit, worry about my hair and everything else.

I pull out clothes I haven't worn in years and fold them into a cardboard box for Mamá to donate. I prefer pants for a lot of reasons; they seem to fit the right way, most of the time. But I do have a couple of dresses I like, like this olive-and-blue shirtdress that buttons all the way down the front. It's been a while since I've felt like wearing a dress in public. Dr. Allyson thinks it's because I'm afraid of what other people will think, and she's sort of right. It's taken me a long time to find a slot I can fit into—where people know my pronouns, the way I dress. I don't want to do anything to mess that up.

I wonder what Sebas would think of me in this dress. Would he like it, or would he think I look terrible? I do want Sebas to see me looking, I don't know, adorable? Cute? Would he think I look cute in this? I'm not sure I'm brave enough to wear it tonight, after having cried on him last night, so I hang it up, a possibility.

I'm so focused on the closet that I realize the alarm on my phone has been ringing for a while before I finally hear it. But the closet is nearly perfect. The only things left untouched are a couple of boxes that have been there since we moved to New Gault, the boxes of my old life. That's not something to dive into right now.

I get dressed, black jeans with ripped knees, a soft navy

T-shirt, and boots. I wear one of the topaz stud earrings Kenzie gave me for Christmas, and I'm ready.

At Sebas's apartment, I wait, rubbing my palms down my jeans because they're sweaty. I'm as nervous as if this were a date, instead of me just driving a friend—a friend who gives incredible hugs—to work. I'm feeling the drag of disrupted sleep and the fall of adrenaline like I'm an unbalanced chemistry experiment, which I sort of am.

"Hey," Sebas says, getting into the car.

"Hey." He looks perfect in his gray tarot card T-shirt. "Wait, is that a skeleton with a jar of pickles?" I ask, pulling onto the highway.

He laughs. "Yeah, Papi sent it to me—it's supposed to be like a tarot card, but funny. He loves pickles."

"Do you love pickles?"

"I guess? But it's kind of a joke between us. And I figured it's perfect for work."

He connects his phone to the Bluetooth. "New playlist," he says.

"Okay. Oh, I like this song."

He smiles, super pleased with himself. "I made a Lu Likes It playlist—every time you said you liked a song, I put that on my list. Now I don't feel like I'm manipulating your music choices."

"Monopolizing?"

"Yeah, you know. Kind of the same thing."

Just like that, it's easy between us. I don't know why I was worried, why I thought anything would change.

Maybe because I hoped something *would* change.

29

Sebas

Sunday afternoon and I'm stressing. There's no reason to be nervous; the most nerve-racking part of today is over—Mom didn't lose her shizz over Lu being nonbinary. I mean, I did preface the whole thing with "If you want my friend to come over and meet you, you must one thousand percent not be a jerk to them."

"Them?"

"Yeah, them. *They/them/theirs.* That's how they want to be addressed."

"I thought her name was Lou?"

"Their name is Lu, *L-U*, and they don't use *her* pronouns, they use *they* pronouns."

"So he's a guy?"

"You're not meeting them, no way," I say, grabbing my phone and heading to the door.

"Wait, wait, Sebby, I'm sorry. I just don't understand."

"You're not trying to understand."

"I am, honest. Just tell me again, okay? Just tell me what I should say. And, like, what I shouldn't say."

I try to be calm as I explain to my mom about gender identity, which is a lot better than making Lu explain, and I cut her off every time she starts a sentence with *I never heard of* or *when I was a kid* or *does your dad know?* In the end, I have no idea if she can handle it, and I'm ready to bolt out the door at a moment's notice, dragging Lu with me, if Mom says anything horrible.

I've done this to myself. I'm the pendejo who came up with this great idea to take Lu on a secret adventure. And I'm definitely nervy.

"I'm sorry you had to meet my mom and it was stressful," I say, getting into Lu's car.

"It was probably much more stressful for you than for me. Though I didn't know what to say to someone who has cancer."

I shrug. "I don't think it's something you need to talk about, unless the person wants to talk about it. My mom gets annoyed when people pretend that it's not happening to her, like they can't see she's wearing woolly hats when it's hot, or that she's lost almost all her hair. Other people in her group get annoyed when people *do* mention it. Everyone is different."

"She's in a group? She doesn't seem like a group type of person," they say, turning onto the main road out of New Gault.

"I know, right? I didn't think she'd go, but now that she's in this clinical trial, there's group meetings and counseling and all sorts of things, and she's doing all of it."

I haven't told Lu where we're going, or even put it into their Maps app, so I have to direct them and keep an eye on the map on my phone. We pass the city limits for New Gault, and I swear I feel like there's more air.

"And she's getting better?" Lu asks.

"I don't know. She's definitely *feeling* better, more positive, less angry. We get into a lot less fights." We haven't fought since we moved into New Gault. I'm not stupid enough to think we're all good now, but maybe things are changing.

"How much farther is it?" Lu asks. I check the app on my phone.

"About forty-five minutes?"

"I didn't realize it was so far away."

"Pfft. I came all the way from San Marcos—forty-five minutes no es nada. And you've got this luxe car or whatever, so the ride is really smooth."

"I get anxious too far away from New Gault."

"Oh shit," I say, and glance at my biosensor, expecting a yellow warning light. But we're outside New Gault, so my word slip doesn't count. "I mean shizz, oh hell, you know what I mean. I didn't think."

"It's okay," they say with a too-wide grin that makes me think maybe it isn't.

"We should go back."

"Like *fuck* we will," they say, lifting their chin. "I want my adventure."

At the sign for Mount Diablo State Park, I tell Lu to turn off.

"Now I know everything. You're gonna ritually sacrifice me at a state park."

"No seas pendeje. I'm trying to show you something."

When I thought of this trip, I just thought about the cool part, the driving and hanging out with Lu. But now I feel like the expectation is too high, and what if they're disappointed, or just not interested? I'm wearing Papi's old band shirt, Los Feos, and a plaid button-up over it, since I didn't want Mom bad-mouthing Dad over the band tee—

"Are you okay in there?" Lu asks.

They've parked in the lot next to the visitor center. And I've been sitting here quietly freaking out for some minutes.

"I was just, um, thinking."

"Cuidado, amigo, you'll turn out like me if you're not careful. Were you obsessing about how many layers of clothing you're wearing, or if you brought hand sanitizer—because I did." They hold up a little bottle in a holder.

"You got me. I was worried I hadn't packed a bottle of sanitizer in a gold lamé unicorn dispenser."

"Travel with me, I have you covered," they say, getting out of the car.

Lu starts walking toward the visitor center, which is, I'll admit, a cool-looking building. It's like a slightly more modern beacon from *Lord of the Rings*, when Pippin sneaks onto the beacon and lights it. Then it looks like Gondor is calling for aid, even though Denethor really isn't, because he's a d-bag. And if I said all that to Lu, they'd probably look at me blankly.

"We don't have time to go to the visitor center; the park closes at sunset. I want to show you something," I say.

Lu walks back to me, hands stuffed into their jeans—the light ones that I really like. "Okay. You tell me where to go."

"I don't know if you'll find it cool or whatever, but I think it's cool," I blab as we start down the trail.

"Like I said, I want to get out of New Gault. Sometimes."

"You? Honestly, you want to get out of Stepford?"

"I've heard you mutter about New Gault being Stepford before, but I have no idea what you mean, so now you have to explain."

"It's a movie— Well, it's two movies, but I'm not counting the 2004 version—that was an atrocity."

"Obviously, original is always better. Although, the 1978 *Invasion of the Body Snatchers* was superior to the 1950s one."

I stop and stare at them.

"Are you . . . are you messing with me?"

"No, or not really. I'm teasing." They grin, full-on. I was wrong about their smile. I thought it was salesy, gimmicky, but it isn't. It's warm and real.

The trail gets suddenly steep, and I stumble, bumping into Lu.

"Sorry."

"No hay de qué," they say.

"Wait, no," I continue, "*The Stepford Wives* was a book first." I remember Anaïs smugly telling me the book was better when I finally got her and Hudson to watch the movie.

"Anyway. Couple moves to a super-awesome-seeming town in Connecticut where all the wives are, like, complacent and perfect and, you know, wealthy and playing tennis or whatever. Turns out the men in the town have replaced their wives with robots."

"So this *is* a horror movie?" Lu asks.

"Yeah."

"Sounds like that horror movie with the sunken place."

"Sort of, but there are no Black or brown people in this

movie—at least, I don't remember any. And no queer people. Basically, the 1970s were white as leche."

"Okay. White people with robots, got it. So why do you keep muttering about Stepford?"

"Don't you think New Gault is a little too perfect?"

They turn toward me. Behind them, the mountains are brown and scrubby, but still look—majestic, I guess? Is that the right word?

"Look," they say, running their hands through their hair. "New Gault has to seem like such a drag to you. I get that. And you were sort of forced to opt in so your mom could be okay. But for me, most of the time, it works. Maybe I'm the robot in Stepford. I feel like that sometimes." They shrug apologetically, then start walking down the trail again.

I feel like a dick.

"Do you even know where you're going?"

They wave a hand ahead. "This way, I guess? Only way is down, right?"

We walk in silence for about ten minutes. I know the burn scar is coming up in a little bit on the left, and I kind of want them to see it before I say anything about it. But I also want to run my mouth and explain things. I manage to keep silent until Lu stops in their tracks. They slip their phone out of their pocket and start snapping pictures. I watch them framing images, taking notes, and imagine the words they're pulling together.

I found out about this place from a short posted on the UCLA film school account—I immediately thought of Lu and the night we drove to the cell tower, when they recited that little piece of a poem, *Now let the night be dark for all of me.* This place seemed to have the same vibe. Maybe it will inspire their own poems. Maybe inspire Lu to share some with me someday. Or not. But I'm convinced that they're happiest when they're shifting words around in poems, not counting them or saving them.

I walk up close beside them, and they jump a little.

"Sorry, in my own world. This is so beautiful. I haven't seen a recent burn scar in person before. It's like another planet."

"I thought you'd like it. It's, like, poetic, right? But that's not actually what I wanted to show you. Follow me."

I'm insanely nervous, like irrationally, out of proportion. As if I'm about to show them a film I made, or a script I wrote. I want them to love it. I want it to make them happy.

I walk into the path of the burn scar, where the ground gets crunchy, looking for the telltale patch of green grass, because that's where the field should start. When I see the grass, I stop and wait for Lu to catch up. When they do, they're still taking pictures of the burnt ground, the twigs and stuff. I wait for them to see the field of orange blooms.

Finally, Lu turns to face me, and I know I was right. Their eyes are shining like fire, and the look on their face, it's like Christmas morning. The sun makes their hair even more golden, their green eyes sparkle like sea glass. I'm lost. *Shit,* I think, looking at their beautiful face, and then, *I'm in trouble.*

30

Lu

At first, I think it's the shadow of clouds overhead, but the sky is clear. Dusk is coming on slowly, just before it tips into night. Then I realize that the dark shape on the ground is a burn scar—the blackened and charred shrubs, twigs, and even carbonized dirt left behind after the intense heat of a wildfire. I start taking pictures, making notes in my poetry file. I completely forget Sebas is there, that I'm here, that anything other than this alien landscape exists in front of me.

When he moves right next to me, I startle a little.

"Sorry, in my own world. This is so beautiful. I haven't seen a recent burn scar in person before. It's like another planet."

"I thought you'd like it. It's, like, poetic, right? But that's not actually what I wanted to show you. Follow me."

Sebas walks off the trail, which makes me a bit nervous, but we're not that far from the car, so I follow him. He walks right into the burnt parts, and I wince as his booted feet crunch on the skeleton shapes of twigs and shrubs. To me, it looks like a delicate filigree of black lace, an underworld of the natural world, a shadowland populated with memories of what the land used to be. Those are just some of the images that went into my poetry file.

Sebas stops next to a patch of green grass. Weirdly, it's not a relief to see the green stalks, it's an affront. Like the green, living things are mocking the land that surrounds them.

Then I see the dots of orange, first just a few, then more and more, floating on the river of green grass that extends far down the slope. The orange-gold petals tremble, like the breeze compels them to dance. In the middle of the burn scar, a ribbon of flowers. It feels like a gift. I turn to Sebas because I realize it is a gift. He's giving this beautiful thing to me.

He looks away down the hill. "Um, uh, they're fire poppies. They're like the coolest flowers ever. The seeds can lie dormant for years, decades, just waiting for a wildfire to wake them up. The smoke and the heat, like, turn them on, make them active, so that a year later, you get these fire poppies showing up right where the hottest parts of the fire were. And they only last a few days, then they disappear again. Waiting until the next, you know."

"Catastrophe?"

"I was going to say *wildfire*, but your word is better."

I bend down to get as close as I can to the fire poppies. They're spindly and papery. They look like they can't last, like it's a mistake they're here, and yet, here they are. The waved edges of their petals shiver just from my exhaled breath. I take so many pictures of the flowers, the spring green of the stems, the filaments, or whatever they're called, that poke out of the base of the flowers.

"Got enough pictures there, Lu?"

I'm lying on the dusty ground, getting close-ups of the flame petals against the backdrop of charred ground and green leaves. I feel like it's a dream, like it will disappear as soon as I stop looking at it. But I pull myself away and stand up.

"Not really. I could look at it forever, you know?"

"But they're not built for forever. Tomorrow or the next day, they'll be gone. And before you ask, it's against the rules to take a wildflower out of the park. Also, there's a fine."

"Me? Break a rule? It's like you don't know me." I look down at my clothes. Bits of gravel, burnt wood chips, and dirt cling to the front of my clothes.

"Let me help," Sebas says, brushing the leg of my jeans to get some of the dirt off—which just makes it worse. "Sorry."

"It's fine, really. Let's get back to the car before they close the park," I say.

"We still have a few minutes," he says, looking uncharacteristically shy. "Will you do something for me?"

"Sure."

"Will you read me some of your poetry?"

That makes me blush hard, I don't know why.

"About the fire poppy?"

"About anything. I love making things, but I'm not good at describing things. Like, how would you describe the fire poppy?"

"Uh, so just riffing, like, making it up on the spot?"

"Can you do that?"

"Maybe?" My voice cracks a little, probably because I thought I was going to say no, but I didn't.

"Could be fun," Sebas says, showing me his smile, the one that hooks me, reels me in.

"I'll try."

I take a deep breath and face the patch of green among the blackened earth. I open my mouth and pour my words out.

Black glass basalt
Shards of earth melted and pressed
Burned away everything but shadow
Until a seedling wakes up to alarm and heat and tragedy
With the message to grow like a weed
An anti-shadow of color against black stains
A firebloom
To show the world that flame can heal
And heat can melt apathy
And danger can ... can ...

"Um." I falter, running out of steam. For a while, the words were just there, like I was reading them, but then I felt like they weren't right, or they were almost right but not yet, and I started hunting for better words—that's why I stopped.

Sebas tucks his hair behind his ears with a rueful little laugh.

"I would really, really like to kiss you," he says. His words echo in my head, and there's a drowning sound in my ears.

"Do you think that's a bad idea?" he asks.

His onyx-and-silk hair glows blue against the gold of the sky. How could kissing Sebas not be a good idea?

"We should find out," I say, and reach through his cool hair, cup my hand against the curve of his neck, and pull him to me.

31

Sebas

I say I'm bad at describing things, but the images that pass through me as I kiss Lu are like an extended montage: colors and heat and taste piling up on top of each other. It's almost too much to process, so I stop thinking.

When I was little and lying in the sun at a beach or in our yard, I'd close my eyes so I could see the red-yellow inside my eyelids. I used to think *that* was the real color of the sun—since it was impossible to look directly at the sun without adults yelling at you, I knew that every picture of the sun, every drawing of the sun (even the crayon color Sun Yellow) was a lie. It didn't have the heat, so it was only kind of sunlike. But behind my closed eyes, I live inside the color of the sun, the heat and the color of my own skin and blood in my eyelids. I used to think that closing my eyes and looking at the sun would bring the real sun right next to me.

That's what kissing Lu is like. I can't open my eyes; there's too much of a drag on my whole body as I pull them closer to me. I can't see them at all, but I can see them better through all the ways they're touching me. Their hand presses on my neck, their fingertips are cold, rough. I feel how hot my skin is in comparison. They taste like lip balm, coconut or vanilla. I pull on the belt loops of their jeans, trying to get even closer. If I keep my eyes closed, if I keep kissing Lu, I'll see them the way they really are, I'll understand them.

Lu pulls back a little, green-tipped curls falling into their face. I could push them out of Lu's eyes, but I'd have to let go of them first, and I'm not willing to do that.

"Fire poppies, huh," they say.

"They're amazing." I laugh.

We hold hands back up the trail to the parking lot and even in the car as they drive. I feel like I have a head cold. I know that's weird and super unromantic to say, but my head is stuffed full of cotton, and it's hard to think of anything but the feel of their hand holding mine. I rub my thumb against the frayed edge of the Band-Aid on their thumb.

"I bite my cuticles, hence all the Band-Aids," they say sheepishly.

"Why?"

"Because bleeding all over the place is frowned upon."

"No, I mean, why do you bite your cuticles?"

"Nervous." They shrug. "Something to do that makes hard things easier, if that makes sense."

I look at their hand in mine. It's a bit larger than mine, squarer and definitely paler, nearly all the fingers tipped with Band-Aids. I wonder at all the worry and nerves that went into causing so much harm.

"Gross, right?" They try to tug their hand away, but I won't let go. I lift their hand to kiss their thumb so they know just how gross I think that is.

Maybe I'm a bit blissed out, but it takes me a few minutes to realize that Lu, cautious, five-miles-under-the-speed-limit Lu, is driving a little fast.

"You okay?"

"Oh yes. Why?" They frown a bit. "Are you okay?"

"I'm not the one driving seventy-five all of a sudden."

They make a funny expression, almost anime-perfect, as if their eyes were bugging. All they need now is for visible beads of sweat to pop out over their face.

"Shoot, I'm sorry. Didn't realize, sorry."

"No hay de qué. Were you thinking?"

"Always thinking," they say as the speedometer slows to a normal speed.

"Okay. So are you freaking out? I'm not saying that as a pendejo. I just want to know. Is this"—I hold up our joined hands—"freaking you out?"

They shake their head, but slip their hand out of mine. It was getting a little sweaty anyway, not that I minded. I flex my fingers.

"I get this feeling, like an internal clock, that tells me I've been out of New Gault too long. That's probably why I was trying to get back faster."

"What's too long?"

"I don't know, it's just a feeling."

"I thought you wanted to get out of New Gault a little." I thought they'd been thinking of me, or at least of kissing me.

"It's not you. It's my own anxiety making me weird."

"You seemed really chill at the fire poppies."

"I seemed chill? My body couldn't figure out if leaping from a rock or crawling under it would be a better move. I was definitely in a state. I took some homeopathic anxiety stuff to help. Guess that worked."

"Well, crap. Now I feel bad."

They give my hand a quick squeeze. "Feeling bad because this was the best I've felt in forever? Because kissing you was like stopping time?" They laugh. "Leaving New Gault and not knowing where I was going? That should have been an easy *no fruiting way*. But with you, I didn't want to say no."

I look at them sideways, like I'm trying to figure them out, but really, I think I already have. Not, like, totally figured out.

"You're like a duck," I say. They look at me for a second.

"I'm a duck?"

"No, not a duck. A swan. Is that right?"

"I don't know, this is your analogy. Apparently, I'm some kind of waterfowl?"

I groan. "I mean, the thing where the, okay, let's say swan, because that's cooler than a duck. You glide on the surface of the water, but under the water it's going gangbusters."

"Gangbusters?"

"My dad uses that word all the time. Like, it's all chaos and, tú sabes, locura under the surface."

"Chaos and locura, that's me." They laugh.

"Ack, I'm not the poet. I'll leave words to you."

Lu comes to a complete stop at a stop sign, even though there's not another car in sight, then puts the car into park. They lean over the gearshift to kiss me, first on my cheek, then my mouth. I lean into them, letting the kiss take over every thought I've ever had. They're right; kissing them does stop time. Until a car horn blares behind us before driving around, cursing us out. We bust out laughing, and I guess time starts up again, because Lu signals a left turn onto the road leading straight into New Gault. Maybe they feel better, pulling closer to that place, but I feel like I've swallowed lead.

Leeza, the home health aide, is dozing in an armchair, a copy of *People en Español* on her lap. Mom is bright-eyed at the kitchen table, doing a jigsaw puzzle. I've gone from an ecstatic experience to just plain weird.

"Sebby!" Mom stage-whispers. "Come sit with me. I can't figure out how to finish this G-D puzzle."

"You can say *goddamn*, Ma, TECH isn't counting your words."

She makes a clicking sound with her tongue. "I don't care about TECH. Leeza hates it when I curse, and I don't want to hurt her feelings."

My mother. Not wanting to hurt a brown woman's feelings. What is going on?

"Is she staying overnight?"

Mom looks at Leeza, snoring lightly in her blue nurse scrubs dotted with monarch butterflies and her white Crocs.

"She's exhausted. This is her second eight-hour shift. She takes really good care of me. You know she lives twenty miles south of here? On those crappy back roads, it takes her forty-five minutes to get home. I called the service and asked if she could stay with me overnight. I told them I was feeling dizzy."

"Are you?"

She waves a dismissive hand. "A little. I have to take fifteen pills every evening, and one of those bastards definitely makes me feel a little light-headed. But there's another pill in that lot that makes it harder for me to sleep. So I'm trying to do a puzzle Leeza brought me. It's all these birds."

As soon as I sit down, she gets up and starts opening cupboards.

"Did you start with the edges?" I ask, scanning the puzzle pieces.

"Obviously," she says, turning on the microwave. A minute later, she puts a mug of something warm next to me. I sniff it, then look up at her with surprise.

"Did you make me cozy chocolate milk?" My voice is tiny, but I can't help that.

She laughs. "I wondered if you'd remember. Yes, warm—not hot, not cold—cozy, you always said."

Cozy chocolate milk was something just between us. Even when Papi and Ma were fighting, the one thing she could always do for me was make me chocolate milk the exact right temperature. I threw the most epic tantrums once Mom left and no one could get the temp of my chocolate milk right. What a little ashhole I was.

I sip, and it's perfect—exactly as I remember it.

"Gracias," I say, and then stop, horrified.

Mom stiffens a little, then laughs. "De nada," she says awkwardly. I'm so shocked at my gringo-ass mother speaking Spanish that I just turn back to the puzzle.

We work in silence for a while, slotting in part of a bluebird's wing, and most of a yellow-gray bird, before she sighs heavily.

"I'm tired. I think I can go to bed."

As I help her get to her feet, stand steady to let her get her bearings, and walk her to the bedroom, I think about how little shouting has been happening in this new place. Maybe it's fake, like how everyone is smiley and cheerful and not total d-bags around Christmas, but it does feel good. Still, Mom doesn't deserve a fruiting medal for not shouting—plenty of people in worse circumstances manage not to be shirty pendejes. No medals for being decent.

Mom sits at the edge of her bed and slips off her hospital socks. Her toenails are painted banana yellow, with little white flowers.

"You painted your toes?"

"Not me, Leeza's daughter, Aracely. She's a manicurist at a salon in New Gault. She makes nail art for celebrity singers!"

I help her into bed, then hand her the TV remote, put her meds near at hand, and make sure the alert button the clinic gave her—it looks like a doorbell on a lanyard—is around her neck so she can call for help if something terrible happens.

"Night, Ma," I say on my way out.

"Sebastian?"

I turn to face her. She probably needs her little glass of water for the pain meds.

"Water, right?"

"No, I got a bottle here."

"Okay," I say, and wait.

"Thank you."

"What for?" I ask.

"For being here. For putting up with me."

"Yeah, it's okay, Ma," I say.

"I got a lot of stuff to try to make right, and I don't know how much time I have left. But I'm gonna try," she says, shifting the pile of pillows behind her. "I just wanted to start."

"Okay," I say, and stop myself from saying *thanks* back, like a little kid.

"Good night," she says, and I nod, not trusting myself to say anything. Because what would I say?

All I know is that I'm wrung out, but too keyed up to sleep. I lie in bed thinking of swans—and kissing Lu—and my mother genuinely thanking me for maybe the first time in my life? I'm even too tired to call Abuela, so I text her lots of hearts and tell her I love her. After watching palmistry tutorials until my eyes burn, I text Lu, expecting them to be asleep, hoping they aren't.

Hey. Can't sleep . . .

Me neither

32

Lu

Monday morning, my phone buzzes with an ambassador message—**new student**—and I'm not excited. Maybe that's because of Sebas. He made me think about every aspect of TECH, question every detail. He pushed back against *everything*.

And he gave you fireblooms.

I'm feeling so disgustingly positive, I nearly choose the olive-and-blue dress. But instead I put on a yellow-and-orange patterned button-up shirt to remind me of yesterday. I pair it with cropped black pants and suspenders.

"You're looking especial—what's the occasion?" Kenzie asks when I pass her on my way to Becker's office. I smile wide and keep walking, even when her expression changes to surprise, then intense curiosity.

"I need details, mije!" she shouts after me.

By the time I get to Becker's office, I'm practically skipping. I take a moment to prepare myself for the encounter. I'm sure Becker will make some joke about how this new student should be easy after finally getting Sebas on board. The man is never satisfied. It's exhausting.

He sits at the spare desk in his office for once, a kid sitting in the chair across from him. A matte black TECH box is open on his desk. Becker's already gotten the new student set up with a phone and biosensor.

"Oh good, Lu, you're here." He waves me in. "I have a new student for you to introduce into the TECH family. I know you'll make him feel welcome, give him all the information he needs. This is Jordan. He's transferred from Palo Alto High School."

The boy turns in his seat and smiles at me. My anxiety monster is all spikes, all razor-tipped tail, thrashing through my insides until everything is shredded. I'm gonna be sick.

"Excuse me," I whisper before bolting out of the office and blindly finding the first bathroom I can. I throw up into the toilet until I'm empty.

Jordan Kingsley is here, in my safe place. In my town. What the fuck am I going to do?

I make it as far as the hallway that leads to the health suite before Jordan finds me.

"Hey."

"I'm—I'm late for class," I stammer, and try to move past him. He blocks me. My heart is racing.

"Sorry," he says. He smiles at me, and the panic in my chest just doubles, trebles, builds like a wall of fire. He can't be sorry, because he's stopping me from leaving. He's making me feel this panic. I move again. He blocks me again. I use my words.

"Can you move. Please."

"Sorry," he says again, his hands up as if he's showing me he's harmless, though he's still between me and escape. It feels like he towers over me. I back up.

"Look, Lu—it's Lu now, right? That's your name?"

"My name is Lu," I croak.

"Yeah, yeah. Lu. Listen. I've been hoping to find you, to talk to you."

This is a nightmare. I feel light-headed, and I hope to God I'm going to pass out. It'd be embarrassing, but I'd take it, just to get out of the situation.

"What are the odds I'd find you here? Like it's, um, the universe or fate or something, right?" Jordan flashes me another smile that makes me feel bloodless. I don't move. I don't breathe. "Mr. Becker says you're the best ambassador at this school. That you would explain everything to me, like, how things work. We could talk."

I'm shaking my head before he even finishes his sentence. "They'll find you another ambassador." I hate that my voice is so thin, so weak.

"I don't want another ambassador," he says, moving closer. "I want to talk to you."

I take a step back, even though it's in the wrong direction. Mamá has a T-shirt she likes to wear that says, I'M A NICE PERSON, PERO NO TE PASES. That's me. I want people to like me, I want to be thought of as nice and helpful. I want to be the solution, not the problem. But I have my limit.

I say the words I never thought I'd have to say.

"Jordan Kingsley—stop following me. I don't want you around me. *You're making me feel unsafe.*"

Immediately, both our biosensors start to pulse in red, and an alarm goes off somewhere. A teacher materializes as if by magic and gets between us.

"What the hell?" Jordan looks confused, and a little of the panic that's flooding my system shows on his face. I take more and more steps away from him as more teachers show up, get between us. I'd run if I could; my legs want me to, my heart wants me to.

Mrs. Ramos, who I had for Chemistry last year, looks at me hard, assessing, questioning. *Don't ask me for reasons,* I beg in my head.

"You okay, Lu?"

"I'm okay," I say breathlessly. "I just . . . I'm not safe."

"What the fuck is this?" Jordan says, angry now. More pulsing lights from his biosensor, and now I'm wondering if he's going to lash out, grab me. I see Luke's face in my mind, a memory that's more like a nightmare, bathed in garish colors. *They grab his arms; they take off his pants. He's crying. I don't do a thing about it.*

I stumble a few more steps back as Mrs. Ramos talks to Jordan, explains. I'm finally far enough away that my biosensor light turns from red to yellow. I would have been the one to tell Jordan this could happen. *In the case of an irreconcilable difference between students, where one or more parties feels unsafe either physically or emotionally when in proximity to another party and expresses those sentiments either verbally or in writing, the immediate and temporary solution will be a six-foot separation zone, which must be maintained at all times.*

There will be a meeting with explanations, warnings, and an offer of counseling.

Classes will be moved around and schedules will be changed. We'll both have to stay away from each other until we resolve our differences. Which means until I say that I feel safe with him again.

That's never gonna happen.

33

Sebas

Before I leave for school, I make Mom green tea with honey, and coffee for myself and for Leeza. They were both up half the night dealing with side effects. She says Mom's okay, that one of the new medications made her break out in a painful rash, which made it hard for Mom to sleep. But that it's nothing to worry about. They both look exhausted. I feel guilty for not doing more.

I drink my own coffee in front of the fridge and stare at the filmstrip from the photo booth in the bowling alley. It didn't matter that Mom only made it as far as the photo booth before we turned around to come back home. She enjoyed the hell out of that photo shoot.

First, she hammed it up by herself, using different filters (adding dog ears, looking like a potato, I don't know what the hell else). Then she dragged me into the tiny cubicle with her so we were sharing the stool. *Pose, click!* Mom grabs my face and puts it right next to hers; we both make fish faces. *Pose, click!* Mom's smile falls a bit, but she still makes rabbit ears behind my head. *Pose, click!* We're both smiling, but Mom is winded, the adventure is over. As we waited for the photo strip to print, Mom leaned against the booth, trying to keep the smile on her face.

"More adventures soon, Sebby, I promise," she said.

I hope that's true.

I saw Lu hurrying down the hallway first thing this morning but haven't seen them since. They weren't in Anatomy in second period, and the texts I've sent have stayed unread. I don't want to jump to assumptions that they regret getting together, that they don't want to see me. So I try not to do that.

"Where's Lu?"

Kenzie pops out one of her earbuds. We're walking to get lunch at one of the food trucks that line the street. I'm aiming directly for queso tots, while Kenzie opts for vegan lettuce wraps.

"I have no idea. Haven't seen them since first thing. But I was out. Dentist," she says, opening her mouth wide to show colorful rubber bands on her braces.

"They're not sick, are they?" I ask. Last night, later than either of us should have been awake, we kept texting back and forth. I asked them for poetry; they asked me to read las cartas for them. We made plans to sit in their guesthouse and not do either of those things.

But now they're not answering my texts.

"I don't think they're sick," Kenzie says, frowning. "But I haven't seen Diego either, so maybe they're together?"

A few minutes before lunch ends, Diego finds us walking across the quad.

"Where were you guys?" He pants like he's been running.

"We were in our various classes, doing our school thing, you clown," Kenzie replies. "Where were you?"

"Helping Lu, like a real friend," Diego says dramatically. "They've been attacked."

"What?" I tense up.

"Who attacked them?" Kenzie asks.

"This new student, Jordan."

"What happened?" I ask.

"I don't know. I wasn't there. But Teagan was in the hallway when it happened and told me about it."

"Is Lu okay?" I ask.

"I don't know," Diego says. "They went home."

"Okay, okay, so when you say *attacked*, you don't mean like jumped, or stitches, or concussion. They're physically okay?" I ask.

Kenzie and Diego both look at me like I'm insane. Have they been in this Stepford town so long that they don't know the meaning of the word *attacked*?

"No one touched Lu," Diego says. "But they felt threatened, so they turned on their distancer."

"What the fu-un is a distancer?" I manage to ask without an f-bomb.

"Didn't Lu explain that to you?"

"Just you explain it, por favor, I'm a little lost here!" I'm shouting at them, I realize, so I breathe deep to calm myself down.

"Distancer is what it sounds like—you feel unsafe, for whatever reason, you say the words *I don't feel safe around*—the person's name—and alarms go off. You both have to stay six feet apart until you reconcile or you get moved around or graduate or whatever."

"What if you're a petty pendejo and you say that just to get back at your ex or something?"

Kenzie rolls her eyes. "It's like you weren't even listening to Lu! If you set off your distancer, there's a whole investigation, and if they find you did it maliciously, you get expelled."

"Okay, okay, expulsion from school is bad." I nod.

Diego shakes his head like I'm a lost cause. "He doesn't understand what *expelled* means."

"*Expelled* doesn't mean you get kicked out of school," Kenzie explains, trying for patience but failing. "It means your family has to move out of New Gault."

The tension between the three of us is something you could bottle, sell as warfare. I want to get back to how Lu is. Not physically hurt is good; mentally, emotionally hurt is bad. Lu is held together by hope and sheer guts most of the time. I have to see if they're really okay—and if I can help.

So I leave campus, not bothering to say anything to Kenzie and Diego, who are locked in some kind of nonverbal fight I don't give a crap about. Not sure why neither of them thought to do the same. I walk to the tram, texting Lu the whole time, just to let them know I'm on my way. They don't respond.

34

Lu

Bad days don't care whether you've just had therapy and are days away from your next session. Bad days also don't care if you're too embarrassed to ask your therapist for an emergency session. Bad days just do not give a fuck.

I don't want to go feral in my room. I want to keep that space clean and desperation-free so that I can walk in and feel like the person who sleeps there isn't on their way to bottoming out. I grab some comfortable clothes and my game console and tell Mamá I'm gonna be in the guesthouse.

"You can stay there only if you check in with me every hour, ¿sí?" Mamá says.

"Okay." She's packing cookies, chips, and soda into a shopping bag—a huge quantity of food that three people couldn't hope to eat, but it makes her feel better.

"Y if I don't hear from you, I might come by and peek in on you, and that has to be okay, yes?"

"Sí. And I know I can't lock the door."

"Okay, you know I love you, right?"

"Sí."

She hugs me, letting me sag against her. She holds me up

and hugs me at the same time. I love the way Mamá smells: of earth and gardenias and coffee and tomorrow. With Mamá there is always a tomorrow, and that's why I love her.

When I get to the guesthouse, I take a shower to scrub off the humiliation of sitting with the school counselor and nurse as I filled out an online form confirming that I was requesting a distancer and they handed me tissues because I couldn't stop crying.

I get dry and put on the softest T-shirt I own—one so full of tiny holes, Mamá threatens to throw it out every time she sees it. It has a sketch of a bat on it and says VAMPIRE FOOTBALL CLUB. I put on a long cotton tank dress that Dad bought me on a business trip to Granada a couple of years ago—he calls it a caftan—and now I'm surrounded by my parents like I'm five, and I don't care if that makes me pathetic. I need to remember them and all they've done for me.

I sit on the bed, cross-legged, to think. But I can only think of two words that won't let me go. *Not again.*

There's a knock on the door, and I wonder if I've lost time like I sometimes do when I spiral, if it's been an hour and I've not texted Mamá a thumbs-up emoji. Another knock. When I open the door, it's Sebas.

"Hey."

"What are you doing here?" I'm startled to see him, in the middle of the day, in the middle of *this* day that's gone to utter shit, so I'm a bit rude.

"I wanted to see you. Diego said you were attacked."

"Did Kenzie and Diego send you?" I wrap my arms around myself like I need protecting.

"I sent myself," he says simply.

"Jordan didn't attack me. I mean, he didn't touch me or anything."

"Good."

"But I really *don't* feel safe around him."

"Is he the kid from your middle school? The one you told me about?"

"You should come inside." I move to make room for him but leave the door propped open in case either one of us needs to flee.

Once we're both sitting on the bed, I feel super self-conscious. My face must be puffy from crying, my hair a mess, and this outfit—not what I'd choose to wear in public.

"I don't know what to say."

"Don't say anything, then. That's okay too."

The silence grows until I feel the pressure to speak, to explain.

"Jordan Kingsley is the kid from middle school. One of the kids. Who bullied Luke."

Sebas nods but doesn't say anything, and it's like he's giving me permission to say all the things I haven't been able to.

"I've been going to therapy forever, talking about this crap, going over it and over it. It's always the same thing—*it's not your fault, you couldn't have known, there was nothing you could do*." I grab the edge of the tank dress and twist it in my hands. "But I didn't stand up for him. I was such a coward."

"It doesn't make you a bad person to not want to be bullied," Sebas says quietly.

"You don't understand," I say, shaking my head. If Sebas is

going to hate me, I want to be the one to give him a reason. I want to tell him the truth.

"I was glad that it wasn't me, that it was someone else. I—fuck—" My sensor blinks red, a word infraction, a hit to my word data. I should be worried. But I couldn't care less. "I was proud of myself. Like I'd gotten it right and Luke had gotten it wrong. I tried to get him to wear different clothes, to like different things. I wanted him to be safe, like me, and I was gonna show him how to do it.

"After he died, I fell apart. The kind of stuff I was helping him with, it was garbage. Nothing he could wear or watch or say differently was going to keep him safe. I was the one who was wrong.

"Coming to New Gault was supposed to fix things. Why isn't any of this better? Why, why?" I struggle to keep my words from turning into gasps, but they get swallowed up by my tears.

Sebas puts his arms around me—it's scary how fast it's becoming my favorite place to be—and lets me cry. We lean back against the pillows, and I roll into him, hiding my face against his chest. It's such a *fucking* relief, the way he doesn't expect anything from me, the way he's comfortable with whatever this is.

I'm so tired, I fall asleep in his arms.

I wake up remembering that I forgot to text Mami. I reach for my phone, but it's not where it's supposed to be. I'm disoriented for a minute, then I remember I'm in the guesthouse. With Sebas.

He sits cross-legged on the bed next to me. He looks up from his phone and smiles. "Hey."

"Hey, um, hi," I say, sitting up.

"Your mom came by with some food. I ate half your ham-and-cheese torta."

"Mami always makes enough food for fifty people."

"Cool. Then I won't feel bad about the fact that I ate your chips too."

I go to the bathroom, check out the damage that crying and sleeping on a boy has done to my hair, and fix as much as I can.

When I get back to the room, Sebas has laid out cards on the bed, three in a row.

He catches my eye, looking slightly embarrassed.

"Sorry, just practicing."

"These are your cards for reading the future?" I ask.

"I'm just quizzing myself, trying to see how many meanings I can remember for each of the cards." He turns over the first one. Four bastos or clubs—two green, two red—one in each corner, their ends pointing to the middle of the card.

"El cuatro de bastos—that's caminos abiertos, like lots of options. But if the client is asking about money worries, then it means be careful, like don't take risks."

"Open road, but don't take risks, got it," I say lightly.

"Unless," he says, turning the card the other way around so it faces me, "it's reversed."

"Then is it 'roads are closed, but take lots of risks'?"

He laughs. "I wish it were that easy, then I wouldn't need the notes I got from Abuela." He scrolls through his phone for a bit. "Okay, here it is. Al revés, it means corruption."

"Damn."

"I know, right? I try to soften it up a bit when I give readings. I want people to feel good about their future. I don't want to give them doom and gloom and all that."

I sit up straighter, push the curls from my eyes.

"Will you do a reading for me?"

35

Sebas

"Okay," I start, nervously shuffling the cards over and over.

"Okay," Lu repeats with a smile. I might have said *okay* already a couple of times. I hand the deck to them.

"First, *you* have to shuffle the cards a little. And while you do, think of the question you have in your mind, the thing you want help answering. Doesn't matter what it is, big or small, or if people would think it's stupid. This question is just for you."

I watch them shuffle thoughtfully, the faded reds, greens, and yellows flashing through their fingers easily.

"Card shark, huh?" I joke.

"Homeschool boredom and internet tutorials," they say, then neatly place the shuffled deck in front of me.

"¿Liste?" I ask.

"Liste," they answer. I pick up the top three cards and lay them out, one by one, face down between us. I point to the first card on my left.

"This card represents the problem, the thing you're worried about or struggling with."

"Got it."

I turn the card over. "Seis de copas. Cups are sometimes

good, sometimes bad. The six means disappointment or fear or trepidation. Not fear exactly, kind of all mixed together."

"Me, every day," they joke. I can tell they're nervous.

"This card is about the past. Like a past hurt or betrayal. And we can stop at any time."

They shake their head. "I'm okay, I promise."

I point to the second card. "This represents the obstacle, the thing that's keeping you from fixing the problem or thing in your past." I turn over the middle card.

"Tres de oros. Coins are, like, chisme, you know, gossip. Or it could be things written about you, or stories told about you. Or it can even be what you think is being said about you."

Lu is quiet, eyes on the cards. They spin the rings on their fingers. When I don't go on to the next card, they look up.

"I'm ready. Go ahead, Sebas. Read the last card."

"I like the way you say my name," I blurt out. It gets a smile out of them.

"You're trying to distract me, but thanks, I guess? I like saying it. Now turn over the last card, Sebas."

I turn over the third card. "Caballero de copas," I say, and smile, relieved.

Lu lets out a breath. "I guess it can't be that bad if you're smiling."

"Cambios favorables," I say. "Good changes are coming."

Lu's mom hugs me and says gracias repeatedly, when all I did was check on Lu, give them a card reading, and eat half their sandwich. Oh, and kiss them until we were both dizzy, but no need to point that out to Señora Hernandez.

Lu stands behind their mom in the kitchen, looking tired but a lot better than they did when I got here a couple of hours ago.

"Mije," Lu's mom says to them, "no te olvides de la invitación para el sábado."

"Oh yeah, right," Lu says, walking me to the front door. "My mom wanted me to invite you to my sister's twelfth birthday celebration on Saturday. I told her you might be working."

"Oh," I say, taken by surprise.

"You don't have to come, it's just a friends and family kind of thing. No big deal at all, absolutely don't have to come."

"I want to."

"Really?"

"Yeah. I can switch my schedule around a bit."

"I can pick you up from work."

"No, I'll get a ride from someone else. Give me a chance to get a shower and not show up with the stink of commercialism on me."

"All that aura reading takes its toll." Lu nods wisely.

"Thanks for inviting me," I say.

They duck their head and glance behind them; then they launch themselves at me, and I catch them in a hug.

"I'll come see you tomorrow after school," I whisper against their neck. I know seeing Lu is how I want to spend my time.

36

Lu

Sebas comes over every day after school, and we hang out in the guesthouse, streaming shows and being interrupted by Mamá or Ofelia on a regular basis. Mami hasn't asked me about Sebas, but Felia makes kissing noises every time she passes me, the toad. A threat to return her birthday gift takes care of that, and by noon on Friday, the week of virtual school I requested ends without incident.

Monday, I'll be back at TECH, worrying about turning a corner and running into Jordan. I think about what next week will feel like, and if I'll be able to function, knowing he's there. Mostly, I get angry. I should feel safe in New Gault, carajo. I shouldn't have to hide at home.

Saturday morning, Kenzie comes over and we go on a run, something we haven't done in forever. It's nice to hang out with just her, though she bombards me with Sebas questions that I don't know how to answer.

"Are you, like, official?"

I roll my eyes. "What does that even mean?"

"I don't know, what do *you* think it means?"

"Uh-uh, nena, I already had therapy this week." I pick up

speed and pull ahead. "If you can't keep up, you can't ask questions," I shout back.

I run flat out for a minute and a half until I've sweat through my T-shirt. It feels so good, the dopamine rush, the laughter when Kenzie finally catches up and smacks me on the butt. We walk back to my house so she can give Ofelia her birthday gift, a mini fridge for her room.

"It can hold six cans of soda and a snack, or"—Kenzie pauses dramatically as she opens the little mint-green fridge—"a whole lot of K-beauty stuff!" Felia squeals over the sheet masks, creams, and other adorably packaged skin care items. She hugs Kenzie extra tight and remembers to thank her as Dad helps her bring her presents to her room, where she's going to painstakingly detail each present in her birthday haul video. She'll be in there, lolling around her presents like a dragon sitting on a hoard of gold, until we leave for dinner. Kenzie sprawls on the comfy blue armchair, exhausted.

"The only reason you beat my run time was because I was up at the crack with Jet this morning," she says, stifling a yawn.

"Why did you have to wake your sib so early? It's Saturday."

"They are heavily invested in this Ultimate Frisbee thing. And Mom and Dad are away. Again. I had to wake them, get them to eat, get them to comb their motherforking hair, and spend an hour finding their team shirt. Then I had to do it in reverse at pick-up time, making sure lunch happened."

"Isn't it illegal to make your eldest kid watch your younger kids?"

"You know it isn't."

"Wait, if you were out with Jet most of the day, and now

you're here—" I check my phone. It's almost two. "Who's picking Sebas up from Dry Town?"

"No te pongas mal, amor, I took care of Sebas. I asked Diego, as a personal favor, to take him and pick him up so I could be Mom's taxi for Jet."

"Since when can Diego drive again?"

Kenzie coils her sweaty ponytail into a bun. "Calm down, he has his driving privileges back, and he's even apologized for being a pendejo lately."

"That's good," I say absently. Grandma Williams, who passed away last year, was fond of reminding me to not borrow trouble. As someone who's got a broken anxiety gauge, it's good advice, impossible to follow. I don't know if this uneasy feeling I have is because I haven't heard from Sebas since last night or because Diego is, at heart, a mess. He tries, I know he does. But he's got anger issues. He's been known to get pissed off and not show up.

"I see you, amor, that hamster-wheel brain of yours cooking up disasters. He's fine. Everyone's fine. Think positively," Kenzie says in a mock-serious tone.

I smile like I'm fine. But history has taught me that thinking positively isn't enough. I can't relax. I have to pay attention. That's how I stop bad things from happening.

37

Sebas

Diego, the flipping ashhole, never shows to pick me up from work. Cabrón doesn't answer his phone when I call either. I know Kenzie is busy, and Lu is getting ready for Ofelia's party. This would be a great time to call a car service or even a taxi—if any of that crap existed out here. It's a two-mile walk to the nearest tram stop, by my old friend the dollar store.

I'm scrolling through my podcast queue—one earbud out, since there's no sidewalk and I don't want to get creamed by a car—when *Poetry 101* pops up on my For You page. Of course my phone is listening to me. I play the podcast, hoping I can learn a little bit about this thing Lu loves—and yeah, maybe impress them a little. Because I haven't been able to stop thinking about them. Even when we're together, I'm trying to figure them out.

"What is poetry?" the host starts, after introducing herself as a poet. *Damn,* I think. *If you don't know, why am I listening to you?* She doesn't answer the question, but instead asks more questions. She recites some poetry, and it's about graves and your mother's laugh. Are you kidding me? Poetry about dead moms? No, gracias.

That's when I hear a car approaching. I have a second to wonder if I should try to hitchhike, and then something hits me hard in the back and splatters all over me, cold and shocking.

The tram driver lets me get on, even though I'm sticky and gross. I don't sit down. I don't want to get this disgusting crap on the seats.

"You okay?" the driver asks. I look bad, dried pieces of fruit and goo stuck to my neck and shirt. I smell much worse.

"Yep. Practical joke," I respond. Don't want to talk about it.

"Need to report something?"

"No."

What am I gonna report? Some ashhole threw a spoiled strawberry-and-banana smoothie at me and drove away? Am I supposed to call the police? If I do that, then I can't go find this bastard myself.

At Lu's house, I climb over the fence into the backyard and text them I'm by the guesthouse.

When they come out, confused and carrying the change of clothes I asked for, I put my hand up to stop them from getting close to me.

"I smell fucking rancid," I can't help saying, and my biosensor flashes red. "And I'm still really pissed, so can I just shower first before I explain?"

They nod and key open the door.

"Door code is 1234, so you can let yourself in anytime," they say.

I stand under screaming hot water, soaping the chunks of rotten smoothie off me, until the water gets cooler. I get dressed in some black jeans Lu lends me and my emergency shirt, which was safely tucked into my bag.

I towel-dry my hair, comb it straight and back into a ponytail. I sniff the ends, thinking I missed a spot, but the sour, spoiled smell is just in my head. It had to be someone I know, right? Someone from New Gault? Or is this part of California subject to random acts of douchery?

"Did I mess up dinner?" I ask when I get outside, where Lu waits for me. They look so good, wearing a tailored button-up shirt over jeans and boots, a long wallet chain at their hip. They hug me, and I tug on the chain, bringing them closer, kissing them.

After a minute, or like a thousand minutes, they pull back.

"Do I smell weird?" I ask.

"What? Not at all. You smell amazing." They blush, then untangle my hand from their waist. "Ofelia has been ready forever, she's so excited. And she's bringing every friend she ever made, so Mamá took the minivan to round them up. Dad's driving us, whenever you're ready."

I meet Lu's dad in the driveway. He's super tall and kinda plump, which makes him look even friendlier with his red-brown beard and curly mop. He looks like a mix between Santa and a guy in a beer commercial. Abuela would say *muy americano*, which really means *Wear your sunscreen, you're gonna burn out there*.

"Two sharp-looking humans over here, making me look like I didn't even try," he says as we get into the car.

"I know you tried, Dad. You're wearing a button-down, but the flip-flops? Felia is going to kill you."

"We've been to hibachi before, it's not fancy."

"It's Ofelia's idea of fancy."

"I've never been to hibachi," I say. "What is it?"

Lu smartly lets their dad explain it. The man likes to tell a long, goofy story—unless his depiction of flaming towers of onions and flying pieces of grilled shrimp isn't an exaggeration.

Lu reaches for my hand, and some of the tension that's been simmering since that pendejo hit me with a smoothie missile eases away.

When I was little, got hurt, and started to cry, Papá said to me, *Let it out, little man. Don't keep those bad feelings in.* Never did I hear any crap from him about men not crying. Hell, I've seen him cry at the movies—usually his stupid movies—but still. So I know I can cry, and it's not any kind of shame. I'm not a freaking fire hose. I don't cry for spoiled smoothie on my back.

But I do lean into Lu, grip both their hands in mine. Mr. Williams, probably clocking what's happening in the back seat, puts the radio up real loud, but it's an acoustic version of a pop song, one where the guitarist, probably due to boredom, goes into full-on flamenco-style guitar frills. I sit up and mime flamenco guitar in time with the song, flipping my ponytail like I'm muy guapo and know it. Lu laughs, and soon we're both losing it, cackling like brujes in the back seat of their dad's car like this is the funniest thing ever. By the time we get to the restaurant, I'm better. Felia and her friends are waving from the front door, telling us they just called us for a table. I reach for Lu's hand, and they look startled.

"No way is this gonna be just for back seats, right?" I say, hoping I am right.

They take my hand, squeezing it. "Right."

There's ten of us, so we get a grill all to ourselves.

"It's so cringe, I can't," Lu whisper-shouts to me. There's no whispering in a place like this, it's so loud. When I'm not actively stabbing things with my chopsticks, I'm grinning and nodding instead of talking. I eat until I'm in danger of exploding, and when they bring out the chocolate lava cake with sparklers on it and sing "Happy Birthday," I'm pretty sure Felia is going to bust too. The eating, the singing, the celebrating all leads up to Ms. Hernandez asking for the check and Mr. Williams presenting Felia with a familiar matte black box.

The joy on the kid's face, the way the whole restaurant seems to stop to congratulate her on this—not her birthday, that was the lava cake and the singing—but this moment of getting the TECH phone. It feels like when you're out in public and you see a quinceañera or a wedding photo shoot and everyone congratulates them, knowing it's something special. A milestone. But for a phone? It feels weird.

"You have to teach me everything," Felia says to Lu as we wait outside for their mamá to pull up the minivan.

"First rule, no curse words," they say.

"I know that! But, like, hacks, I need hacks!"

"I need hacks too," I say to her, looking at my word meter. It had seemed pretty good a few days ago, but now it's under the midpoint. I guess I talk more than I thought.

"Primero you should have learned Spanish," Lu says to their sister.

"Don't be mean, it's my birthdaaaaay," she says.

"Okay, I'll teach you some tricks tomorrow, peste."

"I'm gonna start calling you peste too. At least that word doesn't count."

"Maybe I should have gotten you a book of Spanish curse words—but I hope this is okay instead," I say, handing her the little package I have for her.

"A present? For me?" She bats her eyelashes at me. I laugh, and Lu groans.

"Kenzie helped me pick it out. She said you like stars."

She opens the box to reveal earrings, a trio of dangling stars. They're just like a pair that Kenzie has and Felia coveted. She squeals and tackle-hugs me in thanks.

"How will your mother survive driving back with that bunch of locas?" I ask Lu. The minivan pulls out of the parking lot, loaded up with twelve-year-old girls and presents and pumping K-pop from the stereo.

"She's wearing earplugs—the kind you wear to concerts to not get hearing damage? She knows what's up."

"Ofelia and her friends are having a sleepover tonight," Mr. Williams says regretfully when we get to the house. "You two might want to stay out of their way."

"What could they do to us?" I ask, sort of kidding.

"They could talk to us," Lu says. "The nonsense they talk when they're together is staggering. Okay if we stay in the guesthouse, Dad?"

"Sure. Uh. Will you drive Sebas home later?" he says, holding up the car fob. I'm not sure if he's saying that he doesn't want to have to do it because he's tired, or if he's saying *Don't let a boy sleep over in the shed with you,* or something else.

Lu doesn't seem fazed. "I'll figure it out. Thanks," they say, pocketing the car fob.

We walk through the house to the sounds of stomping and shrieking overhead and a thumping bass line.

"Damn, those little girls are loud," I say.

"And they can stay up real late, like five a.m., no problem."

"I remember doing that."

"I was always the pathetic one that fell asleep first, then had stupid stuff drawn on their face."

"I was the one doing the drawing. One time was with a Sharpie, so I got in a lot of trouble."

"I can see you as a troublemaker." Lu laughs. "And now I know to confiscate all the Sharpies in the house when you come over."

In the guesthouse, everything has been replaced and tidied up. Lu's mother must be supernatural.

Lu sits on the bed and puts on their most serious face. Which I want to kiss.

"Okay, so what happened?" they say, not reading my mind at all.

"What do you mean?"

"You climb over my fence, covered in some sticky goo. You're tense, even though you're really good at covering. Did something happen at work?"

"I like your shirt," I say.

They look down. It always makes me smile when they do that.

"Did you forget what you're wearing?" I grin.

"No, um. I just want to remember what you liked, what you thought looked good."

"I like everything. I think everything looks good. I really like all these cuerditas," I say, touching the strings around their wrist, like grooves on a record, running my fingertips back and forth.

"Sebas."

"Yeah?"

"I feel like you're avoiding something."

"Claro," I snort. "I am. Okay. It's not a big deal. Diego forgot to pick me up from Dry Town, so I had to walk. On the way, some d-bag threw a rotten smoothie at my back." I still feel the cold liquid shoot up my back, into my hair, the shock of it. "It didn't hurt, I was just startled, like a jump scare. Then I was pissed I smelled so bad. I don't smell weird, right?"

"Definitely not. Do you think it was an accident?"

I look at them hard. "You mean, seeing me walking by the side of the road prompted someone to accidentally chuck their moldy smoothie at me?"

"I know that sounds stupid," Lu says.

"I don't really want to talk about it."

"I'm not trying to get into your business," they say awkwardly.

"Really?" It comes out so rude, and I don't mean it to, but the low-level anger simmering in my gut gets the better of me.

"Yes, really. I'm just . . . I want to make sure you're okay. And that it's not someone targeting you."

"What do you mean?"

"This kind of stuff, like, little things, sudden things, that's how the bullying starts," they say. They keep their eyes on their hands in their lap.

"That's not what this is," I say, because it can't be. I can't deal with one more disaster, one more *thing*.

"I'm just saying, maybe you should tell someone at school. It's what TECH is for—" Lu starts, but before they get much further into their public service announcement, I'm up and standing by the door.

"I should go." I don't want to talk about it. I want to forget it happened. "Thanks for dinner and for the pants."

"I can drive you home," Lu says, getting up.

"No need. I'll be fine. I am fine."

I give an awkward wave, and I'm out the door. On the second floor of the house, Ofelia and her friends are silhouetted against the drawn shade of her bedroom window. They're dancing. I can't make out the music, but their giggles are clear as alarm bells. I know I'm being a dick, running away. It doesn't make it any better that I know. But I do.

38

Lu

I'm in school, ambassador pin in my pocket because I couldn't bear to wear it today, but I also couldn't bear to leave it at home. I came late on purpose, so there wouldn't be too many people around when I got my clearance to be back at school from the health suite. I texted Kenzie and Diego on our usual thread, saying that I was fine, that I'd see them at lunch.

I've moved on from biting my cuticles and the skin around my nails to biting my lip so much it's bled, and now I have a weird little scab, which I desperately want to pick off.

My phone buzzes.

I'm here, Sebas texts, and relief floods through me.

outside the health suite, I type back. A minute later, he's next to me, and then he's hugging me. I almost say *thank you*, or *I couldn't do this without you*. I know I could have. I'm just glad I don't have to.

He laces his fingers through mine. "So, once again, I am a d-bag and should not have gotten upset on Saturday. We agree?"

"We agreed that getting hit with a missile, no matter what form, is enough to make anyone pissy. We agreed that you've already apologized enough." He did. The same night, then again Sunday afternoon when I drove him to

Dry Town. We also agreed I wouldn't push him to report the incident, since it was a one-off. Sebas thinks it was some random jerk from another school district letting off steam. I tell myself not everything has to be the start of something bad. I try to believe it.

I get to A period really late, which means that Mrs. Marseglia has to stop the class to show me to my new assigned seat far in the back of the class, since Jordan is sitting up front near the gallery of windows. I try to make myself look at him casually, like I would anyone else. But I can't. I spent last week thinking about what happened to Luke, what I remember and what I don't. There's a shadow made up of grief and guilt that covers a lot of what happened in those months. I've tried to make that shadow smaller, put it in a box where it won't grow. Now that Jordan is here, I have to face it.

When class ends, Jordan is out the door like a shot. I find Mrs. Marseglia standing next to me.

"Hey, Lu. Everything okay?"

"Yup." I make myself put my laptop in my bag, then stand up, proof that everything is okay.

"I put you back here to comply with the distance order. There are a couple of other seats that could work too, like the one right by the door? That way you'd be able to get out of the room first." She smiles at me like this isn't the most excruciating conversation.

"This is fine. Thanks for making the change."

"No problem," she says, and hesitates, waits. Does she think I'm going to confide in her? Tell her what happened? *Just tell us why you're afraid of Jordan Kingsley!* That was the one thing they didn't ask in the health suite as I filled out countless forms.

The next two periods, Sebas is in my classes and Jordan isn't. It almost feels normal. Sebas meets me outside the cafeteria at lunch.

"I got you mashed potatoes because I thought you might have trouble eating. You said you get anxiety stomach." He hands me a white container and a spoon.

I did tell him that. I just didn't expect him to remember it and bring me mashed potatoes. "Thanks, I'm not hungry."

"And," he says, ignoring me, "I thought we could eat them in the quad, maybe walking around."

"Where's your cup of mashed potatoes?"

He holds up a matching cup. "Mine's rice, beans, and chicken. And hot sauce. But still, lunch in a cup."

We walk around the quad, and he talks like it doesn't cost him a thing, describing the plot to a movie about a South American dictator who turns out to be an actual, literal vampire.

"The whole thing was shot in black-and-white film stock, no digital, so it's, like, stark and grainy at the same time, and the storyline is totally bonkers but, honestly, believable in a way. Oh! I forgot to tell you about the renegade nun. Though I don't want to spoil the end of it."

I laugh. "I already know about the renegade nun—you might as well tell me the whole thing."

We walk back to the cafeteria. Both our biosensors pulse, alerting us to the end of lunch period. My cup of mashed potatoes is empty.

"I'll walk you to Psych."

"I know the way," I say, my bottom lip in my teeth before I remind myself not to make the scab there worse.

"I know that." He shrugs. "Don't make it complicated. I just want to walk together."

At the second-floor entrance to the art wing, Sebas leans toward me, brushes his lips lightly against mine, then runs his thumb against my lip, right where the scab is.

"Sana, sana, okay?" he says.

"Colita de rana," I say, finishing the next line of the nursery song Mami would sing whenever I got hurt. He turns and walks toward his Twentieth-Century Film class, and I just watch him go, like I'm dazed from being in the sun too long. He's so thoroughly scrambled my brain, just that little, nothing touch, that only later, when I'm sitting in AP Psych, talking about the sympathetic and parasympathetic nervous systems, do I remember that Jordan is in my next, and thankfully last, class.

When I get to Ceramics II, Jordan isn't there yet, so I sit where Ms. Westin tells me, near the drying cabinets at the back of the studio. Twenty minutes after the start of class, Jordan still hasn't shown up, and I tell myself I can relax. By the time I put my glazed stoneware bowl in the cabinet to dry, class is over, Jordan never arrived, and I've tied myself into knots for nothing.

39

Sebas

Honestly, I can't believe I've been in Stepford a whole-sass month.

I can't believe I'm thinking and *saying* crap like *whole-sass*, but it's my reality now. I'm not that much of an introspective person. I'm not clueless or anything, but I mostly think out, not in; now, not ahead. Yeah, that's always been a bit of a problem when it comes to spending my money, and now spending my words. Overspending them, I should say. Thankfully, it's the first of the month, and my word meter is back up to full.

"Did you move my crochet stuff?" Mom asks, when I hand her a glass of juice and her morning meds. "I need that for my circulation."

Mom is not happy. All it took to set Mom off was to be told that Leeza can't be her helper today. They're sending another person, named Shirley, to make sure Mom has everything she needs.

I take down the basket of hooks and yarn—the crochet things Lu very sweetly brought over after I whined about Mom needing something to do other than her favorite pastime, being crappy to me.

"Leeza always puts your crochet stuff here, Ma, you know that."

"I can't reach up there and if Leeza isn't here, how am I supposed to reach stuff?" Her voice is thin and she's gripping her hands. It could go a lot of ways, crying or shouting or slamming doors. Love that she keeps me guessing.

"And you're always out," she sniffs.

I let that pass, drink my coffee and scroll through the TECH app, ordering my breakfast so it's ready when I show up at school.

"And what about the car we're supposed to get? Why didn't that come?" Mom asks, groping for things to be upset about.

I look up, exasperated. "I can't drive, Ma. You're not well enough to drive. So, who's gonna drive a new car?"

"You can't drive?"

"Never learned."

She pauses for about thirty seconds. "I'll teach you," she says, and stands up, a little wobbly, like she's gonna teach me how to drive right this instant.

"Ma, now is not the time, okay?" She sits down, looking grumpy, agitated.

I try to sound positive, encouraging, like Leeza. "Why don't you try some crocheting? It'll help." The problem is that my mom is starting to feel a tiny bit better, and that just translates to more energy for bitchiness.

"I don't want the damn crochet stuff, Sebastian. I want Leeza to come like she's supposed to." Ah, the mom I know so well is back. Not like I'm surprised.

"She's not at your beck and call, Ma. She's got other responsibilities."

Mom crosses her arms, hunches her shoulders. I recognize the fighting stance.

"I'm gonna be late for school, Ma," I say, hoping for an escape route. But no, she just barrels on.

"All these other pathetic women with nothing to say, they don't know how to hold a conversation. Leeza's the only one I can even stand! She's supposed to be here for me, not abandon me when I need her."

"You'd know about abandoning people."

It's out of my mouth so fast, it's like someone else said it. We look at each other for a second. I wonder which way it's going to go. Is it going to be okay, like the last couple of weeks have been okay? Is it going to turn into a screaming match until we're both exhausted and hurting? Honestly, I can't tell what I want to happen. It feels like I'm ready for this fight, like I've been waiting to have this moment, say these words, forever.

She opens the bin, taking out a length of soft yellow yarn. "I don't know what you're trying to insinuate, but I don't like your tone of voice, kid."

There it is. Denial. It's the spark to the fire that I've been keeping low and rolling since she left me years ago. Finally, *finally*, it's my turn to explode.

"You fucking abandoned *me*." My biosensor flashes red but I barely notice. "I was a kid, eight years old, and you left without a word."

"I told your father."

"You sent Papá a text. You said you'd visit, but you never did."

She sits up, twists the yarn in her hands. "I meant to. I had a lot of things going on. My parents took me in, but they had a lot of expectations. I tried, Sebby."

"You're full of crap! When Abuela took me to my cousin's birthday party, your niece's sweet sixteen, you wouldn't even look at me." Abuela had plotted and planned to take me to this party and make Mom notice me, make the white side of my family acknowledge me. She was so sure that it would work out. It was one of the few times she was ever completely wrong.

"You pretended I wasn't your kid."

I expect more denial, more shouting and going around and around. It's the way Mom has always lost her temper, making you think it was your fault. I'm ready for that.

But instead, she slumps in her chair, the soft wool to her face as she sobs.

I don't know what to do. This isn't how it's supposed to go.

"I know I screwed up. I know it every day. I know, I know."

There's a loud knocking on the door, the kind that when you hear it, you suspect it's been going on a while. I open the door, and a tall Black lady in blue scrubs with a large tote stands there smiling. Her name tag says SHIRLEY, but her face says that, despite her smile, she heard some of our yelling. I don't have any time or energy to fix this.

"She's all yours," I say, slipping on my backpack. "Good luck—you'll need it."

At school, with everyone's word meters back up to full, there's a noticeable increase in volume. I didn't realize how quiet it had become in the last two weeks until now. People are just flexing their words, venting their stories. It's real end-of-the-year energy. I push the thought of Mom out of my head. She's someone else's problem today.

When I see Lu in the cafeteria, I hug them tight, right away, no need to say anything.

"Have I become a ghost?" Kenzie says, pretending to be miffed that I didn't greet her first.

"Morning, K."

"Whatever, loser," she says with a hair toss. I sit next to Lu, take their hand, and place it on my leg, like it belongs there, because I want it to, and they kind of blush hard. It's a bonus that it ever so slightly aggravates Kenzie, since she mumbles something about being a third wheel. That's when one of the servers comes to the table with the breakfast I ordered.

The tray lands with a clatter in front of me, the salsa from the chilaquiles with eggs spilling off the plate. I look up to see that it's Diego in an apron and hair net, looking like the end of the world.

"Hey, Diego," I say, trying to sound friendly. His grim face turns angry, in the way I've seen from him before. Lu grips my hand under the table.

"If you're happy with my service," he says, enunciating *service* like it's a dirty-thirty word, "please give me a positive rating." His face is so red, he looks like he's holding his breath. I think he's gonna say something else, curse at us, but he just turns and walks back toward the kitchen.

"Shizz," Kenzie breathes out. Lu leans their head briefly against my shoulder. "I forgot to tell you not to order breakfast at school for the next week or so. Diego's been put on morning kitchen duty for blowing through his word data, and he hates having to deliver food to us."

"It's a new month, though. Hasn't his word data reset?"

"It would if he weren't such a flipping tool," Kenzie says in disgust. "The infractions he's racked up, the rolling debt from last month. It is pathological the way that boy cannot keep his words to himself."

"Working off a word debt is embarrassing for him," Lu says to me. "Kenzie and I never have to do it, thanks to palabras in other languages. He just feels like it's unfair."

I absorb all that. It does suck, having to watch your words, and I only had to do it for a couple of weeks so far. Plus, I spend my weekends at Dry Town saying all I want and getting paid for it. But Diego has been grounded for stuff at school, stuff at home. I don't even have a clue what his home life is like. What if it's like mine? What if he left his mami or tía sobbing in the kitchen, so full of anger and nowhere for it to go?

"He should get over it," Kenzie says, digging into her overnight oats. Lu tells Kenzie she's being mean, and Kenzie informs Lu that they're being naïve. I only half listen to their back-and-forth. I eat my breakfast looking out for Diego in the crowd. Maybe I should check in on him, see if he's okay. Even if he tells me off, at least I should try. Instead, I see Jordan walk into the cafeteria, grab some cereal, and sit down on the far side of the room. Only the slightest twitch from Lu's hand in mine tells me they've clocked Jordan's entrance too. The way I see it, everyone notices him, while seeming not to notice.

Though it's only Lu and Jordan who have to keep six feet apart, all of TECH High shifts, ever so slowly, away from Jordan.

Just when I think things are going not terrible, I find myself locked in a bathroom on the top floor of the art wing, because some pendejo de mierda jammed the lock.

I try shouting, but all the bathrooms at TECH have full-height doors, and they are *solid*. I try to bust through the door but only end up practically in the toilet. This is ridiculous. I take out my phone and think. If I text Lu, they'll insist I report this incident. And I'm not even sure it *is* an incident. Like, I didn't hear anything. I was just in here doing my stuff—yes, watching video clips on my phone—and when I tried to get out, the door handle wouldn't budge. Maybe it's a lock malfunction?

In the end, I text Kenzie, and, miracle of miracles, she responds right away.

"Sebas?" I hear her outside the stall a few minutes later.

"Yeah, I'm in here."

"Fruiting heck, what have you gotten yourself into?"

"Literally only went to the lavabo like a normal human. This isn't my fault."

"Hold on. There's something wedged against the door."

I hear scratching on the wood and then a smack, and the door opens.

"What the fuck?" I remember to say thank you when the red light flashes on my biosensor. First of the month and I've already got two f-bombs on my tab. Jesus.

"The fruit, as you say, was that someone jammed a block of wood against the outside handle so you couldn't turn it."

"Hijo de la putísima—"

"Exactly," Kenzie says.

I wash my hands with excessive care because I feel gross now, don't know why.

Kenzie leans against the communal sinks, arms crossed, like she's waiting for me to say something.

"I remembered to say thank you, right?" I ask.

"You did. You're welcome. Also, why would someone try to lock you in the bathroom?"

"I don't know."

"I took some pictures of the lock before I opened it so you can include that in your report."

"Ay, Dios y la Virgen, I'm not gonna report it."

"Are you shitting me? Why not?"

I dry my hands and start walking out. Then turn back.

"Because it was probably a practical joke. Not bullying, not the start of something. It's just the usual crap. I know I'm asking a lot, and you probably won't do it. But please don't tell Lu about this."

Kenzie raises an eyebrow at me.

"They're really stressed right now, and I don't want to cause them any more anxiety. I don't want them to worry about me."

"You don't have to treat them like they're made of glass."

"I'm not. I just don't want to make anything worse for them." *Or me*, I don't say.

"I think you're an idiot and asking for trouble. But I won't tell Lu what happened to you. I do suggest, really freaking strongly, that you do."

We walk down the east stairway in silence and meet Lu, who's coming up.

"I was looking for you," they say, smiling. "I thought we could take Diego out tonight, see if we can cheer him up."

Kenzie looks at me meaningfully, like, *I said I wouldn't tell Lu about the bathroom incident. I didn't say I wouldn't make it awkward as hell for you.*

She yawns theatrically. "I'm going home. Tired. You two go have fun," she says, and walks away.

"What's that all about?" Lu asks.

I let out a frustrated breath. There's really no point in keeping this secret from them.

"I got locked in the bathroom."

Lu's expression is blank, then confused.

"Someone locked me in a bathroom stall. On purpose."

40

Lu

"I got locked in the bathroom," Sebas says, pushing his hair behind his ears. My face must show how confused I am, because he continues. "Someone locked me in a bathroom stall. On purpose."

"What?" A wave of alarm hits my whole body. My heart is racing.

"It wasn't a big deal. It was fifteen, twenty minutes, tops, of my life. I texted Kenzie, and she got me out."

Questions crowd my head. It takes me a minute to get words in the right order and speak them clearly. "You need to report this."

Sebas rolls his eyes. "I knew you'd say that. That's why I didn't want to tell you. That's why I didn't text *you*."

He slips past me down the staircase—my heart still thudding, stomach souring. *How bad is this?* my brain asks my body. And I just don't know the answer.

Sebas is waiting for me by my car.

"I'm sorry," he says. I want to say that it's okay, but it isn't.

"Why don't you want to report this?"

He tries out a smile, like maybe it will soften something in me, the way it usually does.

"There's nothing to report. Just someone playing around."

"And if it isn't?" I cross my arms, and he does the same. It's Psych 101, mirroring someone else's behavior. It's how emotions escalate, how fights start.

"This whole place is set up so none of this can happen, right? So, this isn't happening." He shrugs like that's the end of the story.

"Sebas, the system only works if people speak up. I—I should know." I take a steadying breath. "If you don't say something, it will get worse." I just want him to be safe. I want everyone to be safe.

"I have a lot going on, okay? I don't want to deal with this foolishness. I have enough things to feel sick over. I don't need to fabricate something out of nothing."

I wish I were the kind of person who lashes out. Like Diego and his split-second anger, or Kenzie, who can cut someone down with her razor-edged words. But all I have is anxiety making me freeze and his words repeating in my head. *Something out of nothing.*

"You think I'm making something out of nothing," I finally manage to say. It isn't a question.

"I didn't say that."

"You did. You think this is all in my head."

He reaches for my hand, but I take a step back. I don't want him to touch me.

"I'm not a joke. TECH isn't a joke. *Luke* wasn't a joke." My voice carries across the parking lot. I feel the stares of other kids, drawn to this spectacle.

Sebas rubs his hands over his face like he's scrubbing something away.

"I didn't say any of that. You're taking— You— That's not what I meant. I just—"

He reaches for me again, like holding my hand or hugging me might make us understand each other better. But I don't want that soft understanding. I want words that I can hold on to. I take another step away from him.

"Jesus, Lu! What are you gonna do? Set that distancer thing off on me now? Because I pissed you off?"

The blood drains from my face, leaving me dizzy. I get into my car, careful not to hit the clueless human who's breaking my heart. Sebas is yelling something—it could be *sorry*, it could be anything. I make sure I don't hear it.

Life is so random. I should come up with something more original, but that's what's going through my head. It's late, way past my sister's bedtime, but Ofelia is stretched out across my bed, eating my snacks and going through my phone to see how I've set TECH up. And I'm letting her. *Random.* Like the way grit and particles of light stick together randomly in space and eventually, sometimes, make stars, then whole worlds.

"What about social?" Felia says, looking up.

"What about it?"

"I can still use all the same apps, right?"

"Sure, but they automatically default to the highest safety settings on this phone. And since TECH knows how old you are, it knows what content you'll have access to."

"Ugh. That sucks."

"It gets worse. Mamá and Dad get to set up their own parameters of what you can and can't look at that are even stricter than TECH."

Her little face looks so horrified, I almost laugh.

"It doesn't last long. Eventually, they trust you a bit more," I say, sitting next to her and picking up her new phone. Out of its box and without the protective cover that mine has, it looks naked, like a sea creature pulled out of its shell. "Don't break it. Make sure you put the case on it."

"Doesn't matter if I break it, right? They replace it?"

I forgot how much all these questions mattered to me once. How afraid I was to drop the phone or say a bad word without meaning to.

"They do. But you still have to take care of it. It's a big responsibility, Ofelia."

"I know. I'm not gonna break it. I want to use it right but, like, smart too, you know? Hack the things that can be hacked, and the rest I'll be good about."

I lie down next to her, also diagonally.

"Throw me a snack."

Felia looks at our stash, mostly my stuff, and gives me a pack of black licorice.

"Nice," I say, because I love black licorice.

"I almost didn't give it to you, it can cause kidney failure."

"No, it can't."

"Okay, maybe some other failure. But there's something toxic about it, if you eat too much. Not the red ones, just the black licorice."

"Red licorice tastes like plastic—this stuff is the best," I say, chewing a piece that tastes of sugar and herbs.

"You're a weirdo," she says, but she says it like a compliment. "I guess some people like weirdos . . ." She gives me big eyes.

"Don't," I say.

"I mean, Señor Sebas sure seems to like your weirdness." She smiles.

"Not talking about it with you, peste."

"Come on! That's what siblings are for! I'll tell you about all my crushes, if you want?"

"Very generous," I say sarcastically. Though actually, I'm curious. Does she have crushes? I mean, besides the boy band and movie star ones? "Okay. Tell me."

"Really?"

"Not gonna offer again. Or . . . wait. I can guess—Colin Cruz."

Ofelia's mouth drops open, and I can see the sticky remains of sour gummy worms in there.

"Ay, cierra la boca, nena, please."

She closes her mouth and, almost comically, gulps. "How did you know?"

I roll over, trying to shift her so she's not hogging my bed.

"Primero, he's the one that you keep saying has a great smile."

"I say that? Out loud?"

I nod. "Gonna have to watch that now that your words are

being counted. Segundo, when he said hello to you at Sound Café, you nearly choked on your fries."

Felia hides her face in my pillow. Okay, she's kind of adorable right now. An adorable peste.

"And thirdly, your reaction when I said 'Colin Cruz.' Besides, Colin's older sister Alicia is gorgeous—must run in the family."

"Wouldn't it be amazing if I dated Colin and you dated Alicia and it was, like, a family thing?"

I grimace. "Muy creepy. Not interested in Alicia."

"Because of Señor Sebas?"

"Why do you call him that? You make him sound like a thirty-year-old man."

Ofelia looks shocked. "You don't remember Señor Sebas?"

"No? Should I?"

"The *frog*," she almost shouts. "The cartoon? *Señor Sebas Says*?"

I get a flood of memories from the last time we were in Montevideo visiting family. Felia was little, I was bored and uncomfortable around extended family I barely knew. *Señor Sebas* was a show for preschoolers, a sort of Simon Says to get kids off their butts and doing cardio.

"Sebas looks nothing like a frog," I say, trying to sound serious, while she cracks up.

"No, he's handsome. And he really likes you."

"¿Cómo sabes?"

"Because he's here all the time, and you two are always in the guesthouse laughing like lunatics. Isn't that the way you know?"

"Not sure I like him much right now," I say, picking lint off a knobby throw pillow so I don't pick off any more of my own skin.

"You broke up? You were holding hands at my birthday! What happened? Did you break his heart? Did he break yours? Do I have to break his face?"

"Felia! Basta." I laugh. "We— It's not like that."

I'm not sure what it is like, though.

I was anxious, and that sometimes feels like anger, sometimes fear. I can't always tell what the feeling is, just that it's hot and scalding. By the time I calmed down enough to respond to his texts, I could only say, **I need some time.**

Which meant three days of being miserable, catching his eye, and feeling like I wanted to cry. Three days of Jordan keeping his distance, and keeping my distance from Sebas, like we were all in a complicated, exhausting dance.

Meanwhile, Kenzie has been driving Sebas to work at Dry Town, and that's almost the worst part. That was *our* thing.

"You know what happened with my friend Luke, right?" I ask.

Felia sits up, tucks her legs to the side, a mini version of Mamá. "Mami told me. He died because of bullying at your old school."

"That's what I'm trying to get Sebas to understand. If Luke could die that way, anyone could. It's serious. That's why we count words, that's why we take care. It's the whole point of living this way."

"And Sebas doesn't want to live this way?"

"He's here because of other reasons. Good reasons."

"Pero it doesn't mean the same thing to him as it does to you?"

"That's it. And I try, but I can't get him to understand."

Ofelia nods like she's contemplating the situation. She picks through the bag of gummy worms, avoiding the lime ones she doesn't like, then puts the bag down and looks at me with a seriousness that doesn't seem to fit on her face.

"Does it have to be the same thing for him? Does it need to matter the same way, I mean, for you to like him?"

My mouth opens, but the words aren't there.

"I don't know," I finally answer. But I do. Why should it have to matter in the same way? I don't understand what he's going through with his mom. I don't have to understand everything to know how I want to show up for him.

My phone buzzes. Felia peers over my shoulder.

"Is it Señor Sebas? He is spending a lot of words trying to get you to talk to him again."

It's not Sebas; he's at Dry Town and doesn't have his phone. Someone is actually calling me. I look at the number, then at my sister, as my stomach plunges with anxiety.

"It's Sebas's mom."

41

Sebas

Since Kenzie took over driving me to Dry Town, she's been helping Sheila set up, then sitting with me while I do the readings.

"Want a Dr. Limón?" she asks, pulling her red T-shirt away from her neck, where it's sticking a bit. It's hot as hell in here, despite the fans, the ancient AC.

I nod, even though I should probably ask for water to stay hydrated. When she's back with the drink, Kenzie pulls at my tied-back hair.

"You should let it loose, Walter Mercado–style," she says.

"No disrespect to Señor Mercado, may he rest in peace, but flowing hair and bedazzled capes? That's not my vibe at all." I take a deep pull of the soda. Dry Town has one of those soda machines that you can mix to your heart's content. A Dr. Limón is Kenzie's mix of root beer, lemonade, and whatever other nonsense she feels like adding. Sheila complains over the expense of keeping kids entertained without their "TECH meth," as she calls it, but I think she and Ana do a good job. The room is packed with kids from TECH, from Grandview—practically everyone is here. Except, of course, Lu.

"Have they forgiven you yet?"

She's asked me this a few times in the last few days, like she's reminding me each time that this is my mess. At first, I said something stupid, like, *I didn't even do anything wrong*. Then I moved on to *They don't trust me* and *Don't they know me?*

Eventually I was left with Kenzie's merciless stare. *You know what you did*, it seemed to say.

But what did I do, other than let my frustration out?

And okay, I said Lu would be capable of putting a distance order in place for me, just because they were angry. That was so low, I cringe when I remember it.

But getting locked in the bathroom pissed me off, and when I feel attacked, I want to lash out.

I didn't want to tell Lu because I didn't want it to be another thing we had to deal with. Between my mom, and Lu's past showing up to mess with them, it's *enough*.

I don't know, I reached my limit.

The problem is that Lu thinks I've reached my limit with *them*, that I don't want them, their trouble, anymore. That can't be further from the truth.

I got home in the worst mood after school that day, convinced that Mom would just crap all over me.

And what did Mom actually do, the minute I opened the front door?

"Sebby! Glad you're home, kid. Look at what Shirley taught me to do." She flapped a delicate crocheted square at me. Turned out, Shirley was really good at crochet too, and dealt with all of Mom's bull without any problems.

I take my break in the little locker room in Dry Town and video call Abuela. "Hola, cariño," she says when my face appears on her screen. She looks tired, and she's breathing a little heavy, like when she's trying to reach something on a high shelf and refuses to let me help.

"Hola, hermosa," I say, hoping that calling her gorgeous gets a smile out of her.

"Ja, ja, those days are long past, querido. Are you at work?" she asks, peering at the screen.

"Yeah, but I'm on my break. I wanted to ask your advice."

"Por supuesto, mijo. I always want to help if I can."

"You know Lu calls you el oráculo?"

She laughs. "Who calls me that? Your girlfriend?"

"My friend Lu."

"But you like her, ¿no es así?" Abuela says. I don't bother saying *them, not her or him or anything else,* because Abuela's tired and so am I.

"I like them. But they're unhappy with me."

"Ach," she says, like that's nothing. "Well, you will fix it, amor. You know the right thing to do."

"I said something really stupid to Lu. And I apologized. Only, it's still not okay between us."

"Have you asked Lu what would make it okay?" Abuela asks.

"Can't they just understand? I know they're not, like, telepathic, ¿pero no me conoce?"

I take a minute to remind Abuela what *telepático* means, and she agrees that it would be pretty awesome to be able to read other people's thoughts, but dangerous too. Then I tell her about a short film I saw where in the future everyone is telepathic except, like, 5 percent of the population, and it's really horrible to be in that minority.

"That sounds like a terrible future," Abuela says. "Where there is no need for words, and everything is understood in a flash."

"I don't know. Maybe that's a better way than trying to figure out the right thing to say."

"With Lu, mijo, I'm sure you know the right thing to say. Tu corazón sabe," she says, pointing in the general area of my heart.

"Gracias, Abue," I say as she settles back into her pillows. The bright cherry-red shawl she knit herself slips off her shoulders. "Tápate," I say, "you look cold."

"No, mijo, I'm fine. I feel good. Don't worry about me. And I'm not too sleepy, so you can call me if you have any difficult cards."

"In the mood I'm in, I have the feeling all the cards will be difficult tonight."

"If they give you any trouble, ask yourself, *What does this person who sits before me want to know, and what are they afraid of?* Then give them a little bit of both." She gives me a mischievous grin.

"Te quiero mucho, Abuela."

"Nos queremos, angelito," she responds before hanging up.

I just have time to quickly text Lu before going back to work.

> I'm sorry. I'm really, really sorry.
> **Can we talk?**

I stand by the lockers waiting for a reply, but just like the rest of my texts, there's no response. I pull the elastic band from my hair, then braid it, even though Kenzie says the little braid that I produce looks like a crooked tail. If Lu doesn't respond to my text by the time I clock out, I'm having Kenzie drop me off at their house.

I walk back toward my corner. The Tarot Reading area is far away from the vintage-looking jukebox so that people can hear me. I sit on a fancy wicker basket chair that hangs from a chain and swings a little—not the most comfortable setup. The "seeker" sits in a red velvet chair across a table strewn with scented candles on a rainbow shawl printed with astrological signs. A sign Sheila had printed says TAROT READINGS—THE CARDS REVEAL THE TRUTH! which is what Abuela always says.

"What about some extra lights back here?" Kenzie asks, examining my area with an expert eye as I slide into the basket chair.

"Lights could be good," I say, finishing my second Dr. Limón. The last couple hours of the night are always a bit unpredictable. I've already gotten through all the people on the sign-up sheet, so it's down to any final seekers who decide they want a reading at the last minute. Nine times out of ten, it's a question about unrequited love. For a change, I get a question about choosing a college from a blond guy who, Kenzie informs me, doesn't go to TECH. I tell him what the cards say, and he doesn't seem happy or sad, just neutral, which makes me feel like it's pointless.

I take a much-needed bathroom break, resisting the urge to go back to check my texts, see if Lu has responded. Maybe it's better if they don't text back. That way, I have an excuse to go over there tonight and basically apologize better. Kenzie's wrong. I don't need Lu to forgive me. I just need them to know I understand.

I sit back down at the table and concentrate on shuffling las cartas, closing my eyes, trying to remember the subtle difference between a seven of cups that leans toward victory and a five of cups that leans toward caution. Or is it the reverse? When I open my eyes again, Jordan Kingsley is sitting across from me.

"Oh fuck" is the first thing out of my mouth. He winces. Kenzie perks up like she's only here for the f-bombs.

A couple of beats of silence pass. I'm thinking, *This is the bully, the boy who's responsible for driving someone to kill himself?* Up close, he doesn't look like a monster. Which is me being stupid. What does a monster even look like? But he's just normal, basketball-player tall, might be Black or brown or a lot of things. He's got really long, thin fingers that kind of sprawl on the table in front of him.

"Can I, uh, get a reading?" Jordan gestures to the sign, THE CARDS REVEAL THE TRUTH!

"Where's your money?" I ask.

"We take cards or cash," Kenzie chimes in crisply.

"Yeah, okay. How much?"

"For you? Eighty," I say.

"Seems steep." Jordan frowns.

"Take it or leave it."

He taps his card against the reader on the table. And I make a point of waiting till the transaction goes through—in case he tries to get a refund on what I suspect will be a reading that's seriously lacking in customer service.

I push the deck in front of him and tell him to shuffle. It's mildly satisfying to see that he's pretty clumsy at it. Long fingers are good for gripping basketballs, terrible for managing magic cards, I guess.

"Is that good?" he asks after a few minutes of me and Kenzie staring at him.

"Okay." I take the deck back. "What's your question?"

He looks surprised. "I have to have a question?"

"What did you think this was? Texas Hold'em?" I ask.

"No, man, I just thought you'd, like, read my future."

"I will. But you have to ask the cards a question. What do you want to know?"

I know what *I* want to know. What kind of person bullies someone so relentlessly that they don't want to live anymore?

"Okay. Do I have to tell you the question, or can I just keep it in my mind?"

That throws me a little. I've never had anyone not tell me their question. Believe in las cartas or not, but the question from the seeker is important. It guides the reader so we can frame the answers from the cards in the right way. To a lot of people—and to me, in the beginning—that sounds like bull, like one of those TV shows where a ghost gramps shows up through a medium with big hair and a New York accent. All I know is, when done with amor, the cards speak the truth. Not sure I can scrape up any love for this guy. But I can try for honesty.

"You don't have to tell me the question, though that makes it a little harder. Okay, here goes."

I put the first card down in the center, the situation position, then the card to its left, the past. To that card's right goes the future card. Below the situation card is the positive influence card, above it is the negative influence card. I turn each of the cards over in the same order I set them out and contemplate their meaning. When I look up, Jordan's face is a mix of skepticism and disappointment.

"These aren't tarot cards, they're cartas españolas. No skeletons in shrouds here. Just kings, cups, and swords."

"I know these cards," he says stiffly. "My grandfather left my dad cards like these. No one knows how to play with them, though."

I nod because I don't really want to know about his grandfather or anything else about him. Okay, that's a lie. I don't want to know anything *good* about him, anything that will make him seem human to me.

I point to the first card, the six of coins, reversed.

"This is your situation. And it sucks. Ever heard the saying *A lie has short legs?*"

He shakes his head.

"It sounds better in Spanish. But you get the idea. Lies got short legs, meaning they can't run for long. This card says, whatever lies you're telling—to yourself or to other people—they're gonna catch up to you."

I'm deep into the cards now. They're starting to tell me a story, lead me to revealing truths, just like Abuela always said they would.

"This card is in the past position; it's the two of swords. That means disagreement, discord, upheaval. This card leads to the center card. It's how you got here." I look at Jordan, whose face is set like he's listening but he doesn't like what he's hearing.

I point to the future card, the two of clubs. "This card means a decision is coming your way. You're gonna have to make a change, choose a direction, move toward something. Otherwise, you'll stay in shadows and murkiness."

"I'm trying to do that," he starts to say, but I put a hand up.

"I'm just gonna read your cards, and you're gonna stay quiet." Amazingly, that works.

"The three of cups is in the positive position—meaning it's influencing your situation positively. Cups are really good, really favorable. There's a positive energy, a new start, or a possible way forward. The start of a new path." Before Jordan Kingsley can get too excited, I point to the last card, in the negative position above the situation card.

"And this one is the seven of clubs—usually a good card, but in this position, it's working against you. This card speaks to the difficulties you encounter when you don't respect different points of view. This card essentially says, *You're the problem, it's you.*"

I'm watching his face for something, I don't know what, something that shows what he's thinking. But it's still that mask, like he's afraid to show any real emotions.

Kenzie stands behind me, arms crossed and expression set to pissed off, like a comic book henchman. How long have I been doing this reading? The room that seemed full a few minutes ago is emptying out. It's already after midnight.

"Why are you here?" I ask Jordan.

"Lu won't talk to me. I can't get near them."

"Good," Kenzie and I say together.

"I just want to talk. I'm trying to explain what happened."

"They know what happened," Kenzie says, "and so do we." Jordan looks even more uncomfortable than before.

"But I want to tell them that I'm sorry."

"Too bad," Kenzie says at the same time that I say, "What?"

"It doesn't matter why I did what I did. I am responsible for my own actions, I know that. But I never wanted to hurt anyone."

"But you did. Because of you, someone died," I say.

"I'm not saying I didn't do anything bad, no, terrible—I did. I'm not saying anything excuses me." Jordan takes a minute, rocking in his chair, trying to breathe like they do in the chair-yoga classes Mom watches with Leeza now.

"I was a terrible person in middle school. Wait, that's not even fair to the kid I was. I was a confused kid. Scared of everything, especially saying no to anyone I wanted to like me." He puts his hands up like he can tell Kenzie and I don't want to hear it. "I'm not excusing anything, I swear. I just want to be clear, and it doesn't matter if you believe me or not. What we did to Luke made his life miserable, made him feel awful, and I wish to God I hadn't done it. But I didn't know what would happen. And anyway, I'm not that person anymore. I just want the chance to tell Lu that I've changed."

I shake my head and stare at the cards on the table. Someone changes the music midsong, so that the bouncy guitar pop that's been playing through Dry Town all night shifts to moodier downbeats.

"The cards," I say, pointing to the spread between us, "say you're fixated on yourself. Like, severely self-centered." I let that sink in for a few beats. Abuela would probably be sucking her teeth at me right now if she could see me. The cards don't say any of that. I do.

"You won't help me," he says, pushing back in his seat.

"I'm saying, you're making this whole thing—showing up at TECH High School, trying to talk to Lu, coming here to talk to their friends, I see what you're doing—you're making it about *you*. Stop."

I stand up so I know he's paying attention—and yeah, because I'm that drama queen. "This isn't some car wash where you go to get squeaky clean, man. You got to do that on your own. Don't involve Lu."

"They're here," Kenzie says.

"That's right." I nod, riding on my wave of righteousness. "Lu is here now, in New Gault, and you will just have to either live with it, or go."

"No, puñeta," Kenzie says, shoving my shoulder until I look up. "Lu is *here*."

42

Lu

I thought nothing could make me come inside Dry Town. Then Sebas's mom called, and here I am. I've got a death grip on my phone like it's gonna save me from what I have to say to him.

The place looks just like Diego and Kenzie have described a dozen times or more: neon beer signs on every vertical surface, the bar, the wall of tabletop games, a photo booth, and more. Even though it's late and the place is emptying out, I only recognize about half the people. That makes this feel like walking into a room of sharpened knives. Maybe that's a bit dramatic. I can't always tell the difference between real danger, drama, and overreaction. In fact, those things all feel exactly the same for a body steeped in anxiety—like mine is now.

A white woman in a T-shirt with a line-dancing pickle on it approaches.

"No phones, remember?"

"I need to talk to Sebastian Ascencio. It's really important."

"It's very important that TECH crap doesn't come any farther into my establishment than those lockers. Then you can see your friend."

It's just faster to put my phone into a locker, I know that. I've left it before. In Dr. Allyson's basket outside her office. Once when I had to get an MRI. I can do this. But my phone feels sticky, like it doesn't want to leave my hand. Jesus, my imagination. I'm just sweaty.

When I've locked the little door and put the key and band around my wrist, I ask the woman in the pickle shirt where Sebas is.

She points vaguely toward the rear of the open space. "He's in the back, near the photo booth. Have fun."

When I see Sebas reading las cartas españolas in the animated and exuberant way he does, I can't help but smile. Then he stands and his customer stands and the scene looks different. That's when Kenzie sees me and shoves him until he looks over. They both stare at me. *It's not so bad,* I tell myself. It looks like it could be fun to hang out here. Playing games. Not being on the outside looking in. Relaxing without having to worry about what you say.

Then I see Jordan standing across from Sebas, and I freeze. I don't have my phone, but I can still stay six feet away from him.

Sebas runs over to me, hugging me before I can get my words out. His arms around me make me feel so safe, it's almost embarrassing. He kisses me, full-on, and I let myself ignore the wolves at the door—the people, problems, and anxiety that fills me. For only a minute, I let our kiss be the whole world.

"What are you doing here?" he asks, finally pulling away and searching my eyes. Still my words don't come. Behind him, I see Jordan walk away.

"Did you know Jordan was here?"

I shake my head.

"I'm proud of you!" He smiles so widely, it makes my stomach drop in a new, complicated way. I have to tell him. I have to say the words.

"Sebas, your mom—"

Kenzie interrupts by hugging me too, and I've got both of them surrounding me. I should be able to do this one thing. It's the only reason I'm here.

"You jerk! I've been trying to get you to come to Dry Town for literal years! And you show up for this pendejo? It must be amor, eh?"

They let me go, still smiling like my being here is a good thing, like it's something to celebrate.

"Never mind that. I'm such an asshole, Lu. I said—"

I put my hand on his cheek to stop his apologizing, to get him to focus on me. Before I lose my nerve.

"Sebas, I need to talk to you. Something's happened."

He hears me, and slowly, the smile leaves his face. "Is it my mom? She's got the number for the landline. I thought she'd call that if she needed something."

"It's not working, or she couldn't get through. I don't know. It's your abuela, Sebas."

He doesn't let me finish, pushing past both of us to get to his phone, to find out the news himself.

Nothing stops in Dry Town. People keep playing cards, ordering lavender lemonades and energy drinks at the bar.

"What happened?" Kenzie asks, but I can only shake my head.

Kenzie and I get our phones, then meet Sebas out in the parking lot. He's pacing, listening to someone on his phone. It's torture to watch him. Finally, he ends his call and looks at us mutely, tears streaking his face. At least I have a plan.

"We're driving you. We'll be there in about eight hours."

43

Sebas

Kenzie drove the first three hours, until we had to hit a charging station. I leaned against Lu in the back seat like I was ten, and they let me cry on them, zone out, fall asleep, punch the leather seats of their dad's car. They let me do whatever I needed and wouldn't let me go. Thank God. I feel like I could break off into tiny pieces any minute. If that happens, they'll never find all of me again.

"You okay?" Lu asks. They keep asking. I know they know I'm not okay. What they're really asking is *Can you hold on? Can you be okay enough to make it home?* And the answer is always the same. *I'm fine.*

Lu and Kenzie go into the station, which is one of those tricked-out trucker ones with showers, rows and rows of snacks lining the walls, and a twenty-four-hour grill. I stare at my phone, my TECH phone, which works just fine out here, but without any of the restrictions put on it because we're out of city limits. No more messages from Papá. I hope he's getting some sleep, even though I know he didn't go home. He's squashed himself into two of those plasticky armchairs they always have in hospital rooms, three or four thin blankets thrown around him because it's always so damn cold.

I get out to stretch, then realize I really have to pee. Inside the station, the glare of the overhead lights stings my eyes. When I get out of the bathroom, I see Kenzie waiting by the grill counter as a very sleepy girl with a sloppy bun rings up her order.

"I got you a ham-and-cheese, that okay?"

"I'm not hungry."

"I know. But maybe eat anyway?"

"Can I have coffee?"

"Oh yes. Coffee for everyone. Lots of milk and sugar. There's always a fresh pot. That's what Sarabeth here says." She gestures to the sleepy girl, who's on her phone and doesn't look up.

"I'll help you carry stuff."

"Thanks. Oh, I almost forgot." She digs in her shoulder bag until she brings out las cartas españolas and hands them to me. They're loose, and I automatically pluck a black band from my wrist and fasten it around the deck.

"Thank you." The thought of almost losing Abuela's cards makes me light-headed. There are too many things to lose, too many ways to lose them. I put the cartas españolas in my pocket like they have some power to keep me from losing Abuela.

Lu walks over, and together the three of us listen to the sound of the fryer, the country music station that the cook has on low in the back. And we wait for our sandwiches and our coffee. There's nothing else to do. If I were directing this movie, I would cut all of this out, the sleepy teen at the counter, the trucker showers—those are just decorations, eye candy, and they slow down the pace. This is a road movie, right? Or it's a horror movie, or it's a fucking tragedy. No one wants to see the part of the story when the best friend pays for the food, and the damaged kids all trudge out of the rest stop. Maybe they'd want to see Our Hero make himself eat a mediocre sandwich while sitting next to the person he's pretty sure he's fallen completely in love with.

Only, I can't tell exactly what's going on with my heart since it's flown south, to San Marcos, to be with Abuela. *Please don't leave me,* I think.

"You okay?" Lu asks for the thousandth time. I don't mind. They're reminding me that they're here.

"I'm fine."

44

Lu

The UC San Diego Medical Center is humongous, and I'm tired and anxious, so I enter the wrong parking lot—two wrong parking lots—twice. The attendant directs us to the entrance nearest the stroke center just as Sebas gets a text from his dad.

"They're sending her home."

"That's good, right?" Kenzie says from the back seat. But I don't think it's good news.

"It's good that she'll be home," Sebas says miserably. "But it's hospice care."

Sebas gives us directions to his house, twenty minutes away. The sun's rising, a thin orange light over the east that, when it tops the horizon, pours over everything like a searchlight. I pull up in front of his house, a yellow ranch with light blue shutters on the windows.

Sebas gets out, then turns back to say something, and he just can't. I get out of the car, and in seconds, I'm hugging him.

"I don't know what to do. I have to wait for Papi to bring Abuela home, and I hate having to wait."

"We'll wait with you," I say against his cheek. He shakes his head.

"I appreciate it, honest. But I'd rather be alone," he says, pulling out of my arms.

"Okay."

"I'll call you when I know more."

Kenzie and I watch him walk up to the door and let himself in. Then I wait another minute or two before collapsing into the passenger seat like my bones have melted. Kenzie moves to the driver's seat and puts the nearest charging station into the navigation. She got some sleep while I was driving the last four hours, but I couldn't sleep when she drove, in case Sebas needed something. Being able to concentrate on him and what he's going through let me put aside my own raging anxiety dragon for a little bit. Which, I guess, was nice of Nightmare.

We park in the mall lot where the chargers are located. It's so early that only a chain coffee shop is open. She gets me a giant iced coffee that's so full of sugar and milk that it's practically the same shade as my hand. I down it.

"Remember when I used to call my anxiety Nightmare?" I ask when we're seated on the wooden bench in front of the coffee shop.

She shakes her head, takes a sip of her black coffee, then says, "Wait, yes I do! That's the dragon that lives in your stomach, right?"

"Yes."

"I do remember. I just forgot it had a name. So, I take it Nightmare isn't being a good anxiety dragon?"

I shrug, and my shoulders are so tight, they twinge. "I guess they're being nice. They let me get here. So far from home and TECH."

"Jesus, I never even thought of that. I was on autopilot."

"Me too. Now I feel like that one time we all got high off the same vape Victoria had in sophomore year."

Kenzie grimaces. "Both you and Diego greened out, and I had to watch over you so you didn't do anything stupid, like I was tu mamá."

"Have I told you how much I love you?"

She laughs. "Shut up. That's the lack of sleep talking. And I know you love me, idiota, and I love you. Why else would I be here?"

I nod. I could almost fall asleep on this hard, public bench, knowing that I'd be okay with Kenzie.

"Speaking of love . . . ?"

"Como locura," I say. "But I have no idea what's going to happen with me and Sebas now. With his abuela and all the restrictions in New Gault. If I were him, I wouldn't want to go back."

"But he has to go back, right? So his mom gets to stay and get better?"

"And how shitty is that?" I ask, with more venom than I meant. The barista shoots us a look, like it's way too early for this nonsense.

"You went to Dry Town, *Jordan was there*, and then you drove nearly eight hours and hundreds of miles away from the place you feel safest—for *him*. There's got to be an epic poem in that, at least," she says, saluting me with her paper cup.

After checking in with Mamá, Kenzie and I try to get a couple of hours of sleep in the car with the back seats flat. It's almost comfortable. I keep my phone near my head so I'll feel the slightest vibration. Mamá is unhappy that I'm so far away and that she can't track me on my phone anymore. With TECH, my parents never bothered with any other tracking or safety apps. And they never thought I'd willingly leave the safety of New Gault.

I don't remember sleeping, but when Sebas video calls, it's hours later.

"Hey," I say, sitting up and rubbing my eyes.

"You okay?" he asks. He's sitting near a window, his hair pulled back tight.

"That's what I'm supposed to say to you. I'm fine."

"Abuela is here, and she's comfortable."

"Good." I pick through words in my head like they're pebbles on a beach and I have to find the right one. None of them are right.

"Will you come over? I think she might like to meet you," he says.

"Is she awake?" I didn't want to ask, I didn't want to know, but I thought she was unconscious. Isn't that sort of what hospice means, like in a coma?

Sebas shakes his head. "No, not awake. But she's here. I want you to meet her."

45

Sebas

Papá says that Abuela must have known she was going soon, because she spent so much of her time in the weeks I've been gone cooking and freezing meals until the stand-alone freezer en el garage was bursting.

"When she was too tired to do the cooking herself, she made Tía Gladys y la Nonna cook while she sat in her chair directing," he says. I see it like it's a movie I've already watched: my grandmother coaxing with approving and disapproving miradas as her best friends from the neighborhood run around her kitchen, chopping onions finer, then finer still. They bring her spoonfuls of sauce to try, and I imagine my little abuelita like the emperor in *Gladiator*, giving a thumbs-up or thumbs-down. Abuela is all of five feet tall, but there is a bit of the Roman emperor about her. She's always seemed so big to me.

I finish the pollo con lentejas that Papi defrosted for our lunch, then wash our plates. Abuela would hate to see dirty dishes in her sink.

"You gonna try to sleep, Papo?" Pa asks.

"No, I'll sit with her," I say, like I have since I came home. I can't sleep through the little bit of time I have left with her.

Kenzie and Lu show up, and Papá doesn't wait to hear if

they're hungry—he just starts to defrost more of Abuela's food.

"Come meet Abuela," I say, pulling Lu down the hallway to Abuela's room. Kenzie stays with Papá in the kitchen, talking about favorite foods and electric cars.

Before the ambulance transport brought Abuela home, I tried to make her room as beautiful as possible. I opened the windows so the firebush flowers she loves so much, the ones that attract hummingbirds and butterflies, spill inside. I cut other flowers from her little garden—bright pink salvia, seaside daisy—and put them in all the vases we have in the house, then in the blue enamel pitchers she loves, and finally in the plastic takeout containers she makes us save.

I put pictures of all of us, as many as I can find, around the room. Papá put his foot down at all the candles I wanted to light.

"It's not a wake," he said, which made me realize I was set-dressing a death scene like this was a movie, something I could control. I took out the candles, put a TV on to a show Abuela likes, and turned on the radio to the ranchero music station.

"It's beautiful in here," Lu whispers, having no idea how I struggled to get it right.

La Nonna sits with my grandmother, holding her hand. "I should go?" she asks, rising.

"You can stay, Nonna," I say, but she leaves anyway, since we both know I don't mean it.

I sit in the chair Nonna vacated and take Abuela's hand. I don't want her to feel alone for even a moment. She's propped up on a mountain of pillows, hair combed back and behind her ears. I put the cherry-red shawl around her shoulders because the whiteness under her dark, lined skin is killing me.

"Hola, Doña Graciela," Lu says, greeting Abuela with a formality that would tickle her if she were conscious.

"I don't know if she can hear anything. People say hearing is the last thing to go." I choke on the words. Lu sits next to me and holds my hand like we're an anchor for Abuela. I know it's selfish, so I don't say it out loud, but the only thought in my head is *No te vayas. Don't go.*

I think it's the breeze from the window, or maybe a dog barking, that wakes me up. I was resting my head on Abuela's bed, then closing my eyes for a minute, and now, judging from how dim the room has gotten, it's hours later. Lu must have fallen asleep sitting upright, holding my hand. They rub a hand through their curls. But they don't let go of my hand. I watch Abuela for a few seconds. Still breathing, still here. Papá comes in and turns on the little light.

"Almost time for dinner, guys," Pa says, then leaves.

Lu squeezes my hand. "¿Estás bien?"

"I'm good," I say. I think about all the pretending I'll have to do in the next few days, weeks. *I'm fine. Doing okay. Es una bendición, a blessing, to live such a long life.*

"Will you write words for her?" I ask Lu.

"What?" I can tell they were miles away.

"Never mind."

"No, not never mind. You want me to write words? A poem for your abuela?"

"It's a stupid idea."

"It's not. But wouldn't you rather write something?"

"You'd know what to say. How to say it and make it good.

I can't think of anything except *no te vayas*. Kinda selfish to whine *don't go* at someone when they're at death's door."

Lu rubs their thumb against the back of my hand.

"'For life and death are one, even as the river and the sea are one. / In the depth of your hopes and desires lies your silent knowledge of the beyond; / And like seeds dreaming beneath the snow your heart dreams of spring.'"

"Was that Robert Frost?" I ask.

"No, that's part of a Kahlil Gibran poem. I memorized it after Luke died. I thought poetry could teach me how to get past the grief."

"Did it?"

Lu shakes their head. "I didn't get past it, but I knew how to name the feelings I had to sit with. Now poetry is how I say the things that are too sharp, or too bright, for regular words."

"Will you write something? For—for after? You'll know how to say what I mean."

"Are you sure you want me to? I mean, I only just met her, and I don't want to get it wrong."

I think about how Lu uses words—to calm Diego down, to make Kenzie laugh, to make me fall for them. How they put words together in a poem that, when they speak it, plays new movies in my head.

"You couldn't get it wrong," I say simply.

Which makes Lu tuck their head against my shoulder.

"Okay," they say. "I'll do my best. Tell me about her."

Graciela Maria Ascencio dies while we're eating her delicious food, and that seems exactly right. When the visiting nurse comes to check on her, we're eating albóndigas with store-bought tortillas, which Dad insists is sacrilege.

"But my mother wouldn't hear of freezing her tortillas, said I could make them fresh after watching her so many times. I told her, I know how to sing punk songs, how to build houses, and maybe three other things. Tortillas are like rocket science to me!" He's smiling his goofiest smile when the nurse comes back in.

"She's gone. I'm so sorry."

Dad and I are out of our chairs and in Abuela's room in seconds, like we're trying to catch her. She hasn't moved an inch in her bed. She's still got her hands folded over the blanket, her hair brushed back from her forehead. But she's really gone. I watch Dad cry and hug his mamá. I can't cry or move. My brain is stuck on how perfect she looks. Any minute, she'll open her eyes and ask me to make her tea. We'll drink our tea, eat galletas, and talk about unlucky sword cards and favorable coin cards. I'll tell her about Lu, and she'll tell me about when she was a union organizer, and there will be more time.

Tía Gladys and la Nonna are in the room, even though I didn't hear them come in. They gently push us out, so gently, it takes me a minute to realize we're in the hallway. They'll take care of her, wash and dress her, make sure her spirit knows it's okay to leave the room.

Dad's sobbing, hugging me, his shaky breath vibrating through me.

"It's okay, Pa," I say.

"I know, hijo, I know."

Nonsense words, words I wouldn't have bothered saying in New Gault. Back in the kitchen, minutes or hours later, the nurse sits at the table, a folder jammed with paperwork at her elbow, writing about the end of Abuela's life next to the cold meatballs, the packet of store-bought tortillas. It's ridiculous. This whole thing is so stupid, no one would believe it if you put it in a movie.

My phone buzzes with a text from Lu. Somehow, it's almost ten o'clock.

> I'm so sorry, Sebas. Kenzie and I didn't want to be in the way. We're getting some sleep at a hotel. We'll see you tomorrow. Xo

I didn't even notice they were gone.

46

Lu

I have no plans to go back to New Gault, not yet, even without a change of clothes or a toothbrush—though we ran to an all-night pharmacy to get some stuff before we checked in to a hotel. Mamá reminds me that I need my meds, and she needs to see me. She flies down the next morning with bags packed for me and Kenzie.

"I talked to Sebastian's mother," Mamá says as we sit at the little café in the hotel. She's full travel-Ma right now, hair scraped back, wearing a floral baseball cap and the workout clothes she uses only for travel or spin class.

We left Kenzie in the room, in a tense phone conversation with her parents. My folks didn't like it, but they gave me permission to take Dad's car. Though Kenzie had immediately offered to help drive, she never actually told her parents that she was going.

"How is Mrs. Ascencio?" I ask. I don't ask how Mami found and talked to Sebas's mother—mi mamá has her ways.

"She's okay. She was very nice, but worried about her son. She's been talking to his dad too."

"Mami, I want to stay for the funeral."

My mother pauses to finish her café, then asks, "You're okay being away from home?"

I know she's asking if I feel totally safe so far from New Gault and I don't, not completely.

"Okay enough." I shrug. "TECH can't keep me safe forever. I'm not sure it ever could."

Mami gives me a quick, tight hug. "I'll stay for the funeral too," she says, "if you want me to."

"Sí, gracias," I say, and it's not just for now, but for all the times she's been there, waiting to see what I need. She squeezes my hand.

Kenzie comes out of the elevator and walks over to us, looking tired and unhappy.

"I need more coffee," Mamá says, getting up. "Anyone else need anything?"

Kenzie gratefully gives Ma her coffee order. I ask for orange juice.

"I have to go home. I'm going to be murdered when I get there, naturally. But I have to be on a flight that leaves in a couple of hours," Kenzie says.

By the time her parents realized they couldn't track Kenzie's location anymore, they were losing their minds. She texted her parents right before we got to UC San Diego Medical Center to let them know where she was, what she was doing. She did not answer their phone call. They talked to my folks, and Mamá calmed Mrs. Choi down. Everything seemed okay. Until now.

"Thanks for coming down with me," I tell her.

"Don't get squishy. You know I hate emotions."

"I know you don't."

"What are you going to do about Diego?"

"What do you mean?"

"Have you not read any of his texts?"

"Muted him," I say unapologetically. "I couldn't deal with his cryptic abbreviations."

Kenzie tilts her head to survey me. "When you get the chance, read his texts. He's texted all of us."

"Okay," I say distractedly as Mamá comes back with our drinks. "I'll respond."

"You're on the next flight to Oakland, right, Kenzie? I'll drive you to the airport."

"Sos bruja," I say to Mamá.

"I'm not a witch, I just talked to Kenzie's parents. That's what you're supposed to do with people. Communicate."

I hug Kenzie, then head back up to the room to shower and change into clothes I haven't been wearing for forty-eight hours. Only when I'm clean, my hair behaving, and I've checked in with Sebas do I look at Diego's texts.

Shit.

47

Sebas

Lu tells me that it's Diego, ese hijo de la putísima madre—no offense to his actual mamá—who threw the rotten smoothie at me, then locked me in the bathroom stall. I'm not sure how to process it. He was there, his stupid smiling face nodding in sympathy, when I complained about the disgusting smell the rotten strawberry left on my clothes.

And his reason? Didn't like that I was coming between him and his friends. The pendejo is so ignorant, so goddamn up his own ass, that I'm almost more bewildered than mad.

"Want to borrow my ironic bolo tie?" Papá stands at the door to my room, a half smile lifting his face a little. Fuck Diego, honestly.

"Nah, I've got my emergency shirt to see me through." Today is the funeral, the burial. The last time I can be with Abuela. She'd say, *No, mijito, I'm always with you. Wasn't I with you when you were miles away? You can still talk to me, and I will listen.*

In the kitchen, there are two Gansito cakes on a plate, and a mug for me.

"You want your mother to come back and haunt you, Pa?"

I say, sitting down to eat the store-bought strawberry-cream-filled cakes Abuela would never let me get. I use the term *strawberry* lightly—no fruit has been anywhere near this thing. It's delicious.

When I take a sip of what I think is café con leche, I get a shock.

"You made me cozy chocolate milk?" I can't help that my voice breaks a little when I ask.

"That's a little gift from your mom. I spent twenty minutes on a video call with her last night while she walked me through making it. I thought I understood how to make hot chocolate in a microwave, but apparently, I'm wrong."

"It's not hot chocolate, it's *cozy* chocolate. There's a difference."

"Clearly. Did I get it right?"

"Yes." So right, it almost brings me to tears. Mom used to say, "That's a hug for your stomach."

"How is she?" Thoughts of Mom and how she's feeling fell completely out of my head.

"Better, she says. She looks better. And she seems a bit better. Less amargada, you know?"

"Yeah." The bitterness had been leaving Mom these last few weeks. That alone was worth going to New Gault.

That fog I've been in these last days is punctured by a random thought.

"This isn't the funeral I thought I'd be going to, Pa. I don't know what to do." Tears take me over. We cry together in what will always be Abuela's kitchen. Eventually, we pull ourselves together enough to leave for church. Tía Gladys comes into the kitchen as we leave. She'll spend the time we're saying goodbye to Abuela doing the same in her own way: making food for everyone to celebrate Abuela's life when we return.

Church is packed with people who loved my abuela, and that means almost everyone in la vecindad. Anaïs and Hudson hug-tackle me at the door and I'm so overwhelmed that I've got no words. I nod at their condolences, and we go find our seats next to Pa, Lu, and their mami.

"Some people's spirits cast a big shadow," Papá whispers as the priest has to stop the funeral briefly to tell people that there's no more seats, but they're welcome to stand along the back wall.

"Abuela's wasn't a shadow, more like a light," I say as more and more people file into the church. Vivian, the owner of Azúcar, the panadería that Abuela loved; the family she loaned money to so they could open their carnitas food truck; all the women who came to her for cuttings from her garden, advice on herbal remedies or their troubles. The people that she helped, or just listened to.

Now I have to say something to them, up at the lectern after the first reading. I walk up in a daze, like a total out-of-body feeling. I tug at the collar of my shirt and take out my phone. "Um. Any of you who know me know that Abuela was everything to me." I stop, take a breath, try not to see the people in the pews at all, especially my dad, struggling not to cry. "But I'm not good at words, and Abuela deserves the best words. So. Here's a poem. I didn't write it. Someone amazing did, someone who didn't know Abuela, but knows how I felt about her." I find where Lu is sitting next to Pa and Ms. Hernandez. Their eyes are full of tears. Of course they are. It's a funeral. Crying is the freaking love language. "Okay. Here goes."

48

Lu

I wake up like I never went to sleep. Maybe I didn't. Mamá didn't make a sound—she sleeps like she's in a sarcophagus, arms crossed and everything. Still, I'm not used to sleeping with anyone else in my room, even my mom. That's why I'm up at six a.m. the day after being wrung out like a sponge at the funeral. My hand reaches for my phone so I can text Sebas. He's not like me—he doesn't sleep with his phone in his hand. And since leaving New Gault, he's barely looked at his TECH phone. He's not wearing the biosensor anymore either.

I type and delete:

> **You up?**
> **Are you okay?**
> **Hey!**
> **I have to leave today.**
> **Mamá wants me back in New Gault.**

Finally, I fall back on a heart emoji.

As soon as I hit send, the three dots pop up. He must have been staring at his phone too.

Want to get food?

I smile. Always food with Sebas.

Sure. Where?

Diner? and you have to drive, obviously.

15 min

"You're really gonna order Moons Over My Hammy?" We got a booth because it felt somehow more private. When I left Sebas's house last night, he'd been hugged by so many people, even his miracle emergency shirt was rumpled. Family and friends regaled us with stories of Señora Ascencio's past, when she'd organized for farm workers' rights, along with her husband. Photos of a young woman with dark hair and a fierce smile were passed around the friends and family crammed into the kitchen and living room. My mom stayed a little bit, then left me the car keys and took a rideshare back to the hotel.

"The question is, why aren't *you* ordering it? It's punny," Sebas says with his hooky smile. It's good to see it on his face.

"That's not how I make my food choices. And we're not in Miami."

"I'm paying for this, so don't give me a hard time. They don't take your phone nonsense either—you have to actually pay for things here."

"I do know how the world works."

We both snort-laugh. Neither of us really knows how the world works. We only know how we wish it did. I wish I didn't know, completely and utterly, that I'm going home today and Sebas is staying with his dad.

"What happens to your mom if you don't go back?" I ask.

"I have to go back for her to keep her benefits. But I'm here till the end of the school year. I'll do virtual summer school to make up what I missed. Then I'll be back in August."

"I'll look in on your mom."

Sebas chokes on his soda.

"What? It's not like I can't help her with things." I try not to be offended.

"It's not that. You must be psychic. When I told her that I was staying with Papi for the summer but that I could come up every couple of weeks, she said she didn't need me. She said *you'd* help if she needed anything."

"Oh. Ha. Well, I will. Or Mamá will. She's unnaturally organized."

Sebas orders his ridiculously named breakfast. I order scrambled eggs. When the food comes, I don't feel like eating, but every three times I shuffle a forkful around, I make myself take a bite. That's the secret to doing something you don't want to. Like now, I don't want to leave Sebas. But I'm gonna do it anyway.

"What are you going to do about Diego?" I ask.

"¿Ese? Nothing. He's not worth my damn time."

I roll my eyes. "You're still not going to report him?"

"You want me to?" Sebas asks.

"I know I should, but I don't. I thought this system would keep people from wanting to turn on each other. I thought it was enough to protect us. But it only made Diego feel like . . ." I shrug.

"Like he should throw a rotten smoothie at someone? That boy needs more than a system that shames him when he does something stupid. Like, someone to talk to, maybe?"

"I wish he'd talked to me, or Kenzie. I feel like an idiot."

Sebas stops shoveling ham into his mouth for a second as the waitress refills his soda and my coffee.

"Okay, why are you an idiot?" he asks.

"I should have known what was going on with Diego. I should have talked to him."

"Maybe." He shrugs. "But you can't be responsible for everyone's garbage choices."

I eat half my breakfast, which in fairness was enough for two people. We both ask for refills as the waitress clears the table.

"You know what this is?" Sebas asks.

"What?"

"It's the goodbye scene."

Tears have been hanging around, behind my eyes, in my chest, ready to pour out, for days. I wrote the poem for Sebas's abuela in three hours, crying nearly the whole time. Now I don't think I have tears left.

"I know," I say. "But I'm not ready."

"Me neither."

A text pops up from Mamá.

¿Donde estás?

I respond that I'm getting breakfast and tell her I'll pick some up for her.

> We need to leave for the airport by eleven, okay amor?

I text a thumbs-up, then order Mamá's breakfast. That gives us a few more minutes of sitting together.

"Will you do a card reading?"

"For you? Sure."

"No," I say. "For us. Can you do that?"

Sebas looks at me, his face for once completely unreadable. Even his mouth, which is always on standby, ready to speak or smile or cry.

Finally, he reaches into his backpack and pulls out his abuela's cards, sets them on the table. He hesitates for a few seconds.

"I've never done it for two people. And I can't ask Abuela how to do it." He takes a breath, and it hitches in his chest, like it's stuck.

"Forget it," I say, cursing myself for being insensitive.

"No. I want to. Here," he says, cutting the cards into two piles. "You shuffle half, I'll shuffle half. We'll both think of the question."

"Which is?"

"Us," he says simply.

49

Sebas

The next time I enter the city limits of that pain-in-my-ass town New Gault, Papá is driving, so I don't get the chance to show him the spectacle of the bus station.

"Why are the street names so corny?" Pa asks.

"Who knows," I respond. I'm keyed way the hell up. I haven't seen Lu, actually, really seen them, in over two months. We chat, we text, we send each other stuff. I even made them watch the original *Stepford Wives* with me and, well, they didn't think much of the comparison.

"I have better hair than all those wives put together" is what they said, even when I reminded them, again, that I didn't think *they* were like Stepford, just New Gault.

Pa parks right outside Mom's apartment.

"Plenty of parking," he says, trying to sound like being here doesn't freak him out entirely.

"Stop stalling," I say. You would never get me to say this out loud, but I kind of missed Mom. And I'm scared to see her in person, even though she's told us that she's feeling a bit better, that the treatment seems to be working. She doesn't need the oxygen as much as she used to. Her pulse oximeter readings are great.

I drag my duffel bag from the trunk and head for the front door, Papá trailing behind me. Before I can knock, Leeza opens the door, and I hug her. Jesus, did I miss everyone so much I'm gonna tackle-hug them whenever I see them? I need to settle down.

"Good to see you too, Sebas," she says, a little thrown off. She shakes hands with my dad, and then Mom is there, hugging me. It's my turn to be thrown off. She's hugging me tight, not the fragile bird-boned figure I remember from May.

"I missed you, kid," she says when she pulls away enough for me to look at her face. It's still thin and pale, but, yeah, she does look healthier. And she's got a fuzz of hair growing all over her head, and it's *curly*.

"You have curls?" I say stupidly. Mom used to have straight blond hair. She was really proud of her hair, like it conferred some kind of status on her. Which I guess it did.

She passes her hand over her head. "I look like a baby chick, but yeah. It's growing back curly. I don't mind. Leeza said when it grows a bit more, she'll help me figure out how to style it."

"Hi, Kristen," Pa says.

"It's good to see you, Hernán." She says his actual name and not *good-for-nothing* or, with bitterness, *chico*. And she calls him *Hernán* instead of *Herman*, which is what she used to call him—trying to anglicize his name and, I guess, the rest of him. What's more, she tries to put an accent on it, not sounding the *h*, stressing the right syllable. It's kind of a big deal.

I watch my parents hug—probably the first time they've touched each other in years—and even though it's messy and not how I would have written the script, I'm okay with this. I'd call cut, if I could, and put it in the can.

50

Lu

I pick Diego up from his house. We aren't as close as we were, but we're still friends, and that's taken almost all of the summer to navigate. He's not allowed to drive, but this time it's not his fault. Over the summer, he had a seizure while driving. It was one of the scariest things that I've ever witnessed. Kenzie hauled on the emergency brake of his truck and steered us to the shoulder as he slumped over the steering wheel. His biosensor had already alerted emergency services by the time Kenzie and I had fumbled our phones out.

He's okay. He's still a d-bag sometimes, but he's getting better. He's taking medicine, and he's getting therapy.

"I'm like you now, Lu," he says when our phones ping at almost the same time to remind us to take meds. He thinks it makes him sound endearing, but it's patronizing in a very Diego way.

"Thanks for picking me up," he says.

"No hay de qué."

"You nervous about seeing Sebas today?"

I give him side-eye complete with a raised brow. "Since when do you ask me how I feel?"

"I don't know. I just—I thought it would be okay, now that, you know."

"Now that you sorta know how to talk about feelings?" I smile.

"Don't be a dock," he says lightly. So many things have changed over the summer, but Diego's use of fake curse words is not one of them.

"I'm nervous, yeah, but excited. Like, nervicited," I say.

"That's a good word. Did you make it up?"

I nod. "When I first started having anxiety attacks, everything felt panicky, like maybe it could turn into anxiety. I wanted a word to remind me that sometimes feeling like your stomach is gonna leap out your throat is for a good reason. It makes sense, right?"

"I'm gonna use that with my therapist."

"Feel free."

I don't think nervicited *is* the right word. There's so much that's changed and—amazingly to me—so much of it is good. Sebas came to New Gault, and it changed things. Or maybe that's not fair. I was changing already, or at least ready to change. I don't know. I'm still figuring it out. But leaving New Gault shifted something in me. And coming back to New Gault after just a few days away, it felt alien. Nothing had changed. It was me.

We pull into the parking lot of Dry Town, which is packed, as it is most nights, thanks to Kenzie working for Sheila and Ana.

"What night is it?" Diego says as he gets out of the car.

"Spiritualist Saturday."

"Oh, that figures."

Once we're inside, it's a mad crush, and Diego goes off to help Sheila with setting up the video.

When Sebas left, Kenzie took over doing the card readings at Dry Town, with Diego helping out with A/V. If Sebas was like a small business, Kenzie is a freaking multinational conglomerate. She created theme nights, including Spiritualist Saturdays, open mic poetry slams on Thursdays (with my help), and Film Fridays, which was Sebas's idea. When I explained how popular that night is, especially when they project old movies without the sound and make up the dialogue à la *Mystery Science Theater 3000*, Sebas was caught between wanting to see it and thinking it was sacrilege. I can't wait to tell him about last night, when Kenzie showed *The Cabinet of Dr. Caligari* and most of the crowd recited quotes from that early 2000s vampire series. I admit, I almost lost it when Kenzie took the mic and intoned, "Hey, Bella, where you been, loca?" over a hundred-year-old German Expressionist film.

Sebas texted me when he got here, before surrendering his phone to the Phone Jail, so I know he's in the building, and my heart and insides know he's in there too. We've seen each other over the phone all summer long. I know he's cut two inches off his hair so it grazes his shoulders; he knows I've let my hair grow out a bit, so it curls under my ears. I bleached out the green, too, and he said he liked it. We see each other all the time. But we haven't been in the same room since I left after his abuela's funeral. Definitely nervicited.

It's not hard putting my phone in the lockup anymore. I won't say it wasn't hard the second through twentieth time, but it got easier. I nod at Ana at the bar, and Sheila, who's got their little daughter, Alice, in one of those front-loading sling things. The kid's probably almost ready to walk, but she seems cozy in the carrier, big eyes looking around the room like the whole world belongs to her and she's going to pick it up, shake it, and let it make her happy. She's wearing those baby headphones to protect her hearing, because Kenzie is blasting her Mexican synth goth playlist. To match the music and the theme, Kenzie is decked out in black lace and sits on a plush velvet chair that's almost a throne. She uses traditional tarot cards, but all different kinds of decks. One with witches, one with Virginia Woolf as the Empress. I love Kenzie forever.

Like baby Alice, I scan the room, too, ready to shake it and let it delight me, like a snow globe full of what's possible. I like that image, and I reach for my phone to make a note in my poetry file, forgetting for a second that I'm not tied to my phone in here. My hand just hovers by my pocket until I feel Sebas take my hand in his.

"You're here."

"I really am."

I lean against him, forehead to forehead.

When we pull apart, I don't let go of his hand. *Shaking the world for delight* echoes in my head, threading the needle for a future poem.

"I was thinking of a poem fragment, but I forgot I don't have my phone to write it down."

"So, I interrupted genius from happening?"

"Not at all. You're the genius happening to me right now," I gush. Zero chill.

"Since you're not going to always have your phone on you . . ." He reaches inside his backpack and pulls out a little package. "I thought you could use this to write things down."

I unwrap the palm-sized rectangle to find a notebook. It looks handmade, from the printed cover to the rough-edged paper and the staple binding. On the front and back cover, the cartas españolas line up in a grid, ready to tell futures and pasts and even the right now.

"Where did you get this?"

"I made it," he says with the widest grin. "Anaïs is now officially into glassblowing, so she gave me all her papermaking stuff. It's not that hard. It just takes horas y horas y paciencia."

"Which you do not have."

"Agreed. But Papi wanted me to finish my film, which meant no going on building sites with him. When my ass was numb from sitting in the UC San Diego editing suite for hours, I'd go home and stand at the sink, hands in the recycled paper pulp. I scanned Abuela's cartas for the cover and had that printed on my paper."

I hold the little book to my chest, knowing I look like a lovelorn character in a rom-com. I'm owning it.

"Did you finish the film?" We walk through the crowd to where Kenzie sits, with our hands linked, like both our hands have agreed that two and a half months of not touching is enough, carajo, and they're gonna make up for it now.

"Finished. I didn't get the rights to the music, so I'm not using it in the final edit, but it's fine for now, just for tonight."

Diego sets up the little projector in front of a white sheet tacked to the wall. The Bluetooth isn't working, so he scrambles to find a dongle that will connect the projector to Ana's phone—the only phone allowed in Dry Town now. When it's all done, he comes over and fist-bumps Sebas.

"Thanks for setting this up, man," Sebas says.

"No worries," Diego says. Sebas and Diego worked through their stuff and are, if not friends, then not enemies. Diego wouldn't let it go, even though Sebas didn't want to talk about it. He kept texting and leaving messages about how sorry he was for the smoothie, the bathroom. Finally, Sebas blew up and told him that he wasn't there to be, as he put it, his apology bitch. After that, they were cool. People are bizarre.

The blaring music is turned off abruptly, which gets a muted laugh from the audience that's assembled to see Sebas's film about las cartas, about his abuela.

"Whoops," Sheila says, "that was Alice at the controls, sorry about that." She turns away from the sound system to keep her daughter from reaching for any more buttons or switches.

Sebas and I sit in the second row of chairs, armchairs, and benches that have been cobbled together to form seating. Kenzie asks Sebas if he wants to say a few words to introduce his film.

"I'm good here," he says, lifting up our clasped hands.

"Okay, lovely people. Welcome to the world premiere of a documentary by future super filmmaker and hero of anyone's dreams, Sebastian Ascencio!" Kenzie says. Clapping and woo-hooing rebounds in the room. "This is entitled *Cartas*, and it's only fifteen minutes, so if I see you sneak off for a smoke or the bathroom, I will hunt you down and kill you. Okay? Good."

She sits down next to the projector and presses the link on the private website where Sebas uploaded his film. When the title comes up, black background with the word CARTAS in old-timey script, the music starts.

Over clapping and stomping Flamenco music, a voice sings:

Te busco y no te puedo encontrar, te busco y no te puedo encontrar.

Images of his abuela laughing, a long shot that follows la señora through her overflowing garden as she explains plants and flowers, their medicinal uses. The camera lingers on her curled and lined brown hand as it bounces gently at her side, the arm she lost the use of after her first stroke. In the sun-dappled garden, Sebas and his abuela gently argue over what the six of coins means if it's reversed.

It ends on a close-up of Abuela's hands methodically placing cards on the table until she fades out, and the text of the poem I wrote for her scrolls across the screen—Sebas, in voice-over, recites my words.

Nos Queremos
This love between us es una cinta
A ribbon that rests in my hand
while I sleep, and while you dream with stars y ángeles.
Nos queremos.
A place we never search for. We're already here.
Connected—in this space together.
I take your cups, coins, clubs, and swords.
I hear your voice in the birdsong that delighted you in the
morning.
I walk in your garden seeking the smell of hierbas.
I take the tea you turned into medicine for me from a warm
cup.
Una cinta that rests in my hand.

There's a beat of silence before everyone applauds.

"What did you think?" Sebas whispers to me, low enough that his words are almost all vibration.

I think seeing the world through Sebas's eyes has made me less afraid of life outside New Gault. I think loving people, and letting them love and change you, is the story of being fully alive, not just surviving. I don't want to stop this story, even if, in some future version, it might hurt. I think I have to stop protecting myself so much.

"I think you have a bright future, Sebas," I say.

"You mean us, right? C'mon. The future's for both of us." Before Kenzie and Diego, friends, and acquaintances descend on Sebas to tell him how amazing he is, I nod.

AUTHOR'S NOTE

If you, a friend, or a person in your community is being bullied in school, please reach out to your school counselor, your parents, or other trusted adults. You deserve to feel safe where you are, no matter your identity, your background, or the way you look, move, worship, or play.

RESOURCES
Here are some organizations that provide anti-bullying resources for educators, students, and schools.

GLSEN: GLSEN.org
The Trevor Project: TheTrevorProject.org
STOMP Out Bullying: STOMPOutBullying.org

ACKNOWLEDGMENTS

THERE ARE PEOPLE who help bring a book to life, and then there are people who help keep the writer *alive*. The people who didn't let me stop writing, who kept encouraging me through the long, difficult time of bringing *Fireblooms* to life, are some of the truest friends I've ever had. I don't care that I don't deserve you; I'm taking you anyway. I only hope I can be as true a friend to you. Thank you, Mia Garcia, NoNieqa Ramos, and Alison Green Myers for your steadfast faith, your friendship, and your wise words. If anything I write is any good, it's because you three nurtured the writer in me.

Thank you to my agent of muchos años (and hopefully some laughs too!), Barbara Poelle of Word One Literary, for always guiding me *onward*. To my wonderful editor, Stacey Barney, to Sarah Sather, and all the folks at Nancy Paulsen Books, thank you for believing in Lu and Sebastian and for making sure they survived their trial by fire! To Kelley Brady for designing the incredible cover; to Kathleen Keating, Ana Deboo, Aída Bardales, Cindy Howle, and Aaron Burkholder for copyediting and proofreading with such amazing care; and to my lovely publicist, Sierra Pregosin—¡mil gracias!

To author friends who understand the pain and adrenaline of a first draft, thank you for being there for me as I figured this one out—Jas Hammonds, Traci Chee, Anna-Marie McLemore, James Brandon, and Lynda Gene Rymond—you inspire me!

So much gratitude to Mayra Cuevas, Ismée Williams, Megan Jensen, Ines Lozano, and all the wonderful souls at the Latinx Kidlit Book Festival who work tirelessly to amplify the voices of Latinx storytellers and get the stories of our varied and beautiful latinidad into the hands of kids.

The Highlights Foundation continues to be a place of magic and wonder—especially now that I get to help make the magic happen for others. Thank you to George Brown, Emily Rosenthal, Molly Chao, Christina Ousouljoglou, Rebecca Tharp, Bethany Schlaner, Matt Davis, Rona Shirdan, and Bobbie Combs for making such important work joyful.

The last time I published a novel, *The Grief Keeper*, my mother read and reread every word. But she never got to read *Fireblooms*. Though I know she would have loved this book—especially since Abuela, with her midnight pillerías, was modeled after her—it's still a bruise on my heart that she's gone. You never doubted me, Mamá, and that fact sustains me even now.

Gracias, Papá, for your gift of curiosity, your gift of asking more and more questions. It used to annoy me when I was sixteen, but it's the perfect trait for a writer, as it's the engine of imagination.

To my sister, Anamari, I can only say you're my *favorite* sister. How can two people be so different and still love each other so much and support each other when they don't really understand what the other one is doing? I have no idea. But I love you more each day.

Lyra, Rowan, and Tim—you are my heart. If I told you all the ways you make it possible for me to be myself, to write my stories, and to work for better things, we'd be here all day. Instead, I'll tell you that you are in all my stories, all my dreams, and all my hopes for the future.